Brilliant Disguise

RICHARD NEER

A RILEY KING MYSTERY

Richard Neer

Copyright ©Richard Neer

All Rights Reserved 2020

Photo credit ©Andrey Kiselev/123RF.com

Other Books by Richard Neer

FM: The Rise and Fall of Rock Radio

Something of the Night

The Master Builders

Indian Summer

The Last Resort

The Punch List

An American Storm

Wrecking Ball

Three Chords and the Truth

For Vicky

Richard Neer

I

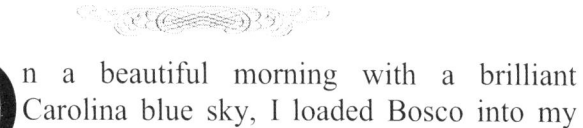

On a beautiful morning with a brilliant Carolina blue sky, I loaded Bosco into my old MDX and cranked up some Eagles and Steely Dan to put me in the right frame of mind. And I couldn't neglect my normal diet of Springsteen.

I was headed to the mountains of North Carolina to camp out with my dog. I needed time to clear my head and decide what I wanted to do with the rest of my life. My private investigator license had expired and well meaning friends were hinting that I was getting too old for this kind of work. Far too dangerous for a man on the plus side of fifty, they said.

Maybe I could live off the grid, become a hermit. A cabin in the woods with solar power. Water from a clear mountain stream. Hunt and fish for sustenance, even though I have never done either. Oh well. Amazon delivers.

To that end, I rented a small cabin to give it a test drive. From the pictures on Zillow, a blind bat could see the place needed work. But I'm good at fixing things and the owner was willing to listen to 'rent to purchase' offers. A month's stay should be enough to tell if I'd be content there.

With the proper tech setup, I could read, watch all those movies I'd wanted to see but never had the time for. Maybe have a go at writing my memoirs, without changing the names to protect the guilty. I could live in virtual civilization without actual human beings, most of whom were becoming an annoyance. And there'd be no lawn to tell kids to get off of.

The car phone shattered my lone cowpoke reverie. I'd barely gotten onto I-95 when everything I'd been planning was rendered academic.

The call came from Jaime, the woman I still harbor a great deal of affection for, despite the fact that she had shacked up with my best friend. Rick Stone had ventured out to California to try his hand in movies. He planned to stay with Jaime until he could find digs of his own.

I was okay with that, never guessing in a million years that they'd fall for each other. After they announced their liaison, I cut them off entirely. A few months later, Rick was dying of pancreatic cancer. We spoke one last time, and I forgave him. They never meant for it to happen and they were heartsick at the pain it had caused me. I had a hard time carrying animosity for either of them after that.

Jaime's voice sounded fresh and upbeat. "Hi there, big fella."

She had never called me that when we were together. I could take it a couple of ways: One, that it marked a new beginning, casting aside old pet names. Or that she now regarded me as an expired old flame, undeserving of affectionate nostalgia from our time together.

I said, "Hey yourself, big girl. Sorry, that didn't sound right. I mean, you're tall and uh, well, big in your industry, but..." I fumbled for a way to make up for a term most women would consider an insult.

But Jaime isn't most women. "I know what you mean. Aren't we past the need to explain gaffes?"

"Uh, sure. Everything okay? It's mighty early out where you are."

"I'm fine. Much as I can be after what happened. I'm up early every day. Because of the time difference, I'm out of bed by five, working out for forty five minutes. At my desk just after six."

When we were together I might have joked something like 'it's about time you get your shapely ass out of bed', but I didn't think that would play well right now. It was strange having to pick my words carefully when not so long ago, I could say whatever came to mind. Neither of us had to worry about a careless jibe being taken the wrong way.

I opted for safe, bland and inoffensive. I said, "I'm glad you called, whatever the reason."

"Well, there *is* a reason, other than to hear your voice." She was feeling the same tentativeness I was. Whatever she needed, she couldn't come right out and say it. It had to be couched delicately, for fear that her ask would come off as presumptuous.

She backed off a bit. "How are things with you?"

It was too soon to tell her of my plans to chuck it all and live in the hills. "I'm fine. Not much on my plate, work-wise. Just getting into baseball season."

Jaime grew up a Mets fan in New Jersey. We had hoped that one summer we'd have the means and time to take in a game at every major league park in America. Now that we both had the means, the gulf separating us had to be negotiated.

She said, "Even though they're so much better than the Metsies, I just can't bring myself to root for the Dodgers. Anyway, I *do* have a favor to ask. Actually, not a favor. More like a job. I'll pay you the going rate."

People often break the rule: *never do business with your friends*. Most of the time, they regret it. With a lover, it's even more parlous. But with Jaime, I had to listen.

I said, "I can't take your money. I'm happy to help you any way I can, but not for money."

"I'm asking you to do what you do for a living. You're a professional. It's not fair that you don't get paid. It's not an easy job and it might take up quite a bit of time."

"Look, you've said a bunch of times I should write a book about my adventures. If I ever get around to it, I'd want you to represent me. Don't tell me you wouldn't waive your commission, because I know you would. So consider this a favor. Someday, and that day may never come, I'll call upon you to do a service for me."

"Thank you, Don Corleone."

I loved that she got the reference. Not many women would.

She said, "We'll figure something out later. If there're expenses, I'll cover them. At least let me do that."

"Like you say, we'll figure it out later. What do you need?"

"Do you know the cable show *Country Fixin's*?"

"I'm not much into cooking shows."

"It's not a cooking show. It's about flipping houses. It's set in South Carolina, near where you live in Hilton Head. It's like that show on HGTV, *Fixer Upper*. You know the one?"

"Oh, yeah. *Country Fixin's*. I have seen it. That's the one with the hot blonde babe and her schlubby husband who rehab houses."

"That's the one, although I wouldn't use that as a tag line. They're shooting the series in a place called Judy's Island."

"I know the place. A sort of Juco Hilton Head. That means junior college."

"I know that. We have a big problem brewing that we've tried to keep out of the press, but that won't last long. The hot blonde babe, as you call her, is missing. And the cops think the schlubby husband killed her."

2

There's no such thing as a local story anymore. Anything remotely newsworthy gets disseminated globally in seconds. It was impressive that Jaime had been able to suppress a hot tabloid story like this one.

I said, "Has Mr. Schlub been arrested? And why do *you* care?"

"He hasn't been arrested, just questioned. And I care because he's my client and I'm responsible for putting the show together in the first place."

"First thing is, you'd better get him a lawyer. If you can't find one on your own, I can probably recommend somebody."

"You forget who you're talking to?"

"Oh, right. Sorry."

"He doesn't want to lawyer up. Thinks it makes him look guilty."

"That might be true. Depends on the cops. So are they sure she's really missing? Sometimes people take marriage sabbaticals."

Jaime said, "Some kids found her car near an abandoned quarry. She hasn't shown up for makeup call for two days."

"I assume they've searched the area near the car. Sent divers into the quarry, if there's water in it. If there's no body, it'll be hard to charge Mr. Schlub."

"Stop calling him that. He's a good guy. It's complicated."

If I was to help Jaime, my mountain experiment would be over less than an hour after it started. But it'd be a great chance for us to reacquaint and see if we could rekindle what we had. That cabin wouldn't be so lonely if Jaime was there with me.

Dream on.

I said, "Jaime, I'm in the car with Bosco. I can be home in an hour. Let's hook up then and you can fill me in on the details. Unless you think it's urgent that I head toward Schlub-land right now."

"Stop with that. They're shooting around her, hoping she'll turn up. I have one of my people on the set, but she's an agent, not a detective. You can liaise with her."

"Damn, you're making this sound like a military op. Let me Skype you when I get home. Meanwhile, put together any info that'll help me. Even the most inconsequential stuff. Rumors, gossip, anything."

Bosco was confused. I'd packed his food, toys, medications and accoutrements into the car. Without a doubt, his travel needs are greater than mine, even though I encourage him to follow my lead and pack light. He expected a long journey, not an hour and a half joyride.

One phone call from Jaime and the mountain fantasy I'd been harboring for the last month flew right out the window. It made me realize how rudderless my life had been lately. Maybe the old man could use my deposit on the cabin to spruce it up some. More likely, it'd get him a better brand of bourbon.

When I got home, it took a few minutes to reset my laptop, after which I Skyped Jaime. From the background, it appeared she was working from home, the beach house I've never seen in person. When we were dialed in, she said, "You look tired, Riles. Not sleeping well? I can relate."

She looked great, as always. Since I'd last seen her when we scattered Rick's ashes, the California sun had favored her with a tawny glow. I was disappointed that her green eyes were obscured by the lo-res image. She was wearing a pink V-neck tee shirt, unadorned by commercial symbols. I assumed she was wearing shorts, but fantasized that she wasn't.

I said, "Let's get to work. Tell me about the man I will no longer refer to as Mr. Schlub, unless that's his given name."

"No, it's Brent. Brent Purdy. Friends call him Boomer. He's a country boy with a big heart, just like he comes off on the show. Four years ago, he was just your average house flipper in the Lowcountry, trying to make a living, doing the best he can."

Jaime's time with Stone had caused her to pick up one of his more annoying habits, quoting classic rock lyrics at every opportunity. I don't mind it as much from her and besides, *Ramblin' Man* by the Allman Brothers is a winner.

She went on. "The *Property Brothers* were filming down by you. Brent got wind of it and went to watch the shoot. He was fascinated. Never spoke to either of the twins directly, but sidled up to an assistant director, who thought he was a natural for his own show."

"Was he wearing a tight sweater at a lunch counter?"

"Ava Gardner?"

"Lana Turner actually, but good guess. Ava was from North Carolina, by the way."

"I never knew that. Anyway, the director suggested Brent make an audition reel and find an agent. Helped him put it together after hours. That's how we became aware of him."

"We? Jaime Johansen, the royal we?"

"I didn't take his call personally. It got routed to one of my staff, who's tight with the DIY people. Based on the tape, she thought he had potential, but needed a co-host, preferably a 'hot blonde babe' as you put it. We were working with an actress who fit the bill. So we put them together, made an demo and the rest is history."

"Wait a minute. So they're not really married?"

"That came later. Strange pairing, a California beach bunny and a southern redneck but during the second season, they tied the knot. We're three seasons in now and the ratings have gone up every year. It's one of our big success stories."

"Of course, you know that when a wife goes missing or dies, the husband is the go-to suspect. This Boomer Purdy have any violent tendencies you know of?"

"When we were shooting the pilot, I spent a fair amount of time with him and he was always a gentleman. A big bear of a man. 'Raised the right way' was how his coworkers put it. Respectful. Humble and kind. Church going."

"Is he as big as he looks on TV?"

"I'd say he's a little over your height, 6-4 or so, but he has you by at least a hundred pounds."

"And the girl, I mean the woman. Is she as hot in person as she is on the show?"

"You try so hard to be politically correct and in the next sentence you show your true nature."

"This from a woman who put them together because the show needed a *hot blonde babe*."

"I don't make the rules and when I can break stereotypes, I do. But the client comes first and if the show needed a co-host who looks great in tight coveralls, that's a proven recipe. Her name is Cami Wordsworth, now Purdy. Short for Cameron. And yes, in answer to your question, she is very attractive. Shorter than me by a couple of inches but much curvier, is all I'll say."

Jaime is 5-10 and not very buxom, but I have no complaints.

"Cami and Boomer Purdy. Happily married? They come off that way on the show, the few times I've seen it."

"The magic of television. They haven't lived together since the end of last season."

3

Moses Ginn said, "Riley King, you are a whole bunch of surprises. You sure you ain't mainlining too much of that CBD oil?"

"Never touch the stuff." This was true, although I'm tempted. Sleep isn't coming easily these days.

He and I sat at the world's most elegant Dunkin' Donuts, just off the William Hilton Parkway on Hilton Head Island. Great coffee, greater doughnuts. What's not to like?

Despite his outward cool, I could tell Moses was unsettled when I told him about my decision to work with Jaime Johansen.

I said, "I need to do this, Mo. This might be my shot at getting Jaime back."

Moses lives in my oceanfront house with a local cop named Alexandra Tomey. On the face of it, Tomey and Ginn could not be more dissimilar. She is a diminutive forty-something, white Baptist, by-the-book, law enforcement officer. He is an older, rules-be-damned, black giant with no particular religious affiliation.

He said, "Have you really thought this through? Yesterday, you tell me you're headed for the mountains to clear your head, don't know when you'll be back. Now you're all gung ho to hook up with your ex. Sounds like romantic bullshit to me. Something you see on one of them Jared commercials. I like Jaime, but after what she done to you, I'd give her a wide berth, brother. Bosco, talk some sense into your dad."

My Golden Retriever was sitting at my feet and his ears perked up at the mention of his name. Normally, they frown on dogs in places where food is served but I know the manager of this doughnut shop, and he lets me bring Bosco during off hours.

Ginn snuck a bit of doughnut to the dog under the table, which I pretended not to see.

He said, "I bet you're planning on using the pup to pull on her heart strings."

"Hey, for a while, I was thinking of driving out to California and showing up on her doorstep with Bosco. Hard to say no to that face and those big brown eyes. Of course, I'd have to book a bunch of pet friendly motels along the way."

"Like a *Green Book* for dogs. Now you know how my people got treated back in the day, like dogs or worse. Still do in some places you'da been travellin' through. Come here, Bosco. I think your dad done lost his mind, buddy."

He sauntered over to Ginn's side and Moses produced another chunk of doughnut, magically pulling it from the animal's ear.

"I don't think Bosco's impressed by your prestidigitation. He just wants a treat."

"Well, I guess you're back in action. That hermit thing you was planning didn't last long. And Ms. Jaime Johnasen is back in the picture. When Alex asks, what should I tell 'er?"

"Just that I'm helping her out as a friend. If things don't work out, I don't want her to think I'm a total idiot."

"That train done left the station some time ago."

4

Later that afternoon, Alex Tomey and I were on my screen porch with Bosco, ocean waves serenading us from just over the dunes. Ginn was out somewhere, doing something. It was a gray late April day, mild and muggy. The overhead fans provided a gentle breeze that the Atlantic wasn't in the mood to supply.

I've come to love my Hilton Head home. Only sand dunes separate it from the Atlantic. It stands high and strong against the sea and its fierce winds. The craftsmanship is superb, every surface carefully planned and executed to an exacting detail. It is a chore to maintain it to the standards it deserves, but it is worth it.

Alex said, "You know Moses was up on a ladder this morning after you left. Putting in gutter guards. I haven't come upon a single thing that he can't fix better than it was before."

I resisted the temptation to throw out the obvious sexual quip. "Yep. The man could have been a builder or carpenter if his life had gone differently. Or a shrink. Maybe a five star chef. As opposed to what he is now, which I can't exactly put a finger on."

"A man comfortable in his own skin. Does what needs to get done and isn't looking to take credit for it."

"That's as good a profile as any."

Tomey had stopped my reconciliation train in its tracks. When I told her that I'd be working with my ex, she said, "Oh, she'll take you back all right. But you won't stay long. I know you, King. You'll revert to form."

"Alex Tomey, you are one mean girl."

She took a sip of hot tea and smiled at me. "I must say I *am* surprised at you, forgiving her for what she and Rick did. I'm not sure I'd be able to."

I said, "That was my fault. She wanted me to move out there with her last year and I said no."

"That's big of you but that doesn't excuse her and Rick for getting together. I know it's bad form to speak ill of the dead, but the man was your best friend. Friends don't sleep with their friend's woman. He knew you still had feelings for her. If Moses and I ever split, you wouldn't dream of trying to hook up with me, thank God."

"That's true for a number of reasons, one of which is, he'd kill me. But with Jaime and Rick, they didn't mean for it to happen. He was staying with her temporarily while he was looking for a place to live and well, ..."

"The only reason you feel guilty for cutting them out of your life is because he died. Sorry to sound so callous about it, but if he'd lived, you still wouldn't be speaking to either one of them. Cancer's an awful way to go, especially for somebody so young."

"His dying taught me what's really important. It's about forgiveness."

"But you *were* justified feeling betrayed. You forgave and took the blame on yourself. Noble, but stupid. My point is ---- you aren't going to be happy with her after what happened. The first time you disagree on something, you'll throw that at her. I know you."

"Tomey, I really want this to work. Maybe *I'm* different. Look, first things first. I may have a murder to solve. You ever watch that *Country Fixin's* show?"

"I do. It's entertaining, but you *do* know those shows are staged. They coach those so-called 'real people' to act like assholes."

"Problem is, it doesn't seem like much of a stretch. It's easy to do when they're typecast in the first place. Jaime reps some of them, so I couldn't avoid them when we were together."

Bosco was asleep in the corner, his occasional bout of snoring overlaying the sound of the waves. His body was entirely on the tile floor; only his head rested on the dog bed. I'd given up trying to coax him onto to the space-age gel cushion (which I'd paid extra for) on the advertised premise that dogs love its cool, nurturing comfort. No, he was happier on the cold, hard tile.

Tomey said, "Well, good luck, fella. If this is what you want, I hope it works out for you."

"Where's Ginn now? Didn't tell me where he was headed after we split."

Tomey said, "Out shopping for dinner. By the way, he and I had an over/under line on how long you'd be gone on your little camping trip with the dog. A week. I won. Now he wants to bet me on how long you and Jaime will be together if you hook up again. Whatever the number, I'll take the under."

5

Country Fixin's is shot on Judy's Island, a jagged expanse on the Port Royal Sound. Hilton Head is south, on the opposite side of the bay. I've gazed across the water at Judy's dozens of times without knowing anything about it. I'm aware that Parris Island, the Marine Training Base is adjacent to it.

I checked out some online listings on Judy's Island and it seemed very nice. Oceanfront houses were available there for well under a million, something that cannot be said for Hilton Head. But when I called my realtor Chipper McKenna to ask about them, he said I wouldn't be happy there.

I pressed him as to why.

"I'm not supposed to bad mouth nobody's listings," he said. "So you didn't hear this from me. You see the local papers online, right? When you see burglaries, bar fights and the occasional homicide, where do most of them come from? 'Nuff said."

Chipper would go no further and said that he only mentioned this because he considers me a friend. All I needed to do was Google the name and lots of interesting things would surface, he advised.

The next morning, I drove to Judy's Island to snoop around the set. It was a forty five minute ride and I was bored with the satellite radio, so I called Ginn, who was tending to a project at the house.

"Alex told me you had the over on how long I'd be gone on my housing trip in the mountains. How much did you lose?"

"Weren't exactly dollars and I'd prefer not saying."

"I hope she isn't going to be denying you her favors since you lost the bet."

"That'd be punishment for her as much as me."

"I'll make a bet on who caves first in that one."

"So you didn't tell me what this case was all about. Afraid I got so caught up in what a fool you was for getting involved with your ex, it kinda slipped my mind. But if this case Jaime gave you is more than somebody's cat is missing, I expect you'll be requiring my services."

"You know the show *Country Fixin's?*"

"Alex makes me watch it sometimes. That's the one with the hot blonde babe married to that Grizzly Adams looking dude."

"The very one. Well, the hot blonde babe is missing."

"They look under that big old flannel shirt her man's always wearing? She could be hiding out there and nobody would know."

"Why didn't I think of that? That'll be my first stop. I'm heading up there now. You home tonight?"

"Apron on, cooking dinner."

"Save me some leftovers. Alex might be able to help too, since she's friends with some of the Beaufort County cops. That is, if she can put her hatred for Jaime aside."

"She don't hate her, just what she done to you, is all. Just be careful, 5-0. If you find that lady and she's not wanting to go back to that hillbilly, don't you get caught up in it. Big as you are, that dude could crush you if he had a mind to sit on you. Just saying."

"I'll make a note."

~~~~

Jaime had given me the name of her emissary on the set and told me to look her up as soon as I pulled in. Iris Walker would make the necessary introductions. She didn't tell me that Walker was a lesbian, figuring correctly that it wasn't relevant. But Iris felt the need to announce it right after we shook hands.

"Is that going to affect our working relationship?" she asked.

"Not unless you were having an affair with Cami."

"That's offensive."

"Joking. But I thought Jaime said that you were a friend of hers and you put her together with Purdy."

She snorted and shook her head. "First off, it wasn't me who put them together. It was Jaime's idea. And why would you assume that because a lesbian has female friends that they're all sex partners? Jaime didn't tell me you were a Neanderthal."

"Iris, I'm just trying to figure out who's who. No need for name calling this early. Wait till later when you get to know me better."

"So you think that because you used to sleep with the boss you have some kind of advantage over me?"

"Why would I need an advantage over you if we're on the same team? Now, are you going to help me or are we going to play power games? Because if that's your agenda, let's call Jaime right now and straighten it out."

"You want to try to get me fired, go for it. I'm billing twice budget projections this quarter. Let's see who she goes with."

"Ms. Walker, I'm starting to get that you don't want me here. But I have no idea why. Look at it this way --- I can help you win. Drop the act and work with me."

"You think you have me pegged --- an insecure little dyke. Is that it?"

"Makes no difference to me who you sleep with. I sleep with a Golden Retriever every night. Listen, we both serve at the pleasure of the queen. Jaime asked me for a favor. The bottom line is, this could turn into a criminal case and that's what I do."

"So I've heard."

"Try to imagine a happy ending. We find Cami, the show goes on, ratings are better than ever. When this is over, we'll have drinks and exchange war stories. It'll be my pleasure."

"I don't drink. You sip your old man's single malt and I'll smoke a joint."

I didn't disguise my surprise very well. How did she know my beverage of choice?

She said, "Looks like I've done more research on you than you've done on me. "

"Twenty one year old Glenfiddich, if you're buying. Frankly Iris, I didn't do *any* research on you. If Jaime trusts you to monitor an important show, that's enough for me. Now tell me about Brent Purdy and Cami. I hear they've been living apart for some time now."

"That's true."

"Any insight as to why?"

We were in Brent's trailer next to one of the houses he was rehabbing. It wasn't luxurious by any standard, certainly less than you'd expect for a TV star. It fit his on screen image. It was neat, compact. Everything he needed, nothing he didn't. It mirrored his actual home, if the one on the show was really the one he lived in.

Iris Walker shrugged. "Cami was considered eye candy and replaceable. She didn't appreciate that."

"And he treated her like that?"

"When it came down to it, his word was final when it came to editorial decisions. Brent has points in the show as an executive producer."

"What does that mean exactly?"

"With most actors, it's a title with no power. It's so they can get royalties and residuals over and above what they'd make as performers. But Brent actually does have say over the editorial content."

"I thought Cami was the key element that made the deal happen. He needed an attractive co-host."

"You remember a show that ran on PBS years ago called *Hometime*?"

"I do. I liked it better than *Country Fixin's*, to tell the truth."

"PBS is different than commercial cable. But the thing is, on that show, Dean Johnson had several female co-hosts. All cute in different ways. Viewers had their favorites but the rotating women didn't matter much. I think Cami felt she didn't have much leverage."

"Didn't being married to the guy give her a little edge?"

"I like Cami and consider her a friend. But she and Boomer were never right for each other. Up until now, they've maintained a happy face for the show."

"Is there any chance Cami is using this somehow to raise her profile in the media? You think her disappearance could be a publicity stunt?"

"I don't think so. Look, I don't want to be trouble for anyone, but Cami's told me more than once that she's scared of Brent. She says he has a hell of temper. Sometimes the least little thing sets him off and he's a big strong guy."

"Any signs of physical violence toward her?"

"No, and I would know if there were. Cami and I are close. She'd never run away without telling me, no matter how much pub it would generate. And that's not something Ms. Johansen would approve of, certainly not these days."

"What do you mean, these days?"

"She's changed since Rick Stone died. She doesn't talk about it at work, but there's something missing. She's not the tiger she used to be. She vanished for almost a month after he died, didn't stay in touch with the office. Very out of character for her. Missed out on a couple of big deals. A lot of us are worried that she's lost the killer instinct."

Iris Walker reminded me a little of what Jaime was like when I first met her. Wary, stand-offish. Naturally attractive but doing nothing to enhance it. She wanted to be taken seriously for her brains, not her looks. I didn't think she was interested in men either. I found out first hand that impression was incorrect.

"I'm sure given time, Jaime will be back to her old self," I lied. If her workers smelled blood in the water, it wouldn't be good for her future dealings, whatever form they might take. "So do you think the main reason she married Brent was to get a bigger stake in the show? Money, power, that sort of thing? And would he be aware of it if she was?"

"You'd have to ask him. I haven't, for obvious reasons."

"He and I are going to have a hard talk. When can I meet him?"

"He called just before you got here. They were shooting at another house about a half hour away. He should be back soon. Just be careful with him. I told you Cami said he has a temper and he's a moose. Played college football. I tread lightly around him."

"Yeah, save your best shots for me, Walker. I can take them."

6

They say that television cameras add ten pounds to your actual weight. That's why many actresses appear downright skeletal in person. With males, there's a different standard. My expectation was that Boomer Purdy was going to look a bit less massive in the flesh.

When Purdy entered his trailer just before dinnertime, he confounded my expectations. He *was* large, but no bigger than an average NFL linebacker. Jaime's estimate of a hundred pound edge on me would mean I weighed one fifty-five, a number I surpassed in junior high.

Television couldn't have added that many pounds. The man had lost weight and the mountain man look was gone --- his beard was short and neatly trimmed. The shoulder length hair had been shorn down to what we used to call a brush cut. It was ginger colored with a few flecks of grey.

Iris introduced us and Brent shook my hand. His handshake could have been painful, but he didn't need to prove how strong he was by crushing my fingers.

He said, "I'll be sure to send Ms. Johansen my thanks for sending you here, Mr. King. You're a pretty big celebrity in these parts, and I'm honored you found the time to help out."

I'm aware that television personalities are not like they come across on screen, but this man must be the

Cumberbatch of reality show performers. I expected a rube built like Haystacks Calhoun with a demeanor to match. Brent Purdy seemed to be a gentle soul, not the aggressive rube who reveled in tearing down walls in the demo phase of construction. He was attired in his customary red plaid flannel shirt over rugged canvas jeans. He looked like a catalogue model for the Duluth Trading Company. I was surprised that Jaime hadn't yet put an endorsement deal together.

"Call me Riley. Who's calling who a celebrity? I might be kind of well known around this area but your fame is national, Mr. Purdy."

"It's Brent. Boomer if you like, but I'm trying to ditch that nickname."

The wide Southern drawl *as heard on TV* was barely in evidence. No doubt, he exaggerated it for his viewership. If your show is called *Country Fixin's*, you'd better sound Dixie.

I called him on it but I heeded Walker's warning not to provoke the man into sitting on me. "You don't look or sound like you do on the show, Brent. I'm no stranger to show biz, but you're certainly not what I expected. I mean no offense by that."

"None taken, sir. I guess you were figuring on meeting the bruiser who was on the show last season. I've cleaned up my act some. Dropped fifty pounds, still working on it. Tidied up my look." He flicked his fingers toward his outsized head.

I said, "They show so many reruns on your network that I'm never sure what season is running. Not like when I grew up and shows ran September to June."

He found that amusing. His childhood postdated mine by a decade or two. "I'm forgetting my manners. Ms.

Walker, can I get you anything? Can I offer you a beer, Riley?"

Iris was uncomfortable around him and it showed. She said, "No thanks. Actually, I have a few calls to make. If it's all right, I'll step outside and take care of some business while you men get to know each other. That okay with you, King?"

"Sure. I have your number if we need you."

Walker left and I sat on the small sofa across from the makeup table. "I'd love a beer, Brent. Amstel, Ultra or Coors Light if you have it."

"Lites are all I drink these days. One Coors Light, coming up."

There was a tiny kitchen at the far end of the unit --- a bar sink, microwave and compact refrigerator. You could eat off the white quartz countertops. There was a futon that folded out of the way when not in use. Its flimsy cushion would be good only for naps or rushed conjugal visits. I wondered how instrumental in the design of these digs Purdy had been. This was one thing that matched the character he played on the show --- attention to efficient design. Some might see it as Spartan.

He handed me a bottle and we clinked the necks. "To your health," he said.

"And yours. Let's get down to business. Tell me about Cami's disappearance. I must say you seem to be handling it pretty well."

"Not bragging but I s'pose that shows I'm a better actor than I get credit for. Fact is, I'm broken up inside. I don't know if you know, but I played some football in college and one thing I took out of it was learning how to compartmentalize. Be a pro and focus on my work. Keep the personal stuff to my own time. I'm just coming off a shoot. A few more of these and you'll see how I really feel."

He held up his bottle and took a long swallow.

"Let's save the serious drinking for another time. Tell me what happened. Can you think of any reason Cami might have gone off on her own?"

"No reason and a hundred reasons, Riley. I don't know what Ms. Johansen told you but Cam and I have been living apart for a while now. That's kind of worked into our shooting schedule. We do a lot of scenes separately and only a few together. They try to schedule those all the same day. We only interact maybe once a week. They edit it all together to make it seem like we're always in the same place at the same time."

Unlike many former football players, Purdy's college education showed in the way he spoke. I was expecting down home expressions, cornball jock clichés and dropped consonants, but he was articulate, with a vocabulary that rivaled George Will's. Well, not really.

I said, "I'm afraid I'm going to have to pry into your personal life if I'm going to do my job. Tell me about the break up. I'm told you were only married a few months when you split."

"That's true. I'll be honest and lay it all out for you. Whatever it takes, I'll do anything to help find Cam. I take the blame for us not being together."

"How so?"

"Cam's a free spirit, a loosey-goosey lady. That's what drew me to her at first. She isn't one for schedules or structure. No plans, very spontaneous. Me, I like order. My football discipline. I like to be on time, meaning a few minutes early. Everything needs to be laid out logically. Jobsite picked up and tidy. The ironic thing is, my appearance was the last thing I paid attention to. I made sure everything around me was orderly, but I let myself go."

He took another swig of beer, draining the bottle. He got up and deposited the empty into a designated recycle bin. That very act underscored his words.

He said, "I always heard opposites attract. But Cam's habits were getting to me. The house was a mess if I didn't pick up after her, which I was always doing. I got on her about it and she just ignored me. I admit I blew my top about it more than once. She was making us late for calls."

"That had to offend your sense of discipline."

"Damn straight. Finally, we started going to the set in separate cars. She'd always trail me by a goodly amount of time, like she was Marilyn Monroe or something."

"Wasn't there a honeymoon period where things were good?"

"Not once we got married and moved in together. I'm sure you noticed that Cam is gorgeous and she's really sexy. Big old slob like me never had a girl like that fawn all over me."

"Even as a football player? Big man on campus?"

"That's for the skill position dudes. I was an offensive lineman. Right tackle. Fat, clumsy guy. All the hot chicks went for the quarterbacks."

"Did Cami and you hit it off right away?"

"Not right away. A few months into the first season's shoot. Ratings were good and the show got picked up for another season. Funny, it's kinda like football that way. When you're winning, everything feels better. You have more fun in the locker room. You spend more time out with your teammates. It was like that on the set. Everybody got along great. Joking around with the crew. Silly pranks.

Birthday cakes. Little unexpected kindnesses. That's when Cam started to appreciate me more."

Once Cami got the notion that it was going to be a hit show with legs rather than just a short acting gig, she started to plot out how she could get a bigger slice of the pie. I'd read between the lines talking to Iris that Cami wasn't satisfied being second banana. Rather than advance that theory, I waited to see if Brent was aware of it.

He went on. "Well, one thing led to another and we started dating, if that's the right word. You need to know something about me. I'm a good Christian. I know I might come off like some fun loving bumpkin, but I'm a man of faith. I wanted to save myself for marriage. Cam seemed to respect that, even though we were sorely tempted. She was willing, but I wanted to wait and we did."

I had heard that such animals existed in nature but had never come face to face with one. The willpower to resist the charms Cami possessed requires powers far beyond those of mortal men.

Purdy was blushing. "I hope you don't think I'm a natural born fool, Riley. I *have* changed my position on that lately."

"By that, do you mean that since you've been separated, there've been other women you've been intimate with?"

"I confess to being weak, yes. But make no mistake. I love my wife more than life itself. I'll do anything to get her back. Anything."

7

I couldn't help but empathize with Purdy. I'd lost Jaime under different circumstances but the effect was the same. I was willing to disrupt my entire existence to win her back. I know what desperation can do to an otherwise rational man. Although we're from different generations, I have a lot in common with Brent Purdy.

After the first few minutes when he seemed unaffected by his wife's disappearance, his voice broke as he spoke about her. From the little I knew of Cami, she seemed unworthy of his devotion. But if Brent believed that she was the key to his happiness, I wasn't going to be the one to dissuade him.

I said, "This is a hard question to ask, but I have to go there. Since the breakup, has Cami been seeing other men?"

Purdy examined the back of his rough hewn hand. "I hear rumors, but that's all. I've asked her about it when we seem to be getting along a little better, but she shuts me down, says it's none of my business. So after a while, I stopped asking. Truth be told, I suspect she hasn't been lacking for male company."

"That must hurt."

"It does. We've been apart for almost a year now, but she hasn't filed for divorce. That gives me hope that she'll come around someday."

You poor lovesick fool. If they divorced now, she'd be entitled to half of the assets accumulated during their marriage. With the show riding a wave of popularity and the possibility of more ancillary revenue from endorsements, side projects and syndication, she'd be limiting her share by ending their legal union prematurely.

It wasn't my job to explain this if he didn't already know it. That would fall to Jaime, and I would bring it up the next time we spoke. The smartest thing for him would be to sue for divorce on the grounds of abandonment to end their financial ties as soon as possible. If by some miracle they did reconcile later, they could always remarry.

I said, "Another awkward question. Is there a prenuptial agreement?"

"No, sir. That's self fulfilling, if you ask me. Talking about the finish before the beginning means you're planning on an end date and negotiating the terms in advance. Cam brought it up, but no way was I doing that."

She had broached the subject, probably knowing full well he'd reject it out of hand. That's who he is. Pretty crafty maneuver if she was planning several moves ahead. She could testify that she had offered to settle for less than half but that he had insisted on her receiving a full share.

Jaime would have her work cut out if she wanted to push him toward filing for divorce immediately. I said, "All right, think hard about this. If there isn't some innocent explanation for her disappearance, can you think of anyone who'd benefit?"

"You think the cops didn't ask me that? I'll tell you what I told them. Someone like Cam is bound to have a lot of folks gunning for her."

"Anybody particular in mind?"

"Other than me, you mean? I know I'm the main suspect if anything happens to her."

"Welcome to law enforcement 101. You're the obvious choice. And honestly, I have to entertain that possibility. But Jaime doesn't think you're built that way and she's a good judge of character. So let me pose another possibility. Cami initially got the job on her looks, and there's lots of good looking ladies out there. Could some actress figure that with Cam out of the way, she might be the new queen?"

"Sure. But I don't like to accuse anyone."

"You're not accusing anyone, Brent. You're just giving me a thread to pull on. If there's nothing there, there's nothing there."

He rumbled over to the fridge for another beer. He grabbed two and handed the other to me. I didn't open it. He took a long pull and said, "I didn't say this to the cops. I don't want to get the lady in trouble if there's nothing there. Things are already a little tense with her. Can I trust you to keep this quiet?"

"Discretion is my middle name."

"'Cause I have to work with this person and if she gets wind I said something, it'd get uncomfortable."

"Tell me who it is. It'll be worth the trouble if it means finding Cami. I'll try to be *delicate*."

That is not a term most people associate with me.

"Okay. Since we split, a lot of scenes I have with Cam are shot with a stand-in. Still getting used to this Hollywood lingo. There's a girl that's built like Cam and looks like she could be her sister. So when they do some scenes of us together, they shoot her a little out of focus or from the back or side. Cam is only in shots where close-ups are involved. They make it look like we're together but most often, we're not."

Anyone privy to the set could make a few bucks by telling a reporter that the public often isn't seeing the real Cami Purdy, but a stand in. Or maybe the public is wise to the fact that much of what they see on these shows is fake anyway and wouldn't care.

I said, "So you think this girl might want to take Cami's place enough to act on it?"

"Again, you gotta keep this quiet. I've been sleeping with her. I ain't proud of the fact I'm doing that while I'm still married, but I was missing Cam so much. Funny thing is, she's the real deal. She's for real what Cami plays on the show. She's a builder. She's from down here in the Lowcountry. And she and I see most things the same."

"Makes me wonder where she was when they originally cast the show."

"She said more than once that we should drop the façade and she should take over for Cam full time. I just sloughed it off but she kept at it."

"Sounds like motive to me."

Brent looked me straight in the eye. "I love my wife and there's no way I'd give her up for an imitation, no matter how compatible we are. It's already caused some tension between this girl and me. I'm thinking I might have to get her fired."

Again his naiveté was showing, along with my erroneous assumptions. An actress on a hit network show had settled for almost ten million dollars in damages because her role had been terminated. She claimed that the show's star made her feel uncomfortable with his constant sexual innuendoes and that he had engineered her demise. Even though *Country Fixin's* had no such resources, this stunt double's case would seem even more valid.

"I'd advise you talk to Jaime before bringing that up."

"Well, I told her that we had to cool it last week. I didn't want her to think there was anything there long term for her. You see where I'm going?"

A blind man could see that. I had a daunting job ahead of me. I recall a famous mystery writer opining that 'the next time a private investigator solves a case the police can't, it'll be the first.' Regardless, Jaime brought me aboard to get to the bottom of this before the news broke.

I couldn't figure out why she was so afraid of the news breaking. A sex scandal and murder mystery would only help ratings, if Brent wasn't involved in his wife's demise. There must be another reason.

8

It was getting dark and I didn't look forward to the drive home from Judy's Island. Even though the set was less than ten miles from my house as the shark swims, it was almost an hour's drive in rush hour. Without the navigation system on the MDX, I might disappear like Cami had. Creeks, rivers, inlets, the Port Royal Sound and the Atlantic Ocean separate the two locations. Water, water everywhere. That's why they call it the Lowcountry.

Alison Reiger, the actress Purdy had pointed me toward, had not been on call that day. The day's action had already broken down and most of the crew had gone to dinner. Afterwards, they'd be off to a motel or wherever they were staying during the filming.

I had picked up some superficial impressions. Brent had emitted no false notes and he seemed likeable, but he was an actor and I couldn't trust my initial impressions without putting them to the test. Iris warned me he had a temper and I needed to see that firsthand.

It wouldn't pay to press him much further now. He would be available to me anytime, he promised. I wanted to explore other avenues before coming back to him. I needed to get an overview of the whole dynamic so I could ask more pertinent questions.

He apologized for not inviting me to join him for dinner, but he'd made plans with a friend he'd met while playing football in Texas. The man was just in for a short time and Brent didn't feel comfortable sharing the limited time he had to spend with him. That worked out fine for me. I was hungry and tired and looking to get home.

His pal was due any minute. I told Purdy that I'd be back in the morning after checking with the local cops to see where they stood. We exchanged contact information and left the trailer. I looked around for Iris Walker, but she was nowhere in sight.

Purdy's friend was just pulling up in a sturdy Ford F-150 pickup, the suspension jacked. Its belly was covered with sand, suggesting it had been driven off-road, likely on a beach.

Purdy said, "That's my ride. I leant it to my bud so he could tool around to check out the area while I'm working. Hey, I'll introduce you quick and then we'll be on our way."

A weathered cowboy, sporting a week's worth of gray grizzle, stepped out of the truck. He was wearing a stained white Stetson pulled low over his eyes, an indigo Western dude shirt with pearlescent pocket buttons. Standard issue jeans, worn at both knees. Expensive looking snakeskin boots completed the look.

Purdy smiled. "Glad you found your way back here. I was getting a little worried. Roads around here are tricky at dusk."

His friend smiled. Underneath the scruff, he was quite handsome and seemed vaguely familiar. Although he appeared to be in his seventies, his luminous white teeth were perfect and all his own. I noticed a Rolex Submariner on his left wrist. This cowpoke had some cattle.

"It's got nothing on Cass County. At least these roads are mostly paved," his friend said.

"Don, I'd like you to meet Riley King. He's a private detective. My agent sent him out to help us find Cam."

"Evenin'. Pleasure. Any luck?"

This guy would make Clint Eastwood seem verbose. I said, "I've just started. Do you know Cami?"

"Never had the pleasure."

Purdy said, "Don and I have pretty busy schedules. I was hoping he could meet her this time around but obviously things didn't work out. Riley, please call me anytime, day or night if you find out anything. Even if I don't answer right away, I'll get back to you in a New York minute."

He grinned at his friend, who was not paying attention. "We'll probably be hanging at a bar somewhere after dinner."

"Sure. I doubt I'll have anything tonight so enjoy your night. Nice to meet you, Don. Take care of our boy."

"More likely he'll be taking care of me."

He tipped his Stetson and ambled over to the passenger's side of the pickup truck. Purdy nodded good night, revved up the engine and pulled away. As I turned to make my way to the MDX, I bumped into a kid who I assumed was some sort of stagehand.

"Sorry, mate," I said, as we untangled ourselves. The kid had been carrying a coil of thick electrical cord and almost dropped it when we collided.

"My bad," he said. "I wasn't paying attention. Got distracted seeing a big star like that."

"I'd think you'd get used to seeing Brent Purdy around. Are you new here?"

"No, not him. His friend."

"The cowboy? He looked sorta familiar, but I couldn't place him. What is he, some kind of old movie star?"

The kid laughed at my lack of knowledge. "Movie star? Nah. There was quite a buzz 'round here when he showed up couple days back. Seems like a man your age would've recognized him."

He started to walk away, hoisting the cable up over his shoulder.

"Hey, kid. Don't leave me hanging. Who is he?"

He turned around and smirked. "Ever hear of the Eagles? That was Don Henley."

9

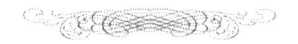

"This is turning into a thing for you, 5-0" Moses Ginn said. "Thought you liked them Eagles. Though the only Eagles I'm into play football in Philly. If Marvin Gaye showed up somewhere I was, I'd damn sure know it."

"He's been dead for close to fifty years."

"I know that. So's the Eagles. Their heyday was in the seventies."

Ginn and I were relaxing, well into our cups, baseball game playing on the big screen.

I said, "Henley's done some nice solo stuff since then. Shame about Glen Frey, though. Those two were great together."

"Yeah well, I had to tell you that the guy you were talking to at the Boathouse a ways back was Springsteen. You just thought he was some biker. And Van Morrison cruised past you a few months back and you didn't bat an eye."

"It's all context, man. You don't expect to see Don Henley on a TV set on Judy's Island. He was wearing an old cowboy hat and Ray-Bans and he wasn't exactly humming *Boys of Summer*."

"Too bad. I guess running into this Henley dude woulda been the highlight of your day if you knew who it was. Grizzly didn't do it for ya?"

"He's not so grizzly anymore." I gave Ginn my read on the *Country Fixin's* scene.

"Sounds like wasted time. Kinda strange, one day you light out to find your private mountain to get away from the weirdoes you used to dealing with. Then one phone call and you wind up working with a mean-ass dyke and a fat old hillbilly."

He sipped his Scotch and smacked his lips. "Call me in when you find that hot blonde chick. Even if she's dead, I'd find her company more satisfying than what you dealing with."

"The glamorous life of a private investigator," I said. "Can't all be seductive blondes with legs up to their neck."

"Or around yours."

"God, Tomey's out one night on police business and that's all you think about."

Mercifully, my cell buzzed. Jaime.

"I'll take this in the other room."

Ginn threw his arms up in the air, the classic touchdown signal as I walked away to talk to someone sober.

"Hey, Jaime."

"Hey. So I heard you talked to Brent."

"I take it Iris reported in. She's a pistol, that one." I let that simmer to gauge how Jaime reacted.

"I know she comes off a little raw, but she's got the makings of a fine agent. She's a hard worker. She said nice things about you."

"Really. Could've fooled me. Let's talk about Purdy. Were you aware he's slimmed down and cleaned up? He looks nothing like he does on the show."

"Iris told me. If he turns into a hunk, it changes the dynamic of the show. Maybe attracts more female demos."

"A hunk with a broken heart. He did this transformation for Cami. To win her back. Sounds hopeless, though. Staying hitched is going to cost him a lot of money if the show keeps getting more popular. Have you told him that?"

Jaime coughed and I heard her take a sip of something. She rarely drank alcohol --- in all our time together, I never saw her soused. Dealing with the likes of me, that was no small accomplishment.

She said, "I put him together with a financial consultant who told Brent exactly that. He fired him on the spot. So don't go there with him."

"That's not my job description. Sounds like Cami has been playing this guy from the start. The reason she married him was to get a bigger chunk of the action."

Another drink of water. "She was deathly afraid of him, you know."

"Iris told me that. Why didn't *you* tell me that from the start? You made him out to be this big old loveable Teddy Bear."

"Riley, she called me one night in tears, afraid he was going to hurt her."

"I don't get it. It's not like you to stick up for a man who abuses a woman."

I had carried the Scotch I was drinking with Moses into the bedroom. Bosco choose to stay with the man who prepares special meals for him, as opposed to his owner, who takes him on joyrides to nowhere and then leaves him alone.

"King, give me some credit. Before I sent Iris out there, I had another spy on the set. The A.D. is an old friend and I stay in touch with him to keep my finger on the pulse of the show. I called him right after she called to make sure she was okay. He told me she was, because he was looking at her. She was at the same bar he was, flirting with some cop."

"And where was Brent?"

"Home sleeping, I found out later. Cami might have made the whole thing up. She told me not to call the cops or anything."

"So is it possible Brent threatened her in an alcoholic rage and she slipped out after he passed out?"

"My director friend said she'd gone straight to the bar after work, never went home between. Brent was off that day, out fishing with a pal."

"Did you ever ask *him* about it? Given he's such a major client, you didn't think to look into this earlier? So are you thinking that Cami's disappearance could be some kind of scam on her part?"

"I want the truth, whatever it is. If there's a chance that something's happened to her and the husband is the first person they blame, you need to go down that road."

"When Cami told you she was scared, why did she call *you*? You've been on Brent's side all along. Why call you?"

"I was the one who cast Cami. She had some baggage and I knew that --- drugs, shady connections and such. But it looked like she'd finally gotten her life together. I thought she deserved a second chance."

"My oh my, you sure know how to arrange things." There it was again. Henley on the brain.

It still didn't make sense. I said, "Why Cami? I mean, it was nice of you, but pretty risky, no? There must be a lot of actresses who wouldn't have brought any negative history to the show. And how did you know all this?"

"Because she's my sister."

10

I had to stop a moment to contain my temper. This was a vital piece of information she had withheld. I felt betrayed all over again. Could I ever trust this new version of Jaime?

When I had calmed down enough to speak, I said, "Jaime, you and I lived together, almost got married, and you never told me you had a sister. Now, you ask me to help Brent Purdy, without mentioning that he's your brother-in-law, married to your sister with a checkered past? What the hell were you thinking?"

"Brent doesn't know Cami and I are related. Neither does Iris. Nobody knows. It has to stay that way."

If this were anyone other than Jaime, I would have quit then and there. When a client tells you a lie of omission of that magnitude, you can't believe anything they say. Fictional detectives get strung along like this all the time; real ones cover their butts. Unless they're in love with their clients. Then they walk on dangerous ground, which is where I was now.

Jaime lived on the other side of the country. Geographically, it would be easy to shut her out of my life. Emotionally, in spite of everything, I wasn't ready to tell her to go to hell.

I was wading into murky waters hiding unknown perils. "Quite clearly you didn't trust me enough to keep your secret. I'm going to need a really strong reason to stay involved with this." I almost added, 'or you for that matter', but I didn't.

"How many times have you met my dad?"

"I suppose this is leading somewhere. Okay, probably a half dozen times. Why?"

"Cami's my *half* sister. You know my mom and dad were never married. They were together a few years and I'm the product of that."

This wasn't news. I'd been hired by Paige White, Jaime's mother, to find a missing author. That's how I met Jaime. Uber-agent Paige got Peterson his first book deal and even though he eventually dumped her as a lover, she remained his literary rep until her death. Jaime took over the agency and continued to work with her father, taking his career to new heights.

I said. "So you're telling me Cami's the result of one of his peccadilloes."

"Of which there were many. My dad's never been married. I think at heart, he doesn't trust or even like women. He always believed that any woman who wanted him was only after his money. So he flitted around indiscriminately. I have no idea how many abortions he paid for or how much hush money he's doled out. That's one reason he's still writing crappy novels when he's pushing eighty."

"You told me he doesn't even write them anymore. He has ghost writers do the work and he just polishes them up."

"Right. There's probably a half a dozen Camis I'm related to. It's not something I advertise. Cami's the only one who's revealed herself to me. So far."

"That's no reason to keep that from me."

"You're right. I'm sorry. I'm ashamed for my dad and I was ashamed of her. Cami's what they used to call a bad seed. She's done things that make your friend Charlene Jones look like Mother Theresa."

Jaime hates Charlene, whom she once saw as the main rival for my affection. The fact she could bring her name up so casually was telling.

I said, "So again, why did you trust her with this big show? Did she blackmail you into it?"

"I told you, I thought she'd changed and deserved a second chance. You see, dad wasn't very discriminating when it came to women's character, just their looks. Cami's mother was beautiful but she was a lowlife. Cami grew up under bad circumstances. To his credit, dad paid child support, even though he could have weaseled out of it. Her mom OD'd when Cami was eighteen. Dad kept the money coming until Cami turned twenty one, in exchange for an NDA. He was old fashioned enough to think it actually mattered."

"So Cami didn't have a happy twenty first birthday."

"True. Like her mom, she hooked up with some rich men, most of them in show business. Weinstein wasn't the only one with a casting couch --- despicable, but it got her some minor parts in a few movies and TV series. I think she even did some soft porn. When I started to do well, I guess she got wind of the fact that I was John Peterson's daughter, too. She showed up on my doorstep one day, told me her story and hit me up for some cash."

"So, blackmail? Protecting your father's image? Really?"

"No. As much as I don't like to see it out there, my dad's like Picasso. Everyone knows he's a cad but as long as his books sell and his movies have big grosses, he's bulletproof. She made it out to be sister to sister, no threats."

"So you gave her money?"

"No. I got her a job. I told her that if she was serious about turning her life around, she needed to prove it. I got her work on a production crew. She needed to show up every day and stay out of trouble, and if she did, I'd get her something better, something on camera."

"And that was *Country Fixin's*. Still seems like you were sticking your neck out pretty far."

"Not really. You have no idea how many pilots are shot and pitched versus ones that actually get made. I liked Brent and thought the show had potential, but I never expected it to turn into the hit that it is. I mean, the two of them were on the cover of *US* magazine after the first season."

"So no one knows about you and Cami. Why hide it now? Might even juice the ratings, no?"

"I made Cami swear not to tell anyone about my dad. Not because of his reputation but now that he's dying, can you imagine all the women who'll come out of the woodwork asking for a piece of his estate?"

"Didn't he have them sign NDAs?"

"Dad was very sloppy when it came to business before I took over his affairs. He never followed through on all of them."

"And you're afraid if real crime reporters or the cops start to investigate Cami's disappearance, they'll find out about your dad. And after he's gone, you'll be up to your neck in lawsuits."

"Yes. And I guess I still didn't trust her to keep it quiet. That's your fault."

"Me? I knew nothing about her until yesterday and now I'm finding out I knew *next* to nothing then."

"You always told me that bad actors almost never change. They revert to the mean when the going gets tough. I was worried that could happen to Cami. I suppose it's like an addiction, being drawn to the dark side. One day at a time. The next day might be the last day clean."

"If I didn't know you better, I'd say you're the main one with motive to kill Cami. Can't blame you for not trusting her. If she did marry Brent to up her stake in the show, it seems she hasn't changed much at all."

"Of course that was the first thing I thought when they announced they were getting married. I asked Cami and she denied it. Now she says she did love him at first, but when she saw the real Brent Purdy, it wasn't pretty. Said that Brent isn't what he appears to be. Kept insisting she was scared of him."

"So far, he's been a perfect gentleman around me. Says he loves her and'll do anything to get her back. Swore he'd tell me everything even if it makes him look bad. He seems genuine on first impression. Even introduced me to Don Henley."

"I bet that made your day."

I didn't tell her that I didn't recognize one of my music heroes. Didn't even try to shake his hand. "Yeah, it was cool."

She said, "With Brent and Cami, it's hard to know who to believe. That's why I keep a spy on the set. My A.D. friend is a man named Ron McLeish. After her call, I told him to keep a closer eye on them and keep me in the loop. They were civil to each other, totally professional at work. Nothing scary or violent when they weren't on camera. But right after that call, she told the showrunner that she wasn't comfortable around Brent. That's when I okayed setting up the stand-in and kept their scenes together to a minimum. It seemed to be working."

"I'll need to talk to this McLeish fellow."

"Does that mean you're still on the case?"

"It does. But don't do this again. Tell me everything you know that's even on the periphery of this. And trust me. You know I'll always take care of you."

"After what I did, I wouldn't blame you if you told me to drop dead. Before Rick died, I wanted to talk to you and explain but you wouldn't take my calls or emails or texts. I know I hurt you bad so I understood why. But it really hurt me too."

"Jaime, right now, you have a missing sister. That's the priority. Let's focus on that and we'll deal with our stuff later."

I could hardly believe my own words. Putting a shady reality show star's wellbeing ahead of our own lives. Business before pleasure. Maybe that's been my problem all along.

II

What the hell is a showrunner? When Jaime and I lived together, I tried to educate myself in her industry but most of what she talked about sounded like Russian. I figured if I knew a few buzzwords, I could at least be a good listener. I could cluck knowingly at the travails showbiz put her through. Most of the time, she was venting and just needed a sympathetic ear, not folksy advice from a well intentioned boyfriend.

A lawyer friend of mine from New Jersey knows nothing about sports. He can't fathom how they play football and baseball at the same time of year, *don't these things have seasons?* He asks me to provide him with a few stock phrases so that when he is hanging with his peers, he can sound knowledgeable enough to fit in with their little boys' club.

I told him to shake his head slowly and mutter, "How 'bout those Mets?". That would cover him most of the year, including the off season when they blundered in free agency. The rest of the time, he could insert Knicks or Jets for the word Mets and be credible.

Like his lack of interest in sports, the television business has no significance to me. The stars I had met through Jaime were so transparent. They quickly evaluated what you could do to advance their career. If you couldn't, they moved on.

Appearances were everything. Check that. Power was everything. You could be uglier than a porch front gargoyle but if you could cast or finance a project, the world was yours.

Jaime recruited a friend of hers who had once run a production company to give me some background on how a reality show works. Winona Sands was semi-retired and living on Daufuskie Island, not far from Hilton Head but accessible only by boat. Jaime arranged for her friend to meet me for coffee at the ferry terminal near the base of the Fording Island Bridge.

The ferry got in at 8:30. We could talk for an hour or so, then I needed to head north for a meeting Alex Tomey had arranged with the detective handling Cami's case. Alex didn't know the man personally, but used her connections with the county force to hook me up.

Winona Sands is sixtyish, a onetime TV anchor who had decided early on she'd rather be a chief instead of a worker bee. Her blonde good looks had stereotyped her with the men who ran the business, even though her business degree from Northwestern should have signaled she had much more to offer. They were only interested in her other assets, but she had made it clear early on that she wasn't playing that game. As such, she was labeled a bitch who was hard to work with. When she formed her own production company, she had little use for the hacks who had tried to seduce her with empty promises.

She *was* a striking woman --- sparkling blue eyes and a flawless complexion. If I didn't know her résumé, I'd have guessed mid-forties. Her dark blonde hair was fashionably cut. She gave the impression of a lady who knew who she was and was comfortable with the choices she'd made. Jaime told me she was worth millions and still worked, but only on projects she deemed worthy of her time, which were few and far between these days.

She was wearing a yellow cotton polo and a short flowery skirt that displayed the tanned legs of an outdoor athlete. The type who played tennis three times a week. Stacked heels, not too high. Lots of expensive looking jewelry --- multiple bracelets adorning her right wrist, a diamond studded Piaget timepiece on her left. A heart shaped ruby on a gold chain encircled her long, elegant neck. No rings of any kind, which I found odd, given the rest of her frills.

"Winona?" I said, as she strolled down the gangplank.

"You must be Riley King." She smiled, revealing an anchorwoman's perfect teeth.

I had planned to take her to a franchise coffee shop just off Highway 278, but her attire made me reassess that decision. I knew of a small café in Old Town Bluffton that would suit her better. My MDX was near the gate and before I could open the passenger side door for her, she popped the handle and let herself in. My attempt at playing old school gentleman was rewarded by a glimpse of thigh that confirmed my evaluation of her fitness regimen. Whichever avenue she had chosen --- be it tennis, hiking, treadmill or beach running --- the results were appreciated.

We spent the ten minute ride exchanging fluff about the weather and Daufuskie Island, which I'd never visited. Properties there were undervalued, she thought, mainly because there was no causeway to the island and the ferry only ran four times a day. The islanders got around by golf cart and there was little artificial development to despoil the beauty of the barrier island. The problem was that beaches are eroding and if the climate scientists are right, the island would be annexed by the sea sometime in the next century.

After we were seated at the bistro and ordered our coffee, I got down to business.

"So, Winona, I suppose Jaime told you about the situation at *Country Fixin's*."

"She did, but I'm still plugged into the industry so I already knew about it. Jaime's been a good friend to me. Steered a lot of business my way when I was more active."

"I appreciate you taking the time to enlighten an idiot like me."

"Hah. Jaime tells me you're far from an idiot, Riley. I'm aware that you two were an item, but then she got involved with a friend of yours. I know he died recently but I'm glad you two are mature enough to still be friends and she can call on you for help."

"Yeah well, stuff happens. Are you married?"

"Divorced. My husband couldn't deal with the hours and demands of my company. Bad timing. Now I've scaled back my work, I'm too old and shriveled to attract much interest."

This was an obvious cue for a compliment and I obliged. "Yeah, I'd say you've dropped from a ten to a nine point nine. Terrible how that happens."

"When I was younger I hated how that 1-10 scale objectified women. Now I'm flattered by it. I used to despise the word cougar, but I guess that's what I've become. There's no equivalent term for guys, is there? Women my age come off as desperate, but men are admired for still being capable of playing the game."

I said, "We could spend hours talking about how the culture has evolved on that score. You're quite a pioneer,

Ms. Sands. As a woman in television, I bet you have lots of stories to tell."

"Jaime's been after me to write a memoir. I've actually started it. I'm fifty pages in."

"Save me an autographed copy. Well, I have an appointment soon with a local cop and no doubt you have plans for the rest of the day."

She gave me the kind of look that made me want to rearrange my immediate schedule. She said, "Let's meet up for drinks sometime and trade stories."

"I'd really like that."

She smiled coyly. "For a minute I thought you were going to invite me up to show me your etchings."

"Adults used to say that when I was a kid. They thought it was clever but I never understood what it meant until this moment. I think I get it now."

Winona is older than I, but we are at the same stage of life. We only work when we want to, but we'll never completely retire. We both have a lot left in the tank. She was smart, attractive and as Jaime said, worth millions.

We could have talked on the phone, there was no need to meet in person. It made me wonder if Jaime was playing matchmaker, setting me up with someone more my speed. A computer dating service would pair me with the elegant Ms. Sands, a mere ferry ride away, more than the younger and more career driven Jaime in Malibu.

My practical side said I should at least explore the opportunity that now presented itself. Winona Sands could turn out to be an interesting diversion, at the very least.

Of course, I might be misreading the signs; it had been a while. Did I fit the bill for her and what was that bill exactly?

Whatever happened to meeting someone and letting things develop on their own? Why did I look at this as a spreadsheet, evaluating the pluses and minuses before committing? Was that part of growing older, or was I just a lost romantic who life had turned into a bitter old crank?

Our time was limited. I tabled my interest in getting better acquainted and got down to the reason for the meeting. "To be continued, Ms. Sands. In the meantime, let's talk television. Tell me everything you know. I'm sort of a fan of these home improvement shows but I know nothing about how they're made."

"Let me give you a little history. *This Old House* was the first show doing renovations. Started in the late seventies on WGBH in Boston and spread to all PBS stations. The station actually bought the house and rehabbed it with the intention of selling it. The profit would cover the construction costs and help underwrite the show. They spent the entire first season on one house, which was the honest way to do it. It can take six months to a year to complete a major renovation."

"It seems like *Country Fixin's* does a new one every week."

"Not really. This Purdy fellow comes off as an honest Joe. He reminds me of Norm Abram on TOH, who I admit I had a crush on growing up. Brent has integrity when it comes to his craft. He wanted to spend at least four episodes on each house; he compromised at three. As it is, he has six houses going at once."

"I have a custom builder friend named Derek Davis and he says that's not uncommon to have that many going."

"In the real world that's true, but this is different. Purdy subcontracts the houses to different builders. The shooting schedule is around ninety days to get them all done."

The waitress stopped by and asked if we needed a refill on the caffeine. We both did. Winona had ordered some kind of avocado toast. Coffee was enough for me.

I said, "Six houses in three months seems like a lot, even for TV. What happens if they aren't finished?"

"The subcontractors are given a rigid schedule and if they don't meet it, they can get fined. And very often, they fake it."

"How can they do that? The last episode usually has a happy homeowner moving in to a finished house."

"On television you only see what we choose to show. They stage the key rooms and ignore the rest. They fill with the homeowners taking their kids to the park with their dogs. They do beauty shots of the most scenic parts of the area instead of going through the actual house room by room."

I said, "I wondered why they do all that extraneous stuff. I watch those shows to see how they transform shacks into showplaces. I couldn't care less about their kids eating ice cream in the park. Those are the parts that I tune out on. Happy shining people with their mutts."

"You don't like dogs?"

"I love dogs. I have a Golden named Bosco who's my best friend in all the world. I spoil him every day."

"Good. Because if you hated dogs, this conversation would be over. I have two rescues and I work with local rescue operations trying to place as many as I can, using my old marketing chops."

Another box checked. She loves dogs.

I said, "Back to *Country Fixin's*. Could Brent carry the show on his own without Cami?"

"Cut to the chase, why don't you? You think Brent had something to do with Cami disappearing?"

"Jaime doesn't think he's capable. I met the man yesterday and I sort of like him but you can't eliminate anybody based on a quick snapshot. He doesn't seem the type to kill for money, but I couldn't rule out a crime of passion. He feels pretty strongly about her. Really wants her back. The old, *if I can't have you, nobody will*, motive."

"Full disclosure. One of the reasons Jaime hooked us up was that I helped put together their original submission reel. I got to know him a little and he seemed like a pussycat. I was coming off a divorce and I was vulnerable to a hunky ex football player. He could have taken advantage but he never showed the slightest inclination. He had eyes for Cami from the get-go. I just can't believe he'd be capable of hurting her or anyone else."

"You and Jaime would make great character witnesses for Brent. But let's talk the big other motive --- money. What's this show worth?"

She bit into a corner of her toast and turned up her nose. "Not the greatest avocado toast I've ever had. To your question --- I don't know. He has a piece of the action, maybe ten per cent. Let's say they have a ten million dollar budget per season. The production company gets ten off the top. His cut probably comes after expenses. And he gets a performance fee. I'd have to see his contract, but I'd be surprised if he nets much more than a million or two a season. The big money would come in syndication if the show goes to local TV stations in a group. There are product endorsements, cap or tee shirt sales. Some of these guys come out with a line of tools. He could have a nice income for a lot of years if Jaime made him a good deal, which is what she does."

"I've heard stories, when it comes to movies, about bogus expenses that production companies charge to make the investors' share nonexistent. Is it the same in television?"

"Depends on the production company. I can tell you that I ran a tight ship. But there are a lot of legitimate expenses. Editing studios charge by the hour. Publicity, marketing. Folks in this business like to travel first class --- they aren't staying in trailers."

"What about the crews?"

"Showrunner. Assistant directors who shoot at one site when the main crew is at another. Generally, we use one steadicam and two fixed or robotic cameras. PAs, that means production assistants. It's not like we're shooting Star Wars with lots of CGI, but credits and show opens cost money. Not much music, we use stock when we can. Sometimes we do need a little original stuff for interstitials."

"Who reviews the budget? I'm thinking about the old 'follow the money' approach."

"Jaime has financial people, CPAs who do audits, especially when her client gets a percentage. But like I said, standards are what they are. We can get local crews cheaper at times, but in the end the more expensive pros can save money, because if they know what they're doing they cut the editing time."

"How is that?"

"A good showrunner can almost edit in the camera, so to speak. Rehearse scenes so that the first takes are the ones they use, rather than make some poor editor sift through dozens to find ones suitable for air."

"Brent told me they have a stand in for Cami. Is that common?"

"No. From what I gathered talking to Jaime, it saves them time and money because Cam is so unreliable. She doesn't like to be around Brent. You can understand that, no? Working with your ex can be awkward."

I said, "Cami seemed to have a wild life before this job. You said you worked with them on the audition tape. Any thoughts about her?"

"I'm not into slut-shaming. But she was, shall I say, willing to do whatever it took to get the job. She seemed pretty cozy with the director we hired to do the filming. More so than Brent, to be honest. She didn't give me the time of day. I noticed that she treated the men on the set a lot different than the women."

"Do you know Iris Walker? The woman Jaime sent to check into this?"

"No comment."

"Come on Winona, this isn't for the papers. Just trying to get some background on the principals."

"All I'll say is, watch out for that one. You can't trust a word she says."

12

Winona and I parted and exchanged contact information. Ms. Sands sure knew a lot about me, much more than I did about her. When Jaime set up this meeting and said I should talk to Winona, I'd merely asked a couple of perfunctory questions about her background.

I wondered how much Jaime had told Winona about me. And why? Just idle chatter between friends or was something else at play? My unease with Jaime made me think she might be playing matchmaker. If she had determined that she and I had no future, she might be setting Winona up as a desirable alternative. *Just my imagination, running away with me.*

I headed to the abandoned quarry where Cami's car was found. Ridgeland is a sprawl of a town of about six thousand in Jasper County, further inland and higher in elevation than Charleston or Savannah. Downtown is comprised of a couple of blocks of squat brick buildings, housing some sleepy old stores and whatever government they consider necessary. Fast food chains and an unaffiliated gas station took care of the vitals. The surrounding area is true rural South --- lots of pine woods pocked by the occasional small farm.

Alex Tomey warned me that the detective on the case didn't like private investigators much and had only agreed to see me as a favor. I expected the marker would be called in short order.

Detective First Grade Martin "Marty" Montanez had light olive skin to go with his darker olive eyes. There was a hint of Creole about him in the way he spoke. The county website listed his bona fides --- he studied at John Jay in New York and had graduated with high honors. He was born and raised in nearby Okatie, which explained why a man with his education had picked such a backwoods beat. His degree and solve rate had already made him a rising star and if this case attracted national attention, his future would be ascendant.

When I arrived at the quarry, he was alone, standing next to a late model Chevrolet Impala, fiddling with his phone. Mid thirties, dressed in a tan suit, its cut displaying an extremely fit copper who spends time in the weight room. I had him by a couple of inches in height but I couldn't match the wide shoulders which tapered down to a 32 inch waist.

I made it a point to sound deferential, despite the age gap. "Detective. Thanks for agreeing to talk to me."

His voice was an unaccented clear tenor. "Alex Tomey thinks very highly of you. My boss respects her judgment; otherwise I wouldn't be meeting with a private dick."

"Again, I appreciate you putting your reservations aside. I'm only here to help."

He sniffed. "I'd be lying if I said that I hadn't heard about you. You're either a crackerjack investigator or you have a great press agent."

"Crackerjack investigator. That'll be on my next set of business cards. Maybe I'll include a free box of snacks with every inquiry."

That didn't invoke a chuckle, just a grunt, so I got right down to it. "The White Page Agency asked me to look into this. They put *Country Fixin's* together and they feel responsible if something bad happens to one of the stars."

"Their guilty conscience is their problem, not mine. I need to find this woman, dead or alive."

"Let's hope alive. What can you tell me about it?"

"Not much. We got our crime scene team here right after the kids called in the abandoned vehicle. If you look down into the quarry, it has some water in it, but it's only a couple feet deep."

We walked over to the jagged cliff. I said, "Enough to cover a body."

"Yep. But it's clear as a mountain stream. No body there or in the woods surrounding it for a half mile radius. We walked the grid."

"This place get much activity now that the quarry's closed?"

"Just kids making out. We did find some used condoms. At least somebody's teaching these kids to be smart about their little trysts."

"Any gators in that water?"

"Too brackish. They tend to avoid salt water although some have been spotted in the Sound lately. They're adapting."

"So it isn't like Louisiana where they dump a body in the swamp and the gators clean it up for them."

"Been known to occur in these parts but not too often. So far, we're not seeing any evidence that anything happened to her, at least in this spot."

The overgrown parking area in front of the quarry hole was a gravel mixture, laced with compacted stone dust to give it a harder surface. Regular traffic would have kept it free of weeds, but teenaged couplings were not enough to keep it groomed.

I said, "So no blood? No signs that someone was dragged? Any usable prints on the car?"

"Her's and her hubby's. We asked him about that. He says that he sometimes walks her to her car after the day's work and probably touched the handle or the glass."

"Plausible. He'd be smart enough to wipe it clean if he did do anything to her. He's fastidious that way."

"And before you ask, too many footprints to make sense of. Purdy wears a size thirteen. Nothing we got in the jumble here matched anything we found in his house or trailer."

"Who was the last person she had contact with?"

"Far as we could find out, she left the set Friday. No one on the crew had any real contact with her after the filming. A couple of them did say that Purdy walked with her to the car and they heard voices raised in anger."

"What'd he say to that?"

Montanez's phone buzzed. He looked down to see who it was and ignored it. "He said they were rehearsing. Going over some dialogue for next week's shooting. Apparently, they were supposed to have a disagreement about the backsplash and the producers encouraged it to get a little heated."

"And the showrunner backed that up?" I was proud to use my newly acquired word.

"Not exactly. She said that conflict makes for good television but she didn't tell them specifically to freak out over the tile."

"So where do you stand with Brent officially?"

"If you're asking if he's our prime suspect, I have to say that it's a continuing investigation and we're not allowed to release that information. Especially since you work for people who have a stake in the matter."

"Save the boilerplate. Just so you know, corny as it sounds, I'm out to find the truth. Despite what you may think about Hollywood, The White Page Agency wouldn't try to cover up a murder for the sake of ratings. The crime angle might actually boost the numbers. Just know that there's no way I'd be a party to it."

"So you say. Scuttlebutt is that you backed up Bobby Bailey, that crooked stockbroker. Blamed his dead wife for killing the old man that blew the whistle on them."

"Bailey's still in federal prison for his part in the fraud. And I *do* believe the wife did it. But I don't think my word influenced the prosecutor at all."

That got a wistful smile out of him. "Maybe, but you brought the FBI in. I'm surprised Alex still talks to you after you big-footed her on that one."

"The feds had resources she didn't. But Alex got her due credit and a promotion. It was a win/win."

He gave me his best tough cop stare and dropped the cooperative façade he'd shown earlier at Tomey's behest. "Word to the wise. Don't try any of that FBI shit with me. I'm on the case and I have more 'resources' than you do. You get in my way and I've got no qualms about nailing you for obstruction."

Not that long ago, I would have fired back at him. Now with the wisdom of the years behind me, I held back. There was no reason to get into a pissing contest. I tried honey instead.

"Well detective, you deserve a lot of credit for keeping this out of the news. A lot of cops would leak it to the press as soon as they got the call, thinking it might be their ticket to stardom."

"That ain't my style. The media only complicates things, bunch of whores. I work under the radar and I run a tight ship. But look who you're dealing with. Hollywood assholes. This'll be out real soon, no matter how hard I try to keep a lid on things. And don't go thinking you'll leak it out there to help your client's ratings."

"Not my style either. That's assuming I have a style."

He smirked and walked back to his car. hadn't given me much to work with. They hadn't turned up anything crucial and my suspicions were as good as his. Montanez had seen me as a courtesy. The courtesy ended when he drew a line in the sand and dared me to overstep.

I wouldn't. Not yet.

13

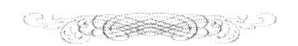

Chipper McKenna had told me that there is a North/South divide in Beaufort County, a mini-Civil War brewing. The lower half has Hilton Head, Bluffton and Hardeeville, and they make up most of the tax base. This more affluent portion subsidizes the Northern half. There is some grumbling amongst the politicians in the south about secession. They've outlined a makeshift plan to band together to form their own county. It might just be for show to gain leverage on taxes and expenditures, but given the state's history, I wouldn't rule it out.

As I drove from Ridgeland to Judy's Island, Chipper's evaluation came to life. There are very few areas in Bluffton and Hilton Head that I'd call seedy, and it would be a stretch to categorize them as such. But Judy's Island had quite a few spots I wouldn't want Jaime roaming alone at night.

I wondered why. The natural topography of the island seemed similar to Hilton Head. It was accessible by a series of causeways, unlike Daufuskie. Chipper boiled it down to one factor --- quaintness. Quaint used to be a term realtors used for 'old fashioned but charming'. The appliances may not be stainless steel, the cabinets might be knotty pine, but there was an authenticity of style to these old houses that was appealing to certain buyers.

Now quaint is code for *'outdated --- don't waste your time showing to anyone other than avid do-it-yourselfers'*. The houses from the seventies on Judy's are 'quaint' but for some reason, no one other than Purdy has shown the will or cash to modernize them.

Hilton Head could have been in the same predicament. There are plenty of outdated properties on my island, but they all sell quickly if they are priced right. Renovation contractors make a healthy living repairing and updating forty year old homes, or if the location is prime, the older shacks are bulldozed to make way for sparkling McMansions. The money people don't see the same potential on Judy's. Brent Purdy seems determined to change that.

I caught Brent between takes. As he took a big gulp of Gatorade, I asked him about the economics, based on my primer with Sands.

He said, "Excuse me Riley, but what's this have to do with Cam being gone? Ain't that why you're here?"

There was no annoyance in his tone, just curiosity. Were our positions reversed, I might have taken greater exception to an off topic question.

"Unless Cami is missing for some personal reason, the other reason would be that money is involved. I'm trying to educate myself on the economics of the show to see who might gain from her being missing."

He put a massive paw around my shoulder and pulled me nearer. "You sound more like a college professor than a private dick. You're talking about that person I told you about yesterday?"

"On a macro level, yes. But there's a lot more at stake here than a well paid acting gig. Millions of dollars flow through your show. I'm like you, I don't want to go throwing accusations around when I don't have any facts, but let's say one of your subcontractors is raking off something on the side and Cami found out about it."

The house that *Country Fixin's* was rehabbing today was right on the ocean. It had been purchased for a half million dollars and boasted twenty eight hundred square feet. It rose up on pilings, which provided an additional fourteen hundred sheltered square feet at ground level. That made for a massive garage/storage/workshop space that would be comfortable most of the year, enjoying ocean breezes in the summer and radiant warmth from the sea in the winter.

Brent wasn't buying into the financial motive, but he was on his best behavior, trying to answer my questions. "Hold on, Riley. Hey, Brenda. How long before you need me for the next shot?"

I couldn't make out the answer but upon hearing it, Brent yelled, "Okay. You want me, I'll be in my trailer. Just buzz and I'll be Johnny on the Spot. Come on, Riley."

"This is a nice spot, Brent. Why didn't someone buy this place when it first came on the market? Looks like it sat vacant a long time before you snapped it up for the show?"

"The drawback is hurricanes. Matthew had caused a storm surge of twelve feet. Anything under the house'd be wiped out. We had to jack it up and put in higher pilings. Most folks wouldn't want to take that on."

Winona had told me that they probably had a one hundred thousand dollar reno budget on this one, hoping to turn it around for a profit. As we walked over to his temporary digs, I said, "So Brent, do you live in the trailer while you're shooting? Or just drive it to the jobsite every day?"

"Not sure what that has to do with anything but no, I usually go home. I live about twenty minutes away. Most days I drive to where we're shooting and a PA brings this around. Sometimes if we work late or I've tied one on, I do sleep here. It's got all the comforts of home."

"I see. Did Cami ever stay here with you?"

"Nope, never. She ain't one for camping out. She insisted on going home every night when we were together."

"How long were you living under the same roof?"

"Less than a year. She's renting now. Has a driver on call."

"Did she leave with her driver the day she disappeared?"

"No, sir. She took off on her own. She really didn't use the kid all that much. Truth be told, it was Brenda's idea to have a PA to drive her back and forth sometimes. I told you, she could be kinda unreliable. When she was real late, they sent the kid to fetch her."

"I'd like to talk to him. Is he here today?"

"They got him doing other things, but he's around, sure. He's just a kid. Don't know what he could tell you."

For the first time, I sensed that Brent wasn't being open with me. Did Cami's driver know something he didn't want me to be aware of?

"Just routine. I'll catch up with him later. So, tell me about how it works. You have enough money on your own to buy up six houses at a time?"

"Oh good Lord, no. Nah, we do eighteen hours of shows. For six houses, that's three hours each. Don't take no math major to figure that out."

He was reverting to the homespun shtick that he uses on the show. When we first talked, there weren't no double negatives.

I said, "Is that common? Don't most shows run thirteen or twenty six weeks?"

"How they break 'em up ain't my concern. Back to your question, the show buys one house that we fix up and sell. The profits, if there are any, get divvied up for bonuses. The other five houses come from folks who already bought places and want us to fix 'em up."

"How does that work?"

"The producers put out feelers, saying that we're gonna be shooting in the area and anyone with a house that wants the *Country Fixin's* touch can apply. Then they check 'em out, make sure they have clear title and the money to do it up right. We only need five, but we usually get ten times that many wanting us."

"I'm not surprised there's that many people eager to get on TV. There's been some negative press about flipping shows lately but I haven't seen anything about how your show lied to them or ripped them off."

"And you never will. Look man, I hire good people and I check out all the work personally. We don't cut corners."

"So your clients have to be pretty well off to afford you."

"No, sir. We make sure at least two of them are affordable housing. See, we get materials at a discount, sometimes free. A trade deal, like me saying on the show, 'this here cement board's a real good siding choice for salt air.' We have a deal to use only Stanley tools on camera. They call it product placement. So they get better stuff than they can afford on their own. And the subs might even work cheaper than the usual going rate. Word gets around they're on the show, they make up for it."

"I see. So how much hands-on do you and Cami actually do?"

"Me? A lot. Not saying I do every job, start to finish, but I get my hands dirty. I might start the baseboard, they shoot that, then the crew finishes it. I pop in at the end to wrap it up and make sure it's done right."

"And Cami?"

"Well, she doesn't like to sweat. She's got no clue comes to budgets, either. Not saying Cam doesn't have some good ideas, but she ain't never been a builder. She doesn't know all the right names for things. Most times we need extra takes it's 'cause she uses the wrong word and looks like she don't know what she's doing."

"And her stand in? Does she know construction or is her main talent that she looks like Cami?"

"Her main talent?" He snickered. "I'm a gentleman about those things so I can't say. But she comes from a builder family. Knows her stuff. Whenever Cam flubs a line, I see her rolling her eyes. If we get together later, I never hear the end of it. 'Cam did this, Cam messed up that'."

"Is she on the set today?"

"I think I saw her on the call sheet for four o'clock. Couple of quick pickups is all."

His phone buzzed. "They need me back on the job. Hope next time we talk, you got some news about Cam, King. I gotta say I'm not seeing much progress."

He gave me a malevolent glare and left the trailer. King, eh? What happened to Riley?

14

The showrunner was a large woman named Brenda Lowrie. Not large tall, but wide. She didn't attempt to hide her girth, in fact, she didn't try to hide anything. She was wearing a short nylon dress, the pattern bedecked with multicolored balloons. It was cut to reveal a great deal of the world's largest bosom.

She was what hippie types used to call an *earth mother*. I don't know the current term for that or even if there is one. Showrunner?

Her hair was a tangle of short, hennaed ringlets. I got a sense of ruthless efficiency from her, one who does not suffer fools who question her dictates. She was used to laying out the final word, no guff.

When Iris Walker introduced us, Lowrie gave me a grudging smile and strong handshake. Her hand felt rough and calloused. "I'll give you five minutes Mr. King, while we set up the next shot. I'm sure that'll be more than adequate."

I'd have to stifle my natural inclination toward witty quips and stick to business with this woman. "I'd think that missing one of your star players would warrant a little more time than that."

"4:40 and counting. Ask me anything but don't waste my time. I've already spoken to the police."

"They don't seem to think that Cami being missing is a big deal. They're treating it like a publicity stunt." I was lying about their attitude to get a rise out of her. "What do you think?"

"I think they're full of shit. I'm not saying we're above grabbing all the ink we can get but they don't understand the industry if they think that. The new season doesn't start airing for months."

"You worked with her the day she vanished. Anything seem off to you?"

"More than normal with that little twat? Nope. She showed up late, like always. When we need her at ten, we tell her the call is eight. That way we have a reasonable chance she'll drift in by eleven."

"How do you tolerate that? Doesn't that throw your whole schedule off?"

She inhaled harshly and spat an enormous greenish wad onto the concrete. She was perspiring heavily and her deodorant had long since quit the case. "Allergies. Damn pollen season. Okay. Cam's a pain in the ass. She thinks she's some fucking diva when she's just a hot little bitch with a thimbleful of talent. I constantly have to work around her."

"Don't you have the power to fire her?"

"I wish. That's part of the problem and she knows it. Long as Brent and the producers dote on her, she gets away with murder. If someone really did knock her off, it'd actually be a blessing."

"Tell me how you *really* feel. Other than yourself, is there anyone you can think of who'd want her gone?"

"How about the whole crew? Well, maybe not the kid we have driving her around. They seem to get along. She treats him like shit but he doesn't seem to mind. Wouldn't be surprised if an occasional blowjob makes up for it."

"You really think there's something going on with them? Wouldn't Brent freak out if he knew?"

"You're down to two minutes, King. Brent is the polar opposite of Cam. Sweet as pie. Nothing he wouldn't do for you. Easily the nicest, most accommodating man I've ever worked with. He sees only the good in people. That's my biggest concern about the bitch being gone --- that it'll affect him."

"Have you seen any of that so far? She's been missing for almost a week now."

"He's a pro. Between takes, I see his face and he's not happy. But once we're rolling, you'd never know."

"Has she ever gone AWOL before?"

"Oh yeah. But only for a day or two. That's why we didn't think much of it until they found the car with her not in it. That's what we get for hiring a damn cokie."

I feigned shock. "Cami does cocaine?"

"Look King, I've worked in this industry a long time and I've seen it all. Have I caught her doing it on the set? No, but all the signs are there. Are you as dumb as you look and I have to spell it out for you?"

"No, ma'am. You have any idea who her supplier is?"

"I do not. It's not like the eighties, when everyone was high. We used to have a dealer on the payroll back then, like an on-set pharmacist. Whatever you needed. Today we work clean, except for greenies when we need a boost."

"So where does she get it?"

"If you know users, it doesn't matter where they are, they find a source. And this hellhole of an island has no shortage of sleazebags."

You'd think since Lowrie knew about Brent and Jaime's support of Cami she might temper her language, although I doubt she'd be more circumspect. She wasn't broken up by her star's absence, and if she was the architect of it, she wasn't doing anything to deflect my suspicion. If anything, she was encouraging it.

"Can you think of anyone I should talk to? Someone who works more directly with her."

"Other than the PA, there's no one. She treats us all like pissants at her beck and call. Your time's up, pal. And King, I don't want you wasting anyone else's time. They all have a job of work to do and we're on a tight schedule. Have a nice day."

15

I realize that I can't charm the pants off all women, nor do I want to. Some are immune to my rugged good looks and sophisticated repartee. Their loss.

After the day's start, a flirtatious session with the lovely Winona Sands, the next two encounters with females were contentious.

After being dismissed by Brenda Lowrie as an annoyance, like the gnats and no-see-ums swarming around the Lowcountry set, Iris Walker was about to serve another plate of comeuppance. She'd been on the phone the whole time I was getting blown off by Lowrie, and I caught enough nasty looks out of the corner of my eye to expect another storm after the first one blew out to sea.

Walker punched my elbow hard and said, "Well Mr. Big Dick, you got your way."

I could have replied that I had no idea what she was talking about. But the look in her eye told me that I'd merely have to wait a beat for her to unfurl the rest.

She did. "Now you have *Country Fixin's* all to yourself. I hope you choke on it."

She stomped away. I followed. I don't like to lead with my jaw, but on the off chance she knew something that might clarify whatever the hell was going on, I went after her.

"Iris," I said, trying to keep pace. "I really don't know what you're talking about."

She strode on with a quick and heavy gait, then stopped and turned on me. I almost tripped over her, since she failed to engage her brake lights.

"King, maybe that wide eyed dumb act plays with the bimbos you're used to fooling around with, but I see through it."

"Iris, I thought we called a truce. What got you so upset?"

"Congratulations for not saying my panties are in a twist. I'm surprised that someone as smart as Jaime would get involved with a snake like you. No wonder she dumped your sorry ass for Rick Stone. I just talked to her. She told me to catch the next flight home. My services are no longer needed at this dumpster fire now that Mr. Big Dick is in charge. This shit storm is all yours now, just like you wanted it."

"Walker, that's news to me. Think whatever you want but I had nothing to do with that. The last time I talked to her your name didn't even come up."

"I don't believe you."

"Jaime asked me to look into this as a favor. She said you'd help me and I sure need help. I know next to nothing about television. There's absolutely no reason in the world I wouldn't want you around to guide me through it. None."

"Bull-shit! How long were you two together? In all that time, you didn't take *any* interest in her job? You learned nothing about what she does? You know actually, I *can* believe that. You're so shallow you can't deal with a woman smarter than you. Explains a lot about why she split. I'm surprised it took her so long."

"Good bye, Iris. Have a nice flight."

I walked away.

16

The 'kid's' name was Bob Walsh. I had to find him on my own, since Iris was no longer going to be of help. It turns out he was the lad who had mocked me for not recognizing Don Henley.

I say lad, but this was no teenager. Had to be mid twenties. Handsome in a scruffy sort of way. Light brown hair, almost shaven on the sides with a longer, kinky mop up top. Never saw the appeal of that *Peaky Blinders* style.

"Excuse me Bob, my name is Riley King. I'm a private investigator looking into Cami's disappearance. I'm told you were her driver."

"So that's who you are. Detective, huh? The guy who couldn't spot Don Henley when he was right in front of him."

"Not fair. I wasn't expecting to see a rock star here. So you're Bob Walsh, eh? Sounds like Bob Welch, guitarist for Fleetwood Mac, before Buckingham-Nicks. *Hypnotized* was a great song. And Joe Walsh is with the Eagles. Henley's band. Six degrees of separation."

He winced at my dad joke. "So you know some classic rock. I bet you were one of the twenty million who bought *Rumors*. Impressive."

His body language said the opposite. Music snobs have contempt for Fleetwood Mac, but they are top ten with me. Call me a dullard. Call me Ishmael, but call me.

I said, "We can waste time talking music trivia, or I can ask you a few questions and get out of your hair."

My dig at his coif went unnoticed.

"Can't talk now, man. Working, can't ya see. Besides, if you're like most of the other assholes 'round here, you're out to make her the bad guy."

"Look, Bob, I've never even met Cami. I'm just trying to find her. I'm certainly not out to blame the victim."

"Cami wouldn't like being called a victim. She's a tough lady." He looked down at the dirt and kicked a stray pebble. "Whatever. You seem okay, just don't patronize me, man." He took a step closer and dropped his voice a few DB. "I can't talk here, dig? I get off at four and there's a pub 'bout a mile down the road. Might be able to meet you there for a few."

I wasn't sure if he meant a few pints, a few chicken wings or a few minutes but it was almost three thirty and an adult beverage or two wouldn't be the worst thing in the world. He gave me the name of the joint and I said I'd be there.

I figured he'd show, maybe because I was the only one willing to reserve judgment on Cami, a woman he seemed to like. I wondered how much.

The tavern he referred to was called the Jackson Creek Pub. From the outside, it looked iffy but a quick check of online reviews said that the food was edible and the bar served decent drinks. All I needed to know. I got there a few minutes early and sat outside on the patio, facing the water. Although it had become overcast, a faint breeze had kicked in and it was refreshing. The inlet looked more gray than blue, but the view was swell.

Walsh showed up a little past four and plopped down across from me. I said, "We can switch seats and you can take the view if you like."

"Pass. I'm cool."

"I ordered a Coors Light. What'll you have? I'll run up to the bar."

"No need, old man. Take a load off. I'll wait for the waitress. She's got nicer legs than you do."

Indeed, the female servers were attired in Hooters style costumes. Short, tight nylon briefs. Form fitting, thin white tees with a swordfish logo encircling the left breast.

Available in the gift shop for only $19.99.

On cue, my beer was delivered and Walsh said he'd have the same. I asked, "So what's your official title, Bob? I just started yesterday and I'm trying to figure out the pecking order."

"I'm at the bottom. What they call a production assistant. It's a glorified gopher on this show. If something falls through the cracks, they dial up Bob Walsh and he takes care of it. Take advantage of my local knowledge."

"So you're from around here?"

"Beaufort. Did a couple of years at USC in Bluffton. Thought a degree would help me get a better TV gig. I was wrong about that."

Even though the reviews said the service tended to be slow here, Walsh's beer arrived in record time. The girl pointed at my half filled bottle and I told her that I'd wait a bit before ordering another. She shrugged and walked away, her shapely young bottom barely covered by the tight shorts.

"So what do you want to do? Act? Direct?"

"Is this how you warm up your suspects? Act like you give a shit about their goals in life?"

"Damn, you are cynical for such a young dude. I don't see you as a suspect, why would I? Just making conversation while we enjoy our beer. But if you have to be somewhere else soon, I can get right down to it."

He gave me a palms-up gesture that I read as an apology. It could have meant 'go to hell'.

He played with a coaster. "So what do you want to know? King, is it?"

"Riley King. Just your take on Cami. Back at the set, seemed like everyone there hated her. You saw another side of her and I'm interested in what that is."

"Cami was *Little Miss Understood*. This was her first big gig in front of the camera and she wasn't real confident. She fucked up a lot and that's hard to do on a reality show."

"How so?"

"The whole deal works on chemistry, how she gets on with Brent. At first, she aced it. They got along great."

"So you've been working on the show since the start?"

"Nope. Started at the beginning of the second season, after they got hitched. Anyway, I picked up that their marriage wasn't going so well. Brent isn't like he comes off on the show. He's more Jekyll and Hyde."

I didn't think most kids his age would know old Robert Lewis Stevenson characters. I doubt they grew up with *Treasure Island*.

"Tell me about the Mr. Hyde side."

"Comes out when he drinks. He's a nasty drunk. Abusive. Constantly belittling Cami. Making fun of how she knows shit about construction. And not just privately, but in front of the whole crew sometimes."

"Ever get physical?"

"Not sure you need to know stuff about her private life."

"Bob, I need to know everything I can find out about the two of them and their relationship. When something like this happens, the husband is who they turn to first. It cuts both ways. Brent tells me how much he adores her and wants her back and how he'd do anything to make that happen."

"It won't. Not ever."

"Why? Because you think she's dead?"

"Didn't say that. God, I'd be blown away if that happened. Just that there's no way in hell she'd go back to that monster."

"So why hasn't she filed for divorce?"

"Some people running the show talked her out of it. I don't get all the legal stuff, but they told her to hold out as long as she could. Accumulated assets they said, whatever that means."

I said, "So when did you see her last?"

"Last Friday. She drove herself home. Didn't need me."

"Did she say anything about when she *would* need you?"

He hesitated. "Uh, no. She never did. See, Cami likes to drive herself. You probably saw her ride, the red Shelby Mustang. She didn't want a driver. The only times I chauffeur her around is when they send me to pick her up because she's late. That's been happening more and more. Part of what I have to do is convince her to put herself together and come in. Lots of times, she didn't want to."

"It was that hard for her?"

"Don't you get it? She hated Brent, hated working with her ex. They set it up so's they didn't have many scenes together but there have to be some. She has to fake it for the camera and that's tough. Those were the days it was really hard to get her going."

"So back to Brent. You think he ever hit her? Was the abuse ever physical?"

He took a deep breath and exhaled, loud. "I never saw any evidence of that but I wouldn't be surprised. He's got some temper, that asshole."

"You say you were at the bottom of the totem pole, yet the star of the show confided in you. Someone with the show thought that you and Cami had a thing. They said if Brent found out, there'd be hell to pay. Knowing how rough he could be, doesn't that scare you?"

"Some detective you are. Not that it's any of your business, but I'm asexual."

17

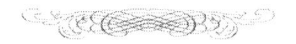

I didn't learn much more from Walsh, but his take on Brent explained a lot. Many public figures who trade on their image are the exact opposite in private, no news there. In his case, is the Jekyll and Hyde syndrome actual schizophrenia? And which side of the subject is the real one, or are they both real? In the end, does it really matter? You can't incarcerate one and not the other.

I called Ginn and filled him in on my day. Moses isn't a 'motive' guy. He often quotes Churchill when I analyze why people act the way they do. After I gave him the rundown, he did it again. "As Winnie is famous for saying, 'I no longer listen to what people say, I just watch what they do. Behavior never lies.'"

"I suppose that works in politics, my friend, but I'm trying to find out who made a woman disappear. Motive's a big part of it."

"Either way 5-0, you gonna need me there. Even though you say the man's dropped a few LBs, he still be a hulk."

"True, but I don't want him to think I'm onto him just yet. And I'm not even sure I *am* onto him."

"You're acting all Hamlet on me now. Man stands to keep a lot more of his bread if his wife is gone. She already hates him. He's getting some on the side. They yelling at each other last day anybody saw her."

"But the showrunner, who works with him all day, says he's a great guy. And she's a tough critic."

"You told me yourself, he's an actor now. Actors make their living telling lies, making folks believe them. They ain't the characters they play, but they do their damnedest to make you think they are. Look at them movie heroes you met back when you was tight with Jaime. Cool on the screen, not so cool off it."

"But those were just snapshots, meet 'n greets. This is a tough woman who works with them both under stressful conditions. No actor can stay in character 24/7 without their true selves coming out."

"Some do, I hear. Hey, I'm making up dinner. When you think you'll be home?"

"I'm on my way. They're done shooting today and everyone's scattered. Maybe you come with me tomorrow morning."

"Right on. Making fresh pesto for sea scallops. Serving 'em over pasta. Mighty fine eatin'."

"Can't wait. Should be back in less than an hour."

It was the middle of the afternoon in California. I called Jaime, hoping she wouldn't be tied up in one of her negotiations.

She wasn't.

"Hey, Riles. What do you need?"

I gave her the latest. When I was finished, she said, "Sounds like you think Brent might be involved in her disappearing."

"Not sure. But seems you have a mighty big conflict of interest."

"That's one reason I brought you into this. You don't have any emotional ties to these people. I'm worried it's clouding my judgment. Truth be told, I like Brent a whole lot better than I like her, but she's blood."

It sounded like someone came into the room she was in. She dispatched whoever it was and apologized for the interruption.

I said, "You feel guilty over the sins of the father. If she wasn't related, you wouldn't have given her the time of day."

"That must be it, Doctor Phil. Like they say, you can pick your friends but you can't pick your family. And since we're analyzing my motives, how about my Father Flanagan impulse to save a wayward child."

"I would have thought that reference would be before your time."

"Film history class. *Boys Town* with Spencer Tracy."

"Yeah, a time when all those little urchins just needed a break and the kindly cops tousled their hair, dispensed some fatherly advice, and sent them on their way."

"Now they shoot first, ask questions later."

"Not fair."

"I was being glib. I've worked with a lot of cops --- technical consultants on some of our productions. I appreciate what they do every day to keep us safe."

"I've known both kinds. Down to business. You said you had someone urge Brent to file for divorce. That wouldn't be in Cami's best interests. How do you balance that?"

"It's a question of fairness. I couldn't advise *her* to divorce him sooner than later. But it didn't matter because he was having none of it. If they got divorced, she'd have to file and he'd fight it."

"Do you think he was physically abusing her, now that we think there's another side to him that nobody else has seen?"

"When she called me and said she was afraid of him, I told you, I checked around. No one else bought it. And this PA who you said was her friend said he never saw any signs."

"Just because she didn't show up with bruises and black eyes doesn't mean it didn't happen."

"I'm well aware of that. I should have done more, but that was right after Rick was diagnosed and I let things slip. Jeez, Riles, I'm just hoping there's something else at work here. That Cami's all right and that Brent had nothing to do with her being missing. I know you have to focus on Brent, but what else do you think it could be?"

"I think we can rule out kidnapping, at least for money. We would have gotten a ransom note by now."

"What about a crazed fan? Someone who's obsessed with her. She comes off as quite the sexpot on the show."

"There's a word I haven't heard this century. That's a possibility but it'll be hard to pin down. We could go through all her fan mail or whatever it's called now. That'd be a good job for Iris. Just don't tell her it was my idea."

"She checks the mail anyway before releasing it to Cami. My half sister is pretty insecure about her acting chops and we didn't want her reading anything negative."

"You can ask Iris if there's any suspicious fan mail, but I'd think she would have already brought that up if there was. You're aware Iris hates me, no? She gave it to me both barrels before she left. Thinks I put you up to calling her back home."

"That's my fault. I'm sorry. I *did* make it sound like since you were on the case, she wasn't needed. Truth is, I wanted her back here to do what she does best. I only sent her there in the first place because she knows most of the folks on the show. It must have come off as 'she should leave the detective work to you'."

Traffic was bunching up on the causeway to Hilton Head Island as drivers were distracted by the colors the setting sun cast over the Intracoastal. I could see a long line of brake lights over the bridge. Dinner would be late.

"Jaime, I have to tell you that I don't much like the people I've met so far. Iris came on nasty right from the start, like I have some history hating gays. Then Brenda Showrunner barely gave me the time of day."

"They're not there for their personalities, Riles. Iris is a great rainmaker in the LGBTQ+ community. And Brenda can be a real badass but she brings the show in on time and under budget. I haven't talked to Winona today and you didn't mention her. Did she rub you the wrong way, too?"

My breakfast with Ms. Sands seemed like ages ago. I reflected on my suspicion that Jaime might be playing matchmaker and this gave me the opportunity to put it to the test."

"Au contraire. She was delightful. Completely open, taught me a lot about the business. Smart, and extremely attractive. I really like her."

"I think she's had a lot of work done."

"It was swell work, whoever did it. I have a good eye for stuff like that and I couldn't tell. She was a real sweetheart to me."

"Maybe she's changed since her semi-retirement. She could be as hardnosed as the other two, if not more so. You think I'm tough when it comes to business; she makes me look like Michelle Obama. I'm glad she was a help, at least."

Her Dolly Gallagher Levi side was nowhere in evidence. If you're trying to hook up a friend, you don't bad mouth that someone, implying their good looks are a result of a skillful blade. Especially by saying that Winona could be nastier than a woman who treated me like a Neanderthal. And another, who wrote me off as dog shit.

That made me feel more hopeful. I think.

18

Cami's Mustang was impounded near the Jasper County Detention Center, just off I-95 in Ridgeland. Across the street was a medium security state penitentiary. The sheriff's office and government buildings were close by. It seemed the entire county ruling body was contained within a quarter mile circle.

I called Montanez. No further news, at least none he was willing to share. I asked if I could check out her car. If I went to the Jasper County Sheriff's office, he'd ask someone there to show me the vehicle. He worked for Beaufort County, but this case crossed jurisdictions. He emphasized this was the last favor he'd do for me, no matter how much he respected Tomey.

I brought Ginn along, rather he brought me along. He insisted we take his 80's Mercedes two-seater rather than my MDX.

"Nothing against your ride, 5-0, but mine's a lot cooler. If we wind up hanging with some TV stars, I think they'd appreciate old Molly here more than that ancient clunker you got. Thought you were gonna upgrade."

"Haven't gotten around to it. Got my eye on an Audi A5 Cabriolet, but even if I get it, I'll keep the Acura. Gets me where I need to go."

We got to Ridgeland and as Montanez promised, a young cop escorted us to the impound yard. It wasn't really a formal facility like the docks in Manhattan or Brooklyn, where towed cars are stored. There aren't many parking violations in Jasper County. I don't recall ever seeing a meter there. This place would be reserved for cars used in the commission of crimes or speeders.

Come to think of it, I've never seen anyone stopped for speeding in Ridgeland. The limit on I-95 is 70, but if that is your top speed, better stay in the right lane and be prepared for cars whizzing by like you're a dead skunk on the side of the road.

There were a few vehicles parked on the grass just off the main parking area for the jail. No security, or even a chain link fence to protect the cars from thieves or vandals. Given the other vehicles surrounding Cami's Mustang, I could see why they weren't too worried. Aside from her Mustang, the rest were a rust bucket collection of old pickups, a ten year old Toyota, a dented up Kia and an SUV from the last century.

The young cop said that he'd been instructed to give us no more than a half hour and to monitor our every move. Nice to know that Montanez appreciated our help.

It didn't take nearly that long. Cami's Mustang was a beautiful mess. It was Ruby Red with a tobacco leather interior, loaded to the gills. Under the hood was one of the largest stock engines Ford offers --- a 5.2 liter V-8 that kicks out 528 horses and 428 lb. ft. of torque. Six speed manual trans, which was the only choice offered with that massive power plant.

Cami liked to drive fast. Every woman I've ever known opted for the ease of an automatic. Did she go racing in the streets after work?

The car was loaded with crap as well --- the seats and carpets were littered with fast food wrappers, plastic grocery bags, Styrofoam coffee cups and old receipts.

"I don't imagine the keys were anywhere nearby," I asked the young cop.

"No, sir. As you can see, it's a push button start. We had to tow it here. There'll be a tow charge and storage fee for whoever picks it up when we release it."

Ginn asked, "Doubt them fees'll bother somebody who musta shelled out 70 grand for this whip. When will you boys be done with it?"

"Can't say for sure. We didn't find anything funky. Doubt you will either, but Detective Montanez said you're welcome to try."

I sifted through the discarded crumpled receipts, hoping to find one that post dated the last time she had been seen. No dice. I went through the glove box. Cami or whoever took care of the car for her had been meticulous at saving the service records. Oil changes and tire rotations at more frequent intervals than necessary.

Odd that on one hand she took such good mechanical care of this ride, yet littered it with all kinds of garbage. Since it was registered in Brent's name, I suspected that he was the one who made sure it was well maintained. If he wasn't so busy with the show, I imagine he'd do the oil changes himself.

I felt around the wheel wells for a key, not expecting to find the large remote control fobs that modern cars favor. I did find something important, something that I couldn't believe the local cops hadn't discovered.

It made me wonder how thorough they had been at inspecting the car. They probably just dusted it for prints and maybe sprayed some Luminol in case there was any blood.

It wasn't the first time I broke the law by withholding evidence. But I didn't trust that Montanez and his crew would put my find to good use. If there was foul play, I could put it back where I found it and tip the cops off so as not to compromise the legal case.

So while Ginn distracted the young cop with small talk about baseball, I pocketed the tiny tracking device I'd found. Between my computer hacker Crain and my FBI friend Logan, I'd have a pretty good idea where Cami had been before she vanished into the Carolina night.

19

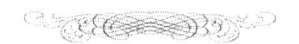

Will wonders never cease? There was something Crain couldn't do. My dark web hacker has always come through for me, even with impossible tasks. Flight manifests? Child's play. Credit card transactions? No problem. Sealed criminal records? Ask him something difficult.

I had a tracker in hand and I wanted at least a week's itinerary for the Mustang to see where Cami had been prior to her disappearance. Moses and I wagered lunch on how long it would take Crain to come through with the goods. I said under an hour and Ginn jumped at the chance to prove me wrong.

We were headed to Judy's Island in his restomod Mercedes. I couldn't interface my phone through the car's aftermarket system, which was just as well. Ginn had never experienced Crain and I wasn't sure how he'd react to this disembodied phantom, who had helped break cases that were hopelessly stalemated.

Crain no longer masked his voice on the phone as he had when we first started working together. He still routed the call through enough towers to make a trace unachievable.

After he apologized for not being helpful, I said, "Just tell me in layman's terms, why you can't do this? Certainly not because it's illegal."

"No comment on that for obvious reasons. The problem is that I would need to lay my hands on the actual tracker, number one. You say it is evidence in a criminal investigation. I cannot tamper with it for fear it could instigate charges against you, if your role in it was revealed. Second, even if I was to obtain said item, there is a limited amount of data that is retained on these devices. The tracking information is uploaded to a server, which is then accessible to the purchaser in real time or catalogued."

I'd always speculated that Crain had a mild form of Aspergers'. He never uses contractions and his manner of speaking sounds like an instruction manual translated from another language.

I said, "So can't you hack into the company's site?"

"I could but it would bear no fruit. You will notice that this device has no serial number embossed on the case. It is encoded inside and there are billions of combinations. There is no physical entry, a USB mini or C port. It might be possible to disassemble it and access the software but I am not a mechanic."

"Do you have any suggestions? Any idea of someone who *could* help?"

"I assume I was your first call. There is a man I am sure you have already considered. I refer to your former FBI colleague, Deputy Assistant Director Daniel Thomas Logan."

He used Dan's formal title and full name. I'm not used to such precision and it took me a second to realize he was talking about my old pal Dan-o.

I said, "What can he do that you can't?"

"Very little on a global level. However, in this particular instance, he can access the data base of the Federal Bureau of Investigation to obtain information from the manufacturer of the device. He can secure a court order to access their records. *You* would be protected under the rules of evidence because you relinquished the item to an appropriate legal authority. I could hack into said database, but that involves considerable risk since they are constantly upgrading their security protocols and the penalties are quite severe."

"Bill me at your normal rate for the call, Crain. Even though you can't do the job yourself, you've been a great help."

"There will be no charge. I am sorry that I could not be of service to you. It is a reminder that we are mere mortals who flatter ourselves, believing that with our advanced technology, we have the power of the Gods. Farewell to the King, until our next encounter."

I don't think I've ever experienced such an over the top send-off. Ginn had caught enough of the conversation to know he had won the bet. He said, "Now the trick be finding a four star steakhouse in this neck of the woods."

20

It was still early morning in California, but Jaime had already been at her desk for hours. Although she isn't one to panic, there was a strained sense of urgency in her voice that I hadn't heard in all the time we were together.

"Riley, you've got to do something. Iris wasn't on her flight."

I put the phone on speaker so that Ginn could hear. "Honey, people miss flights all the time. The way to the airport from Judy's Island is on two lane country roads until you hit I-95. One little wreck and they get backed up for hours."

"That's what I'm afraid of. Iris might have been in an accident. She's an L.A. woman, not used to driving in those conditions, especially with no streetlights."

"What time was she due in?"

"She was booked on the first flight out of Savannah. Leaving at 5:10, your time. Due here around 7. I sent an intern to pick her up. She never got on the plane."

"She might have overslept. Could be as simple as that."

"That was the first thing I thought of. Called her cell and got voice mail."

"You know where she was staying?"

"Ocean View Inn. It's supposed to be on the beach."

"And you called them?"

"Yes. Give me *some* credit, Riles. I wouldn't be bothering you if I didn't try that first."

"And what did they say?"

"Just that she hadn't checked out yet. Check out time is eleven and they weren't going to disturb her, based on a phone call. I said she'd missed her flight and I was worried but they just blew me off. Said if she hadn't checked out by eleven, they'd knock on the door."

"You have the address?"

She gave it to me. I said, "It's almost eleven now. I'm a few minutes away. I'll swing by and see what's up. I'm sure there's an innocent explanation, like she decided to stay over for some reason or was out partying on her last night and overslept."

"Not like her. She's very responsible. She would have called."

"Well, I told you, she was pretty pissed at me and probably at you, too. This could be an act of rebellion. A big 'F-you' to both of us."

"I hope that's all it is."

"I'll call you soon as I know more. Don't worry, babe. I got it covered."

Ginn never took his eyes off the road. He said, "Ain't like Jaime to get all hot and bothered over a missed flight. She a lot more emotional than she used to be. I guess with Rick dying and all, she getting a little fragile."

"She's a tough woman, Mo, but she's been through a lot. Her mother was murdered. Her dad's got late stage dementia. Add that to all the stuff that went down with Stone and me, then he died. And I'm sure her clients aren't the easiest people in the world to deal with."

"That's what I'm sayin'. You gotta cut her some slack, man. Ain't saying I like what she did to ya, but she got a lot on her plate."

"I'm thinking the best thing is for me to take care of business. Much as I'd like to see her, it'd be great if she could stay out there till this whole deal is settled."

The Ocean View Inn was about ten minutes from where they were filming *Country Fixin's*. It was a typical two story motor court. The rooms were accessible from exterior walkways, no inside halls. I suppose you could say it had seen better days, although this is the type of place that had never been much. It *was* close to the beach, but the touted ocean views consisted of glimpses of blue from rooms on the second floor. That is, if the guests don't mind leaving the curtains open, their queen beds exposed to anyone who happens to stroll by. Pulling up to the place, I got the feeling that the patrons wouldn't be seeking views of the Atlantic.

I was surprised that Iris wasn't staying at a nicer place since Jaime's travel agent didn't generally book hot sheets motels. Since this was a last minute trip, it could be that they just grabbed the first available place, unfamiliar with this island as a destination.

I flashed my expired P.I. license to the day manager. The blue haired woman didn't give it more than a passing glance, probably used to people like me looking to catch cheating spouses. I expected her to walk me to Walker's room, but instead she handed me a key and said to leave it on the counter if she wasn't there when I got back.

Walker's room was on the second floor and the curtains were drawn over the large plate glass window. We could see and smell the ocean from there, but the scent wasn't pleasant. Smelled like dead fish.

The door didn't have an electronic card pad like most places these days, just an old fashioned brass key. The chrome plating on the lockset had worn off and the metal underneath was corroding in the salt air. But the key went in smoothly and the metal door swung open without creaking.

Moses and I walked in and he said, "You dial 911, I'll call Alex."

Iris Walker was splayed out on the bed. It didn't take a forensics expert to see that she was dead.

21

I stepped lightly inside the room, careful not to disturb any evidence. There was no blood spatter on the wall, no smear of red on the white sheet where Iris lay. It looked like an overdose of some kind, or maybe a heart attack, which would be rare in one so young.

Walker's handbag was nowhere to be seen. No luggage either, but that might be in the trunk of her rental car. There was no furniture disturbed to indicate signs of a struggle. I couldn't find any other clothes after a quick look in the closet and bath. Someone had cleaned up the scene and removed all traces of Iris' identity.

That had amateur written all over it. Unless she'd rented the room under a different name, it would be easy to establish who she was. I suspected it was someone she had been doing drugs with and they panicked when Iris died. If they had supplied the fatal dose, even by accident, it was at the very least, a case of manslaughter.

Moses knocked on the door. The county cops that Tomey had called had arrived. I wondered if the group would be led by Montanez, especially if they suspected linkage between this and Cami's case.

One of the cops took Ginn and me aside as the forensics team began their work. The county detective who'd gotten the first call was not the young and dapper Montanez, quite the contrary. He was wearing a windowpane sport jacket, brown with blue piping. The yellow shirt and khaki pants reminded me of those ugly old

San Diego Padres uniforms. That wasn't all that was ugly and old about him.

He had the puffy face and bulbous nose of a heavy drinker. The little hair he had was in need of a trim and he'd missed a few spots with his morning shave.

His name was Frank Sancious and his first question was predictable.

He said, "So what are you doing here and how did you discover the body?"

I told him who Iris Walker was and about Jaime's concern that she'd had missed her flight.

"And why'd she call you?"

"Ms. Johansen represents some of the people on the *Country Fixin's* show. I was looking into a situation there for her agency. Iris Walker was helping me."

"Wait a minute. You said she missed her flight. If she was helping you out, why was she leaving? Where was she going?"

"She'd done all she could. She was needed back at her agency and she'd served her purpose here."

"How well did you know her? Do you know anyone who might have wanted her dead?"

I was tempted to say *me* but this wasn't the right audience. "I'd just met her a couple of days ago. I wouldn't know about any enemies."

He mopped his brow. It was muggy and he was sweating heavily, the extra twenty pounds around his waist doing him no favors. "You think she found out something about Cami Purdy and whoever killed her killed this lady, too?"

"I thought you guys were keeping a lid on the Purdy situation."

"With the press, yeah. But the county detectives all know. And I assume that's what this agency you work for sent you out to investigate. I'm working on the theory that Ms. Purdy is demised. So, in your professional opinion, do you see a connection?" He sneered at the word professional.

"Anything's possible but that's quite a leap. We don't know that Cami Purdy's been killed and Iris certainly wasn't hot on anyone's trail. If she suspected someone, she would've told me."

"Well then, I suppose this coulda been a robbery. Or maybe she picked up a guy and he killed her and stole her wallet. We'll put a trace out on her credit cards. If she was some kind of Hollywood agent, I'd guess she was carrying a good bunch of cash on her."

I didn't feel the need to inform him that Iris wasn't interested in picking up men. He'd been fomenting all sorts of theories about the crime with no supporting evidence, just his imagination. The killer would have to walk in and confess for *him* to solve this one.

He'd been ignoring Moses. He turned to the big man and asked, "What about you, boy? You just along for the ride?"

Calling a man of Moses' age 'boy' made me worry that Ginn would slap the man into this century, but he held off. Ginn had been called worse and he didn't need to get arrested over a slur.

Moses just smiled and said, "No statement."

"You hiding something?"

"No statement."

Ginn was calm. Spoke in a monotone. I stepped in front of the detective. "My associate is driving today. We take turns and it's his day."

"So he *is* along for the ride, then. Thought so."

Alex was coming from Hilton Head and wouldn't arrive for at least another half hour. This buffoon was finished with us for now but told us to hang tight and someone would take our formal statement.

Montanez got there five minutes later.

"What's going on, King? Why are you here?" he said. No pleasantries.

I brought him up to speed with what we had so far.

He said, "You stay put. I'm not sure I buy your story about just innocently checking out this motel room. Anyone corroborate that?"

"Jaime Johansen. She's the one who called me about Walker missing her flight."

"And what's her number?"

"I'm sure a detective of your caliber has heard about telephone books. There's even this new gimmick they call goggle or something."

"Thanks for your cooperation. I'll remember that, smartass."

He left to talk to Sancious.

Ginn said, "You really know how to make friends with the locals, don't you? Can't resist them zingers. Careful now, they come back to bite you."

"Sorry, Mo. It's my nature. I'm a man with many shortcomings."

A truck came screeching into the parking lot. A truck containing one Brent "Boomer" Purdy.

"Oh, my God. It's Cam, isn't it?"

He started toward the room, but Ginn grabbed him by the shoulders. Strong as Purdy was, Ginn was stronger.

I said, "Hold up, Brent. It's not Cami. It's Iris Walker."

He stepped back and Moses released him. Relief spread across his face like a cloud passing to reveal the sun. "I'm sorry. I'm just so worried about her." It took him a second to realize he was sounding crass. "God, it's terrible about Ms. Walker. What happened?"

"Don't know. Looks like an overdose."

My hand went to my jacket pocket and I fingered the tracker. At least I didn't have to waste any time trying to find out who had planted it.

22

"Man, I can't abide all that red tape. Statements. Damn. *We come to the motel. Find this lady lying on the bed. She dead. The End.*"

Moses didn't enjoy repeating himself for the woman who took down his testimony. More than once he asked why they just couldn't record it and transcribe it later. It was a valid question.

I said, "You think that's bad, try working for the FBI like I did a century ago. The paperwork there could deforest the state of Idaho."

I wasn't sure how forested Idaho is. Maybe not so much if they have all those potato farms.

"Yeah. Well, don't know if you thought about it, but why did Purdy show up like he did? He got a police scanner or something? Or some kinda inside source in the sheriff's office."

"Simpler than that. We were wondering who put the tracker on Cami's car. Now we know."

"Hot damn. You put that tracker in your pocket and he sees it was on the move. Then it stops at a shady motel. He figures Ms. Cami found out where they was keeping her car and moved it to a safer place. She still had the keys. Gave him the idea she was still alive."

"Or whoever killed Cami showed up with her I.D. and bailed out the car. If Brent killed her, why would he show up when the tracker showed movement? He must have known the car was impounded."

"Do make him look innocent. Unless he hired some cheap hitter to do it and was afraid they were making off with his hot set of wheels."

"Be pretty stupid but most criminals aren't rocket scientists. He seemed pretty worked up when he thought it might be Cami, but I've got to remember, he's an actor. It's not doing us any good to be hanging here. Even if forensics finds something I didn't see, Montanez isn't going to tell us."

"I don't know if you noticed, but that man ain't liking you much."

"Feeling's mutual, partner. Purdy told me he thought Cami's stand-in might be a suspect. We need to get out of here and talk to this body double, Alison Reiger."

"Now that be good duty for Mr. Moses Ginn if her body's anything like the real thing. Be my pleasure to help you on that one while you grill Grizzly Adams."

"I'm sure you would. She's supposed to be hot stuff. Brent was doing her while Cami was away."

"You ain't gonna roust the big boy about the tracker?"

"That's on the list. Crain said there'd probably be an itinerary the days before she wound up missing."

"Sure you thought about this, 5-0. Grizzly had that tracker, he'd know she was at that abandoned quarry the other night. Good place to knock off your old lady if she be hating on you."

23

My call to Jaime was not one I looked forward to making. She has dealt with so much hardship in her life. Her parents split when she was a toddler. Her mother was murdered by a psycho. Rick died young, soon after they had found each other. And now a valued member of her team had fallen victim.

"Jaime, I have some bad news about Iris."

"It can't be worse than I've been imagining."

"She's dead. We found her in her motel room. Looks like an OD. I apologize for not letting you know right away, but the cops held us for questioning. I wanted to try to get as much information as I could before calling you."

"Do they have a suspect?"

"No. I know you said she could be difficult and she sure was to me, but I'm really sorry."

"You said the cops held you. Do they think you're a suspect?"

"Moses and I discovered the body. Found her splayed out on the bed. Sometimes killers call the cops to make themselves look innocent. They're wise to that now."

"Was sex involved?"

"You sound like a cop."

"Living with you did that, I guess."

"Yeah, sorry. On the face of it, could've been a drug deal gone bad. Or maybe a Mr. Goodbar thing, although a female perp in her case, I guess."

"I'll need to get in touch with her relatives. I don't really know much about her family. She never talked about them. God, she was so young. They'll be devastated. I feel so stupid. I never had a clue Iris did drugs."

"We don't know that she did, for sure. This could have been set up. She admitted to me she smoked weed, but this had to be something strong, like Fentanyl."

"I can ask around here and see if she had anyone steady in her life or if she was into picking up strangers in a bar."

"Good. That'd help."

"I'll be there soon as I can. Tonight if I can get a flight."

"Jaime, please don't do that. It's possible that two people associated with this show are dead. We don't know if what happened to Iris has anything to do with Cami disappearing. They may be totally unrelated but if they aren't, I don't want you in the bull's-eye."

"You think someone has a grudge against a reality show? Really?"

"Honey, there are crazies out there. A disgruntled homeowner who thinks the show didn't do them right. Someone lusting after Cami. Maybe she and Iris might've done some blow together."

"Are you sure Cami was using again?"

"According to the showrunner."

"McLeish never told me that."

"Maybe he didn't know. I'll get together with him later."

"How's Brent taking this latest? Does he know?"

"Didn't seem to affect him too much. He rushed to the motel after we found the body. He was afraid it was Cami. Was relieved more than anything." I didn't tell her about the tracker. I wanted to confront Purdy about it first.

"Riley, I really want to come out there and help."

"Jaime, there's nothing you can do and it may not be safe. Best thing you can do now is notify Walker's people, help set up arrangements. I'll stay on the cops about releasing the body, soon as they're done with it. If I think there's a way you can help here without sticking your neck out, I'll let you know."

"Okay, I'll do it your way. For now."

"You know I really want to see you. But let's wait until we know more about what's going on."

~~~~~

Alison Reiger *was* a dead ringer for Cami Wordsworth Purdy, although using the word dead at this particular minute might not be the best choice. Based strictly on her looks, I couldn't blame a man like Brent for drifting in her direction once Cami was unattainable.

Reiger's physical resemblance was remarkable, but her background couldn't have been more different. When she extended her hand, I felt calluses borne from hard work. Although I'd never met Cami in person, on TV, her curves struck me as soft, the type that might give way to bloat over the years.

This woman would never let it come to that. Her arms were sinewy, on full display in a cut off tee. She was wearing loose fitting cargo shorts and her calves were those of a Tour d'France rider. The glimpse of her abs that the tee revealed when she lifted her arms was impressive.

After Ginn and I introduced ourselves, I asked, "Is there a place we can talk privately?"

Her fist tightened. "I don't rate a trailer. But the tent they have set up for food ain't busy now. That should do."

Alison looked to be a decade older than Cami, who was twenty six. Her voice was low pitched and Southern.

We sat at a long, unsteady folding table that seated ten. My chair was at the end, flanked by Ginn and Reiger. She offered to grab us a Gatorade and we accepted.

When she returned, I said, "Have you always wanted to be an actress, Alison?"

She smiled. She was really cute in a farmer's daughter kind of way. "I don't consider myself an actress. I'm a prop. I got the job because I look like someone else. They would have used a cardboard cutout if they could have sold it to the viewers."

"How did you come to get the job?"

"I was working as a construction supervisor in the second season. Brenda, that's the showrunner, picked up that I looked like Cam and asked me if I'd be interested in some extra work. In fact, she told me that I was everything Cam was supposed to be."

"So you never auditioned for the female role?"

"Nope. I'd heard they were looking for a female co-host but I never followed through. My dad's a builder, one of the contractors they hire to do the other houses. You don't think Brent does all that work himself, do ya?"

Ginn said, "Man can only do so much. So you had designs on replacing Cami?"

"No. I was planning on taking over my dad's business when he retired. He wasn't exactly thrilled I was doing this gig. I convinced him that I could still be his project manager and make a little extra cash on the side."

I said, "Wasn't it frustrating?"

"Kinda. I mean, I watched her mess up one take after another. She was jive and I knew I could do it better. If I'd have got in earlier, I coulda been the fake Mrs. Purdy."

"Or the real Mrs. Purdy."

"Thought crossed my mind. Look, I'm no fool, bit by the acting bug. Woman my age isn't going to Hollywood to star in movies or nothing. Even if that's what I wanted, I'd be starting too late."

"But you could be a star on a reality show. Brent said you were pushing to take Cami's place. Both on and off the set."

I could see she was hurt by that. "He told you that, did he?"

"Well, not in so many words. He said what you just told us. That you were the real deal and that Cami was faking it."

"Look fellas, I don't need this show. Yeah, it pissed me off seeing somebody doing a job I know I could do a whole lot better, but before I worked on this, I was fine doing what I was doing."

I glanced over at Moses, who sat with his arms folded. I was taking the active role asking questions, while he observed her reactions. I was the provocateur, Ginn the analyst.

"Ms. Reiger, I don't want to embarrass you, but I have to ask. Brent did say you were having an affair. But you were pushing so hard to replace Cami that he had to back off."

"And I suppose you're going to tell me he said that I'd kill Cami so I could get what I wanted."

"Would you?"

"Okay gents, fuck it. I'll tell you the truth and you believe what you want. Yeah, I thought he was a good guy and he really wants to make this island a nice place to live again. We're in the same line of work --- had that in common. But I was the one cooled it, not him."

"Because he still loves Cami?"

"That had a lot to do with it. But I told you, I never was after Cami's job."

"Why not? Acting on this show's got to be easier than building houses. Probably pays better, too. And Brent's a cash cow. And now he's in better shape, he's not a bad looking dude."

"What are you, his publicist? I agreed to talk with y'all to help find Cami. Didn't want to get into any of this personal shit. He's a good guy and has some real interesting ideas about Judy's Island and I wanted to help him with those. But he's so hung up on Cami that I couldn't keep seeing him the way we were. Now if you'll excuse me, I got work to do."

24

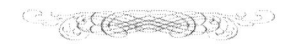

Reiger had provided an alibi for last night, so after verifying that, we could cross her off the list of suspects in Walker's murder, if that's what it was. After we left her, Moses said, "I believe her. That girl don't take no shit from no one."

"That's for sure. But I still think she has motive. Cami's job has a lot more sizzle than a lifetime of building houses with your father."

"For some folks that may be true but this chick ain't afraid of honest work. She mighta been all starry eyed about TV at first, but once she got behind the scenes, I bet she don't find it to her liking. Where to next?"

"I'd like to talk to talk to Jaime's spy, that assistant director, Ron McLeish. Gotta be careful there because Jaime doesn't want him to know I know that he's working for her undercover."

"That's where you like to be."

"Ah, that sharp sense of humor returns."

"Just lightening things up after finding that dead body. Don't blame you if you got shook up after seeing that. Knock you off your game. But don't fret. I got your back if you start slipping. Let's seek him out."

"Seek him out? Wow, being around showbiz has you talking like a Penny Dreadful."

"Who's this Penny Dreadful lady and why you say I sound like her?"

"*Penny Dreadfuls* were cheap magazines or books in England in the eighteen hundreds. Characters like Sweeny Todd, the demon barber of Fleet Street. Grisly, sensational crap, sometimes supernatural. There was a TV series a few years back with the gorgeous Eva Green."

"Eva Green, Eva Destruction, whatever. You talking trash, man. Let's go find this McLeish cat."

I had no idea what McLeish looked like or where he might be. Iris Walker wasn't around to introduce us. A picture of her dead body flashed in my brain. I wondered if word of her death had reached the set.

Ginn and I walked around, trying not to trip over cables or tip over light tripods. I spotted Bob Walsh and he pointed us toward McLeish, who was sitting in the shade on a director's chair, looking over some notes.

I introduced ourselves. McLeish barely looked up.

I said, "Jaime Johansen sent me out to look into the Cami Purdy situation. She's a friend, CEO of the White Page Agency."

That didn't seem to register one way or another. He looked like a veteran of the television wars. He'd been around the block a few times, reversed course and went around a few more. He had a full head of graying hair and lived-in face, kind of like William Holden in *Network*. I smelled liquor on his breath.

"I'm working on some setups now, King. Can this wait?"

"I'm afraid not. I have some bad news. Iris Walker was found dead this morning."

That got his attention, but only on the margins. "Sorry to hear that. What happened? Overdose?"

"Why do you say that?"

"Struck me as a druggie. Pretty common in this business."

"Could be she was murdered."

"Hmm. That is horrible." He said that without conviction. "Didn't know her well. She hung with Brent most of the time she was here. Does he know? If he doesn't I'd appreciate it if you wouldn't tell him until we're done shooting. Don't want to throw him off his game."

I pretended to be as insensitive as he was. "If his wife disappearing didn't do that, I doubt this will. But he already knows. In fact, he saw the body."

"Oh Jesus, so that's where he took off to."

"Right thoughtful of you to worry that a little thing like this might throw him off his game," Moses said.

"Forgot for a second who I was dealing with. Anybody else, I'd give 'em the day off. But Brent's a real pro. He'll work through it."

I said, "You've been working on this show since the start. We want to get your take on things with Brent and Cami."

The liquor smell was overpowering. His ill-kept yellowing teeth made me think he was a smoker.

He whispered, "Not here. Not now. Won't do for people to see us talking."

"What people?"

"Gimme your number. I'll be in touch when the coast is clear. I'll text you a time and place. Now get lost."

25

Ginn's phone buzzed and he glanced down at the number before answering.

"Tomey," he said, taking a couple of steps away.

He listened for a moment, then turned to me. "She's at the motel where we found Walker. Sheriff's people are wrapping up."

"Can she meet us here?" I said. "I'd like to compare notes in person."

He asked and she agreed. He texted her the address.

"She'll be here in fifteen minutes. Getting to be late in the afternoon, though. Your dog be wanting his dinner. And we skipped that lunch you owe me."

"The big man has a rumbly in his tumbly?"

"You *do* remind me of a bear with little brain," he shot back. "Winnie Churchill, Winnie the Pooh. Same deal."

I said, "I'd like to try to hook up with Purdy, see if I can coax him out for a few drinks. Maybe catch a glimpse of that dark side. You could go back home with Tomey and I'll take your Benz."

"You know there ain't much I won't do for you 5-0, but lending you Molly to go out boozing is off the table. I don't know how Tomey got to the motel, but if it was in her Honda, I might be persuading her to let you take that heap.

That way, you wreck it, she get something more stylish, dig?"

"It would have been nicer if you said her car has modern airbags and is safer than your little chick magnet."

"'Course, if you wanna insult Molly you can Uber it home."

"That might be the smartest way. Let's see what Tomey says. You know me, Ginn. I can pretend to match someone drink for drink and pour mine into a potted plant."

"Waste good Scotch? That ain't like you."

"Who said Scotch? If I'm going to fertilize a plant, bourbon'll do just fine. Maybe you can check out Reiger's alibi and do some digging into her father's business."

"Telling you, that girl is legit."

"Wouldn't be the first time us he-men are fooled by a pretty face. Look, Cami's disappearance and Walker's murder may be totally unrelated, but other than Purdy, the only common thread is Reiger."

"You thinking Reiger and Brent in it together? Cami being gone means they get the whole pie. And like you say, she's more his type than Cami was."

We went silent for a moment as young Bob Walsh walked past, carrying several small corded microphones. He gave me the stink-eye as he went by, as if I had stuck him with the bar bill the other night.

After he'd passed, I said, "We need to find out if Iris was seeing someone here or if she was picked up by the wrong stranger. Rule out that she was dosed on purpose."

Ginn nodded in agreement. "I suppose they wiped the place down so there weren't any prints."

"Based on what they have or don't have so far, I bet they'll rule it an accidental OD and move on. They'll say was she was doing drugs with her connection and overdid it.

He or she then stole her stuff. Her phone might have their number in the favorites section or at least a record of their calls."

"Woulda been a lot smarter to leave the purse, just take the phone."

"Yeah, and who knows what DNA might have been on her clothes or possessions. No luggage either. Even if this wasn't deliberate, someone has something to hide."

26

McLeish was spot on in his evaluation of Brent's professionalism. The big man went through his paces as if he didn't have a care in the world, smiling patiently as he showed a homeowner how to tile a kitchen backsplash. The man he was instructing was getting mastic all over the face of the tile and laying it in crooked rows. Purdy corrected the homeowner's early mistakes on camera, then turned things over to a subcontractor to clean up the rest.

I grabbed him before he moved on to the next task --- installing custom racks in the master bedroom's walk-in closet.

I said, "Hey, buddy, let's go out for a couple of pops after you're done shooting today. We both could use it."

"Say that again. Anything new on Iris?"

"Yeah. I'll bring you up to speed later. How long do you think you'll be?"

"Got a closet to do, then hanging a chandelier in the dining area. I'd say an hour, maybe hour and a half more likely."

"Great. We'll meet up when you're done. Call me if I'm not here. Might have to chase something down."

Tomey had lent me the keys to her Accord and driven back to Hilton Head with Ginn. Moses and I didn't tell her about my plan to ply Mr. Hyde with liquor. If I wasn't successful at staying sober enough to drive, I'd either stay over or Uber it home.

While watching Brent expertly assemble the closet shelving kit, I got a text from McLeish. He was at one of the other houses, setting up for the next day's shoot. Could I meet him there in ten minutes?

It was only five minutes away so I texted that I'd be there. Brent had priority but I figured I could get what I needed from McLeish still be back in time for our boys' night out.

The crew had broken down and pulled out so he was there alone. His Jetta was in the driveway --- engine running, AC up full blast, classic jazz playing at high volume. He saw me pull up behind him and motioned to join him in his car.

The interior reeked of cigarettes and booze. I noticed a paper bag in the back seat, the kind that usually conceals a pint bottle.

He wasn't slurring as he spoke. "Don't have a lot of time. I talked to Johansen. She said you knew I was her spy on the shoot. I'm okay with that but please, please, please, don't tell anyone else. I get along swell with the cast and crew and I don't need 'em looking cross-eyed at me."

"I don't know what you're talking about. Who're you spying for? The Russians?"

My little joke seemed to work. "Forget it, King. Okay, what do you need?"

"I've heard that Cami was afraid of Brent. True? And if so, was there reason to be?"

"You get right down to it, don't you? The answer is no. I did catch them arguing one time. Afterwards, he told me that I didn't see what I saw, that it was staged, like they were rehearsing. He bought me a few drinks and I went along with it, but it was a load of crap. They weren't rehearsing. It was real."

"Did he threaten her? Did you ever see it get physical?"

"Never saw him hit her. Look, husbands and wives argue all the time and this one wasn't anything out of the ordinary. Only telling you 'cause she's missing."

Jaime had made a poor choice for intel gathering --- a man who could be bought off for a few drinks or the face of a pretty girl.

I said, "I'm told the show worked because of the chemistry between them. Didn't their relationship falling apart threaten that?"

"Ah, that was my magic touch, if I don't say so myself. I coached 'em up. Made it look like that chemistry was there even after it was long gone. I'd take shots of him with Alison Reiger's hands caressing his back, then cut to a close-up of Cam. Looked like they were together, when in reality, the takes were done separately, sometimes not even the same day. Had to be real careful with continuity. Same clothes, hair and jewelry, stuff like that."

"Speaking of Reiger, did you get the impression she was hot for Cami's job?"

"Oh yeah, no question. Even said it out loud to Brent when Cam wasn't around. We'd do a quick take and she'd say, 'see how much easier it is with somebody who knows what she's doing?'"

"If Cami was so replaceable, why didn't you replace her?"

He coughed, a smoker's hack. "Above my pay grade. I'd have shit-canned her but the powers that be kept her on, despite all the chaos. It isn't PC to say it, but Cam is white trash. Brent's a patient guy, but he must have had it up to here with her antics."

"He swore to me he loved her. Still does."

"Oh, I don't doubt that. He was always making excuses for her when she first started pulling her stunts. He covered for her a lot. The time I caught them fighting, they thought it was in private. He always believed that he could straighten her out in time."

"And you didn't?"

"We put up with that diva garbage from women like Taylor, Monroe, Diana Ross. They were giants, big draws, stars. But twats like Cami are a dime a dozen. The show would be just as good, if not better, with Reiger. Whenever Cami was on the outs with the showrunner, which was always, Brent saved her ass. Ungrateful little bitch didn't appreciate it."

"Why was he so devoted to her when she treated him like that?"

McLeish laughed. "You're supposed to be a detective? You need glasses? Look at her. Piece of ass like that's hard to quit. And when she was straight, she had a kind of vulnerable quality that was hard to resist."

"When she was straight?"

"Brent'll deny it, but she was a cokie. Probably not in front of him or with him. He drinks. I'll bet he never even got a contact high from grass. But she was into the white powder in a big way."

"Where'd she get it?"

"I don't know for a fact, but I suspect that kid who drives her around. And also, not to speak ill of the dead, but Iris Walker wasn't above sharing a line or two when she was around."

27

It made sense to meet wherever Purdy felt at home. He'd be more comfortable opening up if he felt he was among friends. When he called, I told him to pick a place and I'd meet him there.

The Jackson Creek Pub was his choice. I suppose some supersleuth would set up the bistro in advance, in case I couldn't handle Brent's ugly side. Like in *The Godfather*, taping a gun to the back of a toilet tank so that Michael could knock off Sollozzo and McCluskey. I didn't figure on needing a weapon, but it would have been nice to find a compliant barkeep to water down my drinks.

Purdy had gotten there before me and was seated at the bar. Two empty shot glasses and a half filled beer mug were in front of him. The staff and patrons were treating him like the prized celebrity he was.

He said, "Someone told me you were a Scotch drinker, King. I'm a shot and a beer guy myself. Bourbon. Makers Mark. What's your pleasure?"

"I'll start with a beer. Coors Light."

Brent's presence ensured us first class service. "Hey Joe, another round for me and a pisswater for my friend."

He hadn't disparaged my choice when we shared a couple of Coors in his trailer. Said that was all he drank these days. Was this his other persona coming out? I said, "Hey man, if you don't mind, can we grab a table rather than sit at the bar? I slept funny last night and my back's a little stiff."

He was fine with that and said he'd carry our drinks over. I found a booth in the quietest corner of the room, a conveniently located potted plant nearby. I was in luck. It was an artificial Ficus tree that was impervious to alcohol. Planticide would be off my conscience.

The smell of beer-dampened sawdust pervaded the place. Happy Hour was in full swing, mostly guys in work clothes. There was a steady rumble of semi-inebriated conversation that I'd have to raise my voice to talk over. I would have preferred a calmer setting but this would do.

"Next round's on me," I said when Brent sidled over to the booth, drinks in hand.

"Our money's no good here. I just leave a big tip. Cash. That way it goes to the folks who need it most. Way I look at it, local folks know I hang here. The owners get a boost for the business and don't need my money. Kinda like product placement on the show."

"You're a one man economic stimulus."

"I know you're kidding but that's kinda how I see myself. I look at this island and I can see why it's in sorry shape. Bad planning. A lot of yahoos with no government or building experience been running the place for years. I've actually made friends with the current mayor. Nice older man, but clueless when it comes to plans for the island's future. They let things deteriorate. I'm trying to change that. One house at a time."

"More like six a season."

"Six a year is a drop in the bucket, but if the show keeps on growing, we can make this a cool destination. Get folks to check it out. Bring in some Yankee currency."

"I suppose in time, you're thinking it could be Hilton Head North."

"Nah. I think big. I'd like to make *that* place, Judy's Island South. But that's a dream, long way off. Next step is to get myself elected mayor."

"Politics? Really?"

"Yeah, really. See, there *are* some investors hovering around, partly because of the show. But they're vultures. They don't want to revitalize the island. Just want to exploit it. If I was mayor, I could get them to spend the right way. Build a community with roots that'll be self sustaining. The guy in office now is retiring and he's said that if I want his endorsement, he'd be happy to give it. I'm planning to do just that."

Purdy's agenda seemed authentic. He hadn't uttered a word about making money for himself. He went on about how Hilton Head had been developed with the environment in mind and he wanted to do the same for his special island. Planned communities, laid out to take advantage of the Lowcountry's natural beauty, that Pat Conroy had written about so eloquently. He taken courses in civil engineering and urban planning in Texas, and was wary of greedy developers taking advantage of lax zoning regulations. He was passionate about it, almost as passionate as he was about Cami. He hoped to use his celebrity to sway star struck investors into doing the right thing.

I said, "What about the show? Can you do both?"

"Mayor is a part time gig, pays twenty five grand. I've been working out a way they can shoot around my civic duties. Hell, I'll work sixteen hour days if that's what it takes. And we only shoot half the year anyway."

He tapped his bourbon glass against my frosty beer mug and gave a solemn toast. "To Iris Walker. May she meet her heavenly reward."

"Amen," I said. After a silent moment, I explained what we had so far.

"Iris was a drug user. Cocaine. Her connection might've figured she was a rich Hollywood type and ripped her off."

"So what happened had nothing to do with Cam?"

"Don't know that for sure. Her wallet and phone were missing. No clothes or luggage. That could mean robbery was the motive or that someone wanted us to *think* it was the motive. My cop friend told me that Iris had turned her rental car in already. So she must have Ubered it to the motel or come with someone, and that someone was likely the one who got her the drugs."

"It could be she met the wrong person online and the hookup went south. Can't they get DNA from man juice?"

"Iris was gay."

"No shit. How do you know that?

"She told me. Made it a point, first thing when we met. She never told you?"

Brent started in on his beer and signaled the attentive barman for another round. I'd barely put a dent in mine.

He said, "Truth be told King, I thought she had a thing for me. Not my type and I was going hot and heavy with Alison at the time. You sure she wasn't bi-sexual?"

"Didn't seem that way. They'll swab for sexual activity and we'll find out."

He finished his beer chaser. "By the way, did you talk to Alison?"

"I did. She claims not to have any interest in replacing Cami, on the show or in real life, despite her contempt for your wife's construction skills. If I were you, I'd be nice to her. She's really someone better suited for you than Cami."

His tone changed from friendly to combative. "How do you come off saying that? You think you know what's best for me?"

"Alison is the real deal. Just like you. Honest, hard working. Clean. Cami has a pretty unsavory past and more than one person on the set told me she was into her evil ways again. Did cocaine with Iris."

"Watch what you say about Cam. You're full of shit if you believe those rumors."

"Brent, keep it down and watch your language."

"Who're you to tell me to watch my language? My mother? I don't give a shit who hears me." Mr. Hyde was emerging after three shots and a couple of beers. Like flipping a switch.

I pushed to see how far he would go. A stress test. "Your wife was doing blow. I know you think she walked on water, but you couldn't miss the signs. She's a stone junkie. It could be her connection killed Iris."

"Who's side are you on, King? You blaming Cam for what happened to Walker?"

"Very possible. Calm down, Brent." Another test of the theory that telling someone to calm down usually has the opposite effect.

It did.

"*You* fucking calm down. You were hired to find Cam, not run down her good name."

"Don't be an idiot. You were blind to who she really is. You're a big boy, Brent. Too smart to fall for such an air head like Cami. Open your eyes."

Instead, he tried to close one of mine. He shoved the unmoored table at me, and only a quick reaction kept it from breaking some of my ribs. He hurled himself toward me. I didn't have time to stand so I went low, aiming at his left knee.

The old football injury. He yowled in pain and crumbled to the ground. I jumped up and hovered over him, ready to shove him down if he tried to get up. Before I could, two of the bar's patrons grabbed me from behind and held my arms back. I was in the process of breaking their hold when a massive fist collided with my jaw.

Next thing I knew, I was pinned to the ground. Three big guys were holding me down. I was prepared to be punched and kicked to Kingdom Come when I heard Brent's voice through heavy breathing.

"That's enough, fellas. Let him up. Just a little misunderstanding, is all."

28

The huddle of redneck goons around me dispersed and Brent Purdy extended a hand to help me to my feet. I ignored it and got up on my own.

He said, "Let's take a walk, King. Outside."

If this was an invitation to take him on one on one, I was all in. A little salt air would clear the cobwebs and I'd be ready for round two. I bit my lip and walked toward the door. The tip be damned.

When we had cleared the pub's patio and reached a sandy expanse leading to the water, I turned to face my adversary directly.

"Your move, Boomer," I said.

"Please accept my apology, King. I'm sorry I flew off the handle at ya."

An unexpected peace offering that I was in no mood to accept. I said nothing.

He spread his arms and offered his jaw. "Okay here, you want a free shot. Take it. I'll turn the other cheek."

I was tempted. But, bruising my hand against his rock hard chin wouldn't accomplish anything, other than a moment of satisfaction followed by an evening of throbbing until I could find some ice. Besides, his makeup girl would have a challenge if I gave in to my instincts.

"I'll say this and then I'm out of here, Purdy. The cops see you as the number one suspect in Cami's disappearance. But Jaime Johansen thinks you're a good guy and asked me to look into it, hopefully prove the cops wrong. You sure didn't help your cause tonight."

"I know that and I'm sorry. But you gotta believe me. I love Cam and I had nothing to do with her going away."

"So you never let that temper we just saw get out of hand around her?"

"Okay, I'll admit it. I let things get out of hand sometimes. But I never hit her. I swear. I'm getting help. I'm seeing a shrink."

He voice broke as he said it. It took courage for a man with his background to admit he was a damaged soul.

He said, "See, my mom gave me up when I was five. My dad had left her with me and my baby brother and she couldn't support us both, so she foisted me off on someone she said were related to us, an older couple who wanted kids but couldn't have any of their own."

He walked a tight circle while continuing. "They took care of me. There always was food on the table, clothes, decent schools. Nothing fancy, but they gave me what they could. I called them my aunt and uncle, but to this day I'm not sure they were.

"They were real devout Christians. Didn't let me date in high school. My aunt made me hate what she called Jezebels. She was real plain looking and my shrink says she musta been jealous of any woman better looking than she was, which was just about everyone. So I grew up not trusting any female with even a hint of pretty."

He was having a hard time getting his words out. I could relate to an extent. I said, "And they taught you that sex is dirty. Not something you talk about. I get that. I was raised Catholic."

"I hope yours wasn't as bad as mine. I went away to college. I was on the football team. You know the deal. You played hoops. Even though the cheerleaders went for the skill position guys, I had my chances. But I never gave in to it. I saw all them football groupies as sluts. It kinda confirmed what my aunt was saying. I told you I was saving myself for marriage. That was true. Can we walk a little? Would that be okay?"

This mountain of a man was asking my permission, his voice reduced to a constricted whimper. We started toward the water.

I said, "So how was Cami different?"

"She had her own scars. She was honest about those. She never really knew her dad. Her mom wasn't religious but she was hard on her like my aunt was. Physically abused. I guess we had pain in common."

From what I knew about Cami's history, that much was true. But I also knew that she wouldn't be above using stories of her own hardships to manipulate him.

He said, "Fact, it was on a walk on the beach on a night like this when she poured her heart out to me and I guess that's when we fell in love. She was so vulnerable but she gave off this vibe of being a tough cookie. Just like me, a hard-ass football player turned builder. But inside, I was a hurtin' pup."

"How does this explain your temper?"

"My shrink said I thought I deserved to be punished for betraying my raisin'. She says that even though I found someone I could love and respect, deep down I needed to pay the price for going against what we learned growing up. So when Cam wanted to do what married people do, she turned into a slut in my eyes and I lashed out. Later I knew how crazy that was and apologized but I was fighting against years of brainwashing. I've made a lot of progress. Shouldn't say this, but things was good with Alison."

"Did you ever think you took it too far with Cami? That she was afraid of you?"

"I never touched Cam that way. But I'm twice her size so I s'pose I can see how she'd be scared when I'd fly off the handle."

"She told other people she was deathly afraid of you. Did she tell you that was why she left?"

"No way. She just said she didn't love me anymore. 'The love has died' was how she put it. I pleaded with her to tell me what I could do to make it right. I'd do anything. Counseling. Separate bedrooms. She wouldn't budge."

"If it were me, I'd think there was another man."

"She swore there wasn't. I believed her. It would have been an easier out if she told me there was someone else."

"Maybe she was afraid you'd hurt whoever it was."

We'd reached the water's edge. The tide was going out, revealing a muddy bottom caked with all manner of shells and debris. Although we could look out to the ocean, this beach was on the Sound and tidal.

He said, "I wouldn't do that. I ain't that kinda man."

"You didn't do anything to follow her? Try to catch her in the act with someone?"

He shook his head and gave me a weak, "No."

"You know Brent, you had me going for a while. I was really starting to feel bad for you. But then you lie to me and blow all your credibility."

"What did I lie about?"

I pulled the tracker from my jacket pocket.

29

"What's that supposed to be? Looks like some kinda part off a computer."

"Come on Purdy, don't deny it. You planted this on Cami's car."

"What is it?"

"The more you play dumb, the more you lose me. You know it's a tracking device. And I know it's yours."

He kicked at the sand. His impulse was to stonewall and keep feigning ignorance, but he needed to keep me on his side. "I was just wanting to see where she'd been hanging out is all. Maybe I could run into her somewhere away from the shoot and we could talk."

"Brent, you withheld evidence. You should've told the police you had this on her car the minute they asked you about her."

"How'd you get a hold of it? Do the cops know you have it?"

"I'm going to turn it in tonight. I was hoping you'd have some kind of log as to where she was in the weeks before she disappeared."

He wasn't sure he trusted that I'd protect him and I couldn't blame him. He said, "Gets downloaded in real time to my phone. Kinda like how you know where your Uber driver is. But the history syncs to my laptop and that's at home."

"I need that history. It could help me find out what happened to Cami."

"Then you're gonna give it to the cops. If you do, they'll arrest me. Like you said, withholding evidence. They already think I'm guilty. Please King, I'm begging ya, don't give it to them."

"That makes it sound like it's been an act all along, pretending to care about Cami. You're holding back something that could help find her to save your own skin. Makes you look guilty as sin."

"I swear to you I'm not. I love Cam and I'd do anything to get her back."

"So why didn't you tell them upfront about the tracker?"

"Like you said, it makes me look guilty. Look, the cops were banging me hard with a lot of questions, acting like I did something to her. I reckoned if I told them about the tracker, that'd put it over the top."

He had a point. "So why didn't you tell *me* about it?"

"Because you'd tell 'em and the same thing would happen."

"You were a jealous husband who was worried his estranged wife was stepping out. That was a given with the cops, right from the start. If you'd told them about the tracker up front, it'd look like you were doing everything you could to help. It would've boosted your credibility with them."

"Or they could have just booked me on the spot."

He started pacing, looking out over the water. "The problem is, if I'm arrested, even if I'm cleared down the road, there goes my chance of winning any election. And my plans for Judy's Island go up in smoke."

He wanted to make his island a better place and that was a righteous cause. As it was, I'd already stuck my neck out by not immediately giving the cops the tracker. Montanez wasn't a fan and he could make a case that *I* had obstructed justice.

"Brent, give me that history log. Then I'll turn the tracker in. I'll tell the county guy that I was going to give it to him right away but Iris Walker's murder got me sidetracked. There's a chance they'll believe that."

"But if you tell them it's my tracker, they'll come for me."

"I don't *have* to tell them that. I can say I found it and I have no way of knowing whose it is. The only person who knows otherwise is Ginn and he'll never talk."

"How *did* you know it was mine?"

"When you showed up at the motel. No one on the show could have known that Iris was murdered, unless they were the killer. I gave you the benefit of the doubt on that."

"Thanks. I don't s'pose it matters if I tell you I had nothing to do with killing Iris. I do have someone who can back me up on that. Henley's last night in town."

"Unimpeachable, in my eyes. You saw that Cami's car was on the move and thought that whoever abducted her had bailed it out. Or maybe she'd hijacked it herself. No security in that lot and she loved that red Mustang. You figured you'd find out on your own before calling the cops."

"Yeah. If I called them soon as I picked up movement, they'd know I'd been tracking her. Damn it. I thought I had it covered."

"Once they have the tracker in hand, they're going to try to find out who bought it. That won't be easy because I tried with my computer geek and he came up empty."

The cops wouldn't necessarily put together that he rushed to the motel where Iris was killed. If they did, he could claim someone heard about it on a police scanner and told him about her. He'd have to convince someone to lie for him.

As it was, he said, "I bought it online from a black market site. It could get 'em in a passel of trouble. They'll never admit they sold 'em to me or anybody else."

"For your sake, I hope you're right."

"I'm telling you the truth, man. Follow me back to my place and I'll print out that log."

In Tomey's Honda, I followed his pickup along a back country road to his place. The ten minute ride gave me time to make two phone calls.

The first call was to Montanez. I got his voice mail. I told him I had found the tracker and I wanted to give it to him personally but Walker's murder happened and I'd forgotten all about it in the furor. When and where could we meet?

The second was to Ginn. I told him that I'd hidden the tracker under the rear carpet of Tomey's car, next to the transmission hump. If he didn't hear from me by ten this evening, assume that Brent had killed me in an attempt to recover the tracker and save himself.

30

My fears were unfounded. I could tell instantly that Purdy was no computer whiz. It took him a bunch of *hunt and pecks* until he found the history log of Cami's movements. It took him even longer to locate his printer queue and send over the pages.

"You want me to email this to you, King?"

"Nah. This'll do fine."

In case matters came to a head, I didn't want an electronic trail leading to my inbox.

I said, "You shooting tomorrow?"

"Yep. Different house. Actually two different ones. I'll give you the addresses. And hey man, I am sorry about before. I'm working on anger management. Got me a temper that's hard to shake."

I shook his extended hand. "Lot of us tough guys suffer from that. I'll be in touch."

I was home less than an hour later. Ginn and Tomey were cuddled up on the sofa, watching Kevin Costner in *Yellowstone*. They paused the DVR when I entered.

Bosco was asleep at their feet, only his head on a dog bed. He looked up when I came in, gave me his "oh, it's you" look and went back to his doggie dreams.

Moses said, "Quarter to ten. I was about to call out the cavalry in a few minutes."

"I'm glad you said cavalry and not Calvary like most people do these days."

Ginn said, "More kids into religion now than Westerns. Always count on old Costner to weave us a good cowboy story. So, what happened with Purdy? When we talked, sounded like you thought he was luring you out to the country to chop you into little pieces, like in *Fargo*."

I told him about the altercation at the bar and the subsequent peace talks.

He said, "Damn, King. I missed a chance to mix it up with some rednecks?"

"It was four on one."

"Me there woulda evened up them odds. You ain't looking no worse for wear."

"Tell my jaw that. Lucky, Purdy called off his dogs when he did."

Bosco's ears perked up at the mention of dogs. I wasn't sure if it was because it sometimes was followed by the word 'food', or that he harbored a wish that I'd bring home a puppy to be a companion.

Alex said, "Did Montanez get back to you?"

I checked my phone in case I'd missed a voice mail or text. "No. Strikes me as an 'early to bed, early to rise' type."

"No such thing in our biz, Riley. Turn the tracker in to me now. I'll fudge the time a little if it helps."

"What tracker? I don't want to put you in a position to have to lie to protect Boomer. I can prove I called Montanez tonight to turn it over. I expect he'll give me some guff about not doing it right away, but unless they're really out to get me, it shouldn't matter."

Ginn said, "What I don't get is you not wanting to tell 'em it's Purdy's. Why you covering for him?"

"Thing is, I think the guy really wants to do some good." I told them about his plans to run for office. "Purdy was right that an arrest would kill his political future."

Tomey was frustrated with me. "You're withholding information about a crime on the hunch that Boomer's innocent. Your neck is stuck way out, bud. Now we know, too. We're co-conspirators."

Ginn agreed with his woman. "Before he printed out that log, you could say you suspected Purdy but couldn't prove it. Now you got proof in your hands, 5-0."

"Legally, you should divulge it," Tomey said. "I should divulge it. No one can prove you told us, but you're pushing me over the line again and I don't like it. I think it's highly possible Boomer's playing you."

"I think he has a good heart. He wants to do good for his community. He just got involved in a bad situation with a bad woman."

Tomey shook her head. "You haven't heard her side. She was afraid of him. You saw his temper tonight. I think you picked the wrong horse, King."

31

Decades ago with the FBI, I participated in pre-dawn raids. I didn't like them then, I like them even less now.

It's one thing to crash a drug lord, or a human trafficking czar. Surprising them when they're in the buff is a justifiable way to bust a bad guy before he and his minions can lock and load or flush away evidence.

But a lot of dramatic raids are done for publicity purposes or to scare the living daylights out of a white collar criminal who would have surrendered peaceably. There's no need to traumatize the family, especially when young children are involved.

It wasn't exactly a predawn raid that awakened me that morning, but 'Marty' Montanez and two uniforms armed to the teeth was not how I wanted to start my day. At least they just pounded on my door instead of crashing through it.

Montanez said, "Who else is in the house, King? And are they armed?"

"My dog Bosco is armed with a ferocious set of teeth but never uses them on humans. Scares the hell out of the local squirrel population, though."

"This isn't funny. Who else is here?"

"I haven't checked upstairs but Detective Alexandra Tomey has been known to stay over with her boyfriend."

On the spur of the moment, I couldn't come up with a better description of Ginn. *Boyfriend* is so inadequate.

Montanez smirked. "I need you to come with me."

Here goes the dance. "Am I under arrest?"

"Not yet."

"If you just want to ask me some questions, I'll be more than happy to answer them. Why don't we do this in a civilized manner? Cop to ex-fed-cop. Got some fine Kona."

"I could arrest you and *make* you come in."

"You could, but that'd be embarrassing. For you. Look, I get the whole intimidation thing but it doesn't work with me. Why don't we sit down and talk? Coffee'll be ready in a jif. I *would* like to put on some real pants, if you don't mind."

I was wearing pajama bottoms, my torso on display. The two cops with him didn't sound any wolf whistles, so I took it that they weren't impressed with my six-pack.

Montanez weighed his options. He had to save face with his men, but whatever he thought he had on me had to be flimsy. He'd wind up owing an apology and no cop likes to do that. He said, "I'll need to come with you when you change."

"No peeking. Okay, right this way. Bosco, I'll take you out in a minute unless one of these gentlemen wants to volunteer."

I thought I heard a stifled sarcastic laugh from one of the uniforms. My act wasn't playing well this early.

In my room, I pulled on a pair of jeans, a *Dire Straits* tee shirt and running shoes that had no intention of running this morning.

Montanez and I came back out to the breakfast area. I started a pot brewing and the coffee was ready almost instantly.

I said, "Help yourselves to milk and sugar. I was hoarding that box of doughnuts on the counter but my momma taught me to be a gracious host. Don't eat 'em all, though. Bad for the tummy."

"Shut up, King. Sit down."

I didn't heed his sit command, but I was polite about it. "Yes sir, Detective Montanez. Now what can I do for you?"

He took a sip of coffee. As much as he tried to suppress it, his face told me it was an upgrade over what he was used to. His two colleagues went over to the sofa in the great room, coffee and doughnuts in hand. Bosco followed them, figuring the newbies would be easy marks. Failing that, they might be careless eaters prone to dropping crumbs.

Montanez said, "Let's do the easy part first. What's the story with this tracker you called about last night?"

"You agreed to let me inspect Cami Purdy's Mustang. I found it attached to a wheel well."

"Why didn't you turn it over immediately to the officer who showed you the car?"

"I thought I told you on the message I left. I wanted to give it to you personally. The kid was Jasper County and looked a little raw. I wasn't sure he'd handle it the right way. It's your case so I didn't want to tie it up in a turf battle."

"That's no excuse. You broke the chain of evidence, you should know that."

"The other part is, this tracker looks to be black market. I have a computer geek who I thought might be able to trace it through means you may not have access to. Struck out on that, unfortunately."

I was standing at the kitchen island, across from Montanez. "The tracker's in this drawer. I'll take it out slowly, in case you're afraid I'll throw a butcher knife at you. Okay?"

"Not okay. I'll take it out myself."

I said, "Your lack of trust is very hurtful, detective."

He slipped on a latex glove, opened the drawer, and looked over the device as if it had cooties. He dropped it into a plastic evidence bag.

Moses Ginn was padding down the upstairs hallway. The footfalls were too heavy to be Tomey's. "Uh, sounds like Detective Tomey's friend is coming down. Don't let his looks scare you. He comes in peace."

"Boys, keep an eye on that guy. Guns ready."

I said, "Wait. No need for that." I called up, "Moses, detective Montanez is here with two other officers. Come on down with your hands in plain sight. They're a little antsy for some reason."

Ginn came down the stairs and for once, followed my instructions. It was likely that he had a gun, hearing noises coming from the great room.

Moses said, "Morning, Detective. We meet again. Officers. Digging them doughnuts, I see. Hope you haven't drunk all the coffee. I need my morning Joe, else I get cranky."

Montanez looked wary of my giant friend. "The infamous Moses Ginn. I didn't put it together at the motel. Jason, pat this man down. Just a precaution. Please cooperate, Mr. Ginn."

Ginn was trying to be as obsequious as a man of his dimensions could be. "Yes sir, detective, sir. What's this visit's all about, might I ask?"

Ginn reached the bottom of the stairs. Sure enough, he was packing. Not his go-to weapon, just a smaller backup. He said, "Licensed, concealed carry permit. Always have it on me knowing the way trouble follows my man King around."

Officer Jason brushed the doughnut crumbs away and removed Ginn's gun from the small of his back and placed it on the island in front of Montanez.

Montanez said, "We'll need to confirm that later. Do *you* happen to know why King didn't turn this tracker in sooner?" He wanted to see if we had our stories straight or were improvising excuses.

"He was fixing to, but King here got a call about a girl who missed a flight. Her boss was real worried something bad happened so we had to run over and check it out. Turns out it was that Walker lady."

"Is Detective Tomey upstairs now? And if she is, why did you come down first and not her?"

"She ain't here," Moses said

"A shame. She'd be much more pleasant to deal with and look at. So. Iris Walker might have been murdered and the tracker became low priority. Is that your story?"

Ginn and I nodded in unison, like Alvin and the Chipmunks.

Montanez said, "Ms. Walker's TOD was one a.m.. Where were you both then?"

I went first. "I was here, sleeping. Moses and I turned in around eleven, I think. Separate bedrooms, in case you were wondering."

"So you're sleeping with Alexandra Tomey, Mr. Ginn?"

"Ain't seeing how's that's none of your concern."

"Can you swear King was here at one a.m.?"

"Damn. Normally, I check his bed every hour just to make sure no bogeymen be bothering him, but that night I plumb forgot."

I said, "Bosco'll vouch for me. Come on Montanez, are you insinuating that *I* killed Walker? Why on earth would I do that?"

"I don't *insinuate* anything. I stick with facts. Bottom line is, we have a very credible eyewitness who states that you and Iris Walker had a very heated argument that afternoon on the *Country Fixin's* set. Says you had a look in your eye like you were ready to kill her on the spot."

32

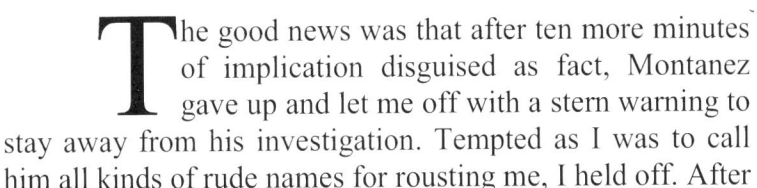

The good news was that after ten more minutes of implication disguised as fact, Montanez gave up and let me off with a stern warning to stay away from his investigation. Tempted as I was to call him all kinds of rude names for rousting me, I held off. After this early morning jam session, it was clear he'd be more of a hindrance than a help.

Ginn was on the same page. He took everything in stride, as always. "Well 5-0, so much for professional courtesy."

"What, I wasn't nice enough to him? I offered him our finest coffee and his guys cleaned out our doughnut stash. You were on your best behavior. *Yes sir, no sir*. What do I have to do the get that kind of obedience from you?"

"I doubt even Bosco be willing to do that, Massa. Enough jive. What's our plan today?"

"If Montanez hasn't got someone tailing us, I'd like to check out some of Cami's movements the last days before she vanished. Got the print out from Purdy but I haven't really looked it over yet."

"Why don't I scare up some breakfast while you take the pup out for a walk? Maybe you and him come up with some ideas."

That was just what I needed --- a brisk walk on the beach with Bosco tugging me in the direction of every seagull who dares to cross his path. It would give me time to organize my thoughts and come up with something that might break the stalemate. Ginn told me to come back in half an hour and he'd have prepared a fine breakfast, both on the table and in the doggie bowl.

Bosco always darts away when I reach for his harness. I don't know why he does it. He loves his walks and knows that when I leash him up, he's about to go out. Perhaps he does it to get my blood circulating. Or maybe he just likes to play hard to get. Even when I threaten to leave without him, he dances away. He calls my bluff and I give in. Who's the smart one?

Today, the beach was sparsely populated: a few joggers, bicyclists, and other dog walkers. The ocean was cloaked in a dense fog which extended over the beach until it reached the dunes. It was dissipating in slow motion. Visibility was less than a hundred feet, so I had to be on the lookout, lest some careless biker run over Bosco. Most of them cautiously navigate the packed sand, but there always are a few crazies, high from the previous night.

On the walk, I struggled with the default assumption that Cami Purdy is dead. No ransom demand yet. That made kidnapping unlikely unless her captor was after something other than money. A beautiful TV star might attract such depravity, some INCEL who wants to make her his sex slave, thereby punishing all the women who had rejected him. The type of psychological damage that might inflict might make murder a more desirable outcome in the mind of the victim.

If she had been killed, her body might never be recovered. Woods, swamps, and abandoned farmland are all within easy reach. It was easy digging in the sandy soil and easy to cover up signs of excavation. Even though we weren't in the bayou, there were plenty of gators who'd relish dining on a sushi-ed actress.

I knew that Cami was living in a large rental house while filming *Country Fixin's*. That would be a must-see before scoping out the itinerary of her last days. I didn't have a key, but that's never stopped me before.

My dog did his business and I bagged and disposed of it. Upon returning home, I gathered up Purdy's printout and carried it over to the kitchen island, figuring I'd peruse it over breakfast.

Ginn had prepared a feast. Blueberry pancakes, bacon, chunks of seasonal fruit and a fresh pot of Kona blend. He mixed some crumbled pancake and bacon with Bosco's kibble, which the dog polished off before I'd had my first sip of coffee. He'd be alone until Tomey got back, but with a full tummy and an empty schedule, his day would likely be more pleasant and productive than mine.

33

Ginn insisted on driving again. Although my MDX is much roomier, he has added so many modern conveniences to the old two-seater that it was more advanced than my more recent SUV. The heated and cooled perforated leather seats enveloped us in luxurious comfort. But to him, the key factor was that his vehicle was more stylish than mine.

I said, "This *Driving Miss Daisy* bit doesn't bother you?"

"The Benz don't have no back seat but I do see the resemblance 'tween you and that Daisy crone. Difference is Morgan Freeman wasn't packing like I am."

"I doubt they'll be much need for it. Folks on Ribaut Island tend to be pretty genteel."

"Yeah, a black man never had much to fear from rich white folk."

"Good point."

Ribaut Island is a small gated community within the larger Hilton Head Plantation. Since the gate automatically opens both coming and going, it is strictly ornamental. It's elegant and reeks of exclusivity, but it's as useful as snow tires in Florida.

Ginn said, "Didn't one of them stock defrauders live on this here island? That Bailey woman we tried to save before she drowned in that storm."

"They did have a house here at one time. Boy, that Bailey caper was a close call for us, wasn't it? We almost bought the farm. Rising water and rats in that dark tunnel. Yeesh."

"Yes sir, don't exactly bring back a ton of good memories, 5-0. But we got the job done."

The graceful gate swung open and we entered the private enclave. Ribaut Island only has a few dozen homes, but each one is spectacular in its own way. The places that face the marsh are more affordable, if you consider a million bucks affordable. The houses along the Sound start at two mil and soar close to eight figures.

Cami's rental wasn't visible from the street, so lush was the tropical landscaping. Each tree and shrub was meticulously cropped, not a leaf out of place. The maintenance costs must be astronomical. The house itself was impressive --- three stories of beige stucco, a tall dual staircase leading to a copper roofed entry porch. The backside faced the marsh and had to cost the production company over five grand a month.

There was an older black man trimming a tiny patch of Zoysia grass. As Moses parked the Benz in front of the house, the man didn't look up from his chore. He was wearing a bulky headset and didn't hear us pull in. The gas powered trimmer he was using was louder than a Black Sabbath concert.

Ginn tapped him on the shoulder. The man put the tool into the idle mode and pulled the headphones down to his neck. From the chunky green earcups, I could make out an old Temptations song.

I said, "We're with the *Country Fixin's* show and we're here looking for Ms. Cami Purdy."

The old gardener smiled at Ginn, displaying a couple of gold incisors. "Don't know as I know 'bout country music or whatever you're talking about. Lady rents here. Barely says hello. Like I'm invisible. I don't keep her schedule or nothing."

"Has she been here in the last week?"

"Not so's I know. But that ain't no big thing. Only way I'm sure she's here is her car's parked outside. Can't miss that red whip."

"You have a key to the house?"

"No key but I got the garage code. That's where they keep the tools. Blowers, mowers and such."

"You don't bring your own equipment?" Moses asked.

"I do, but not for this job. Boss drops me off here three days a week. I use the stuff comes with the house. Just bring a gas can so's I can fire 'em up."

I said, "Does Cami have many visitors? Parties?"

The man took a big red handkerchief from his back pocket and wiped his face. It was warm, the humidity was high. He was sweating a great deal; his stained grey shirt soaked through.

"Don't see no one else here most times. I'm just here during mornings and truth be told, ain't none of my affair. Lady could have folks staying with her at night and I wouldn't know. Never saw nobody with her 'cepting that young dude that drives her around sometimes."

"Bob Walsh?"

"Don't know his name. Friendly fella. Always says hello. Tosses me a bottle of water on his way out sometimes."

"Young guy? Strange haircut. Mid twenties?"

"Be about right. Now if you excuse me, I got work to do."

"Sure. What's your name, sir?"

"Percy Mayfield."

I said, "Percy, take my card. If you see anyone at the house, please give a call. The show is paying a pretty steep price for the rent and other than Ms. Purdy and her personal guests, no one is authorized to stay there."

"Askin' me to snitch?"

Moses said, "To protect your boss. Any damage gets done inside, there could be a nasty fight over who pays and you wouldn't want to get caught up in the middle."

"That case, I'll keep my eyes peeled."

I thanked him and we walked around the house. One of the three garage doors underneath the house was open. Since the foundation was raised, there was room for a dozen cars if the owner chose to keep the area open. This tall crawl space was more cut up --- there was a designated garage that could handle three cars, maybe a fourth if parked in tandem. There were two steel doors on opposite sides of the back wall. We tried the left one first, which led to a cavernous workshop. All kinds of professional woodworking tools and equipment were arrayed in neat rows.

The door on the right opened to a small vestibule with a wide staircase leading up to the living area. There was an elevator controlled by a security keypad. Since we didn't have the code, we used the stairs.

When we reached the top, the door was unlocked, so the gardener or anyone else with access to the garage could enter the main house. My lock-picking skills were unnecessary.

Ginn said, "Before you open your mouth, you ain't in no position to ask why one woman living alone needs a house this size. Look at the shack you be living in."

"I have a dog. Bosco needs his space."

My place was larger and had nicer views, but this was no slum. Every detail was top of the line, actually a bit over the top. The furniture was oversized and a trifle gaudy for my taste. Lots of gold fixtures. White marble. Wallpaper. Heavy molding. Faux painting on the ceilings. A place built or last updated in the nineties. A poor man's concept of the high life.

I said, "Give me some credit for taste, Ginn. Your grandma might be happy here, but a twenty-something like Cami? I suppose it's only a rental. Kind of doubt she'd buy a house like this if it was up to her."

"Has good bones, though. I bet your pal Davis could do a number on it and make it real cool."

I had run the address through Zillow and noted it had been on the market several times over the past decade. No takers. Finally the owner decided to defray some of the carrying costs by renting it out.

Ginn said, "This kitchen looks like no one ever cooked in it. Cami not very handy with pots and pans. Although someone looks like her, who cares?"

"Lucky I have you around for that." He gave me a sour look. "Let's check out the bedroom."

The master bedroom was on the second floor, a definite no-no is this area. Most people want the master on the first floor. That was a big reason that a house with this kind of potential hasn't sold to a rehabber. Even Brent Purdy would have a hard time flipping this place for what it had cost to build.

The bedroom had a marble fireplace and a generous sitting area. An enormous walk in closet, full of frocks. I took a picture of the contents of the closet with my phone.

On the double vanity, I saw a thin layer of whitish dust. "What do you make of this?" I said.

Ginn dabbed a finger to his tongue and rubbed it across the countertop. He sniffed. "*Peruvian Marching*

Powder, they used to call it. Jes' keeping with the 80's theme of this pad. Cocaine."

I rummaged through the vanity drawers. The first thing I learned was that Cami isn't a natural blonde. She suffered from digestive problems, evidenced by several brands of over-the-counter remedies. There was a host of cosmetic products that women consider necessities for purposes beyond my comprehension.

No prescription bottles. Initially, that seemed unusual because most of my contemporaries are on doctor recommended medications. At Cami's age, that wouldn't be the case. Ah, the sweet bird of youth.

As we went back to the bedchamber, Ginn's nose was twitching like a bunny in heat. I said, "Better rinse that junk off your snout, man. Who knows what kind of crap she was snorting."

"Not that. Cologne. You smell it?"

"Not really."

He went into his bloodhound routine, focusing on one of the pillows on the left side of the king bed.

"Got me a keen sense of smell, 5-0. That's one reason why I's such a good chef. This pillow reeks. Take a whiff."

He handed me the pillow and burying my nose in it, I did smell *something*. A little cloying, but not unpleasant. He went to the other side of the bed and lifted the top pillow to his face.

He wasn't exaggerating about his highly developed sense of smell. Last year, he had picked up that Jaime had been in my house when I thought she was on the West Coast with Stone. He smelled her perfume on my dog.

As he put the pillow down, I asked, "Well, Sherlock, what do you think?"

"Couple things. This here other pillow was the woman's. Same shampoo, face cream, feminine shit. And somebody used it recent-like. Last two days or so. And the one you got was used by a man. Old Brent's after shave?"

"My nose isn't as sensitive as yours but I was in his trailer with him. And his house. Close quarters. Never noticed any cologne."

"Hand that over. Let me smell it again."

"You don't need to cleanse your palate? Does that work for smells, too?"

"Got any sherbet?"

He forced a heavy exhale to clear his nasal passage and took the pillow from me. "Definitely a man. I smelled this same stuff the other day. Trying to think of where. If I can, we might find out who was porking Cami."

34

Ginn had put it crudely, but his question might be a key to what had happened to Cami. If she was stepping out on Boomer, the behemoth might have killed her in a fit of jealous rage. It was also possible that she had taken on an unhinged lover.

In the middle of a fruitless investigation, doubts creep in. I question why I got involved in the first place, although this time, I know why. The list Brent had printed out was useless. Cami had either been on Ribaut or at one of the houses they were rehabbing. If she was out catting around, it wasn't in the Mustang.

As we drove away from the rental on Ribaut, I shared my misgivings with Ginn. "You know, Moses, we're getting nowhere on this. Letting Jaime down."

"I know you trying to win back your girl. That's why you taking this so personal. Usually you got a thing for truth and justice."

"You forgot to add the American Way, whatever that is nowadays. Yeah, getting Jaime back was what got me started but now I'm into it. I just don't know which way to turn."

"Seems to me like ole Brent's the logical choice, 5-0."

"True, but in spite of everything, a big part of me wants to see him be innocent so he can keep up the good work and fix up Judy's Island. Make it a cool place again.

It's like Asbury Park, back in my old stomping grounds in Jersey."

"All I know about that is that postcard on the Boss's first LP."

"You wouldn't know the history, living down here. Asbury had fallen on hard times. Became a real slum by the sea. Nobody wanted to live there, despite it being close to New York City and right on the ocean. Race riots, crime, drugs."

"And your boy Springsteen turned all that around?"

"He had a part in it. Lit the spark, made it sound like a neat place, even when it wasn't. But what really happened was the gays came in and revitalized the town. Rehabbed houses and shops, one by one and now it's a mecca."

"What you saying, you think Brent wants Judy's to be Asbury South?"

"I don't think Brent cares who comes to the island, in terms of orientation, sexual or political. Long as they have money to spend. And it doesn't seem like he wants to do it to make himself rich. There's something honest about the man, Moses. Pure. He knows he's got a problem with temper and he's trying to fix it. His weight was an issue and he's taking care of that. I think he sees himself like the houses he works on. Good bones, but in need of a few small repairs to make things right."

"You always telling me you can't let feelings affect your judgment comes to crime. Man has a violent streak. Big time jones for a lady who dumped his ass. Dude put a tracker on her car so's he knows where she is all the time. That don't strike you as obsessed?"

"It does. He's got to be the number one suspect, I know that. But if he was really out of control, he would've let those goons kick the crap out of me. Instead, he told them to stop before they did any real damage. He lost it quick but pulled it back just as fast. That counts for something."

"That's you, not a woman he's hurting about. What if he followed her to that quarry, where she be necking with some dude she picked up at a bar? He kills 'em both and feeds 'em to the gators."

"If Cami met somebody at a bar, why go to a make-out place like that when you have a house like the one we just saw? That might work for teenagers living at home with their parents but adults don't do it in the back seat anymore."

"Speak for yourself. Maybe she don't want no dude she picks up at a bar knowing where she live. But the scent I picked up at that house was new, 5-0. Either someone was there using Cami's woman stuff, or she's alive."

We stopped at Dunkin' to replenish our doughnut supply and while we were there, a quick cup of coffee. We'd had a heavy breakfast a few hours ago, but a couple of old fashioned doughnuts called our name. We sat in one of the small booths and contemplated our next move.

I said, "I printed out pictures of the cast and crew of *Country Fixin's*. Might do you some good to familiarize yourself with the names and faces."

"Hand 'em over."

He sipped his coffee and thumbed through the photos and short bios. He stopped at one, scratched his chin and pursed his lips. "Seeing this picture jogs my memory. He's the one with the scent I picked up on that pillow. When he walked by us the other day, I couldn't miss it."

He passed me the photo of Bob Walsh.

I said, "Lots of guys probably use that cologne, not just Walsh. It's not exactly proof. That guy Percy said Walsh had been there."

"Didn't say when. That smell on the pillow was recent. Last couple of days."

"Come on. The FBI lab guys can't even put a date on that kind of thing."

"You always tell me you don't believe in coincidences. This kid wasn't just her driver. He was sleeping with her."

"Mo, he volunteered to me that he was asexual."

"You need me to explain how that works? Someone like Cami who knows her way around the feathers could come up with a way to give a fella like that a happy ending."

"Say no more. Okay, I'll go with it. We'll talk to Walsh again. Sounds like you think he's hiding Cami against her will."

"Or with it. I'm thinking they definitely been there after Cami went missing."

My phone buzzed. A text from Winona Sands. Someone had leaked the news that Cami was missing and a reward had been posted. A quick check of my news feed confirmed it.

I told Ginn. "Who'd be stupid enough to do that? Now the cops'll be chasing their tail with all kinds of false leads."

Ginn said, "Might be able find out on my phone." His thumbs flew over the tiny keypad. I could never type on a full size keyboard using two hands, much less text with my thumbs. I use the *voice to text* mode and correct it when it messes up, which is at least half the time. I'm amazed someone with massive hands like Ginn could master that skill, but he is a man of many talents. He has yet to reveal a good many of them, I'm sure.

"No luck," he said, after a minute of pecking. "Ain't the po-po, so I guess it's maybe your squeeze or someone else with the show."

"I don't think Jaime would do that without asking me first. Let me call her."

She sounded a little out of breath when she answered. "Hey, Riles, what's up?"

"I'm sure you know the media's all over the fact Cami's missing now."

"That's what I've been doing all morning. Trying to spin it."

"What're you telling them?"

"Just that Cami has done this in the past. Personal issues to deal with. She doesn't tell anyone what they are because they're private."

"They buying it?"

"For a minute they did. But then goddam Brent put out that ten thousand dollar reward. It'll come out real soon that they've separated. That's not so bad but people have seen enough *Law and Order* episodes to know he's the prime suspect. Kills his nice-guy image. It's in the damage control stage now."

"You can't finesse that?"

"Not easily. There's a thing in our business called the *Streisand Effect*."

"What's this got to do with Babs Streisand?"

"It about something she did years ago. There were some pictures of her house that she felt invaded her privacy. She made a big deal about trying to suppress them. Fact is, the pictures were nothing special and nobody would have noticed them. But because she whined so much about it publicly, it became a cause célèbre and everybody saw them. So if we try to cover up, they'll keep digging and more damaging details will come out. If we admit that they were going through a rough period and living apart, maybe that'll be enough."

"It'll boost the show's ratings, won't it?"

"I really hate going down this road but once it starts rolling you have to massage it to your benefit or it can work against you."

"Well, the reason I called was to tell you that I'm thinking there's a chance Cami's alive."

I told her about Bob Walsh and Moses' intuition. "Thing is, Walsh told me he wasn't into sex. With anyone, male of female and I bought it. We think he shared a bed with her though. Do you know anything about this kid?"

"Never met him. He's really just a glorified gopher and chauffeur. I have no idea what his story is. Isn't he from around there?"

"Yeah, he's local. Something I can look into."

"Riles, I know you said not to, but I need to get there. The set will be crawling with media, looking to dig up shit. I need to manage it hands-on and I can't do that very well from three thousand miles away."

"I get it. You can come, on one condition."

"Love you Riles, but you're really not in a position to set out conditions. But okay, what is it?"

"That you stay at my house. Tomey and Ginn are there and if there *is* some wacko around, they can protect you."

"What about you?"

"I'll be there, too. Of course I will."

"In that case, condition accepted."

35

We were a half hour's drive to the house where Brent and his crew were working. Jaime had told me they were halfway through filming for the season, and the disruption caused by Cami's absence would soon reach critical mass. Her stand in could only do so much, especially in the two-shots where she and Brent compare design ideas. I mentioned that to Ginn as he drove his pride and joy through the Lowcountry.

He said, "Why can't they just put a baseball cap on her. Wear shades. She look enough like Cami that I bet people won't know the difference."

"What about the voice?"

"Don't expect you hip enough on music today to know about what they call auto-tune. They say it can make even your croaking sound like Sinatra."

"Like you're into hip-hop. I noticed all your playlists are old soul --- Motown, Philly, Stax/Volt. But aside from whether they could pull it off or not, it's downright fraudulent. Deceiving them into thinking they're seeing one woman when it's really an imposter. Heaven forbid."

"I know you're funning with me, but think about it. Ain't that what acting is all about? Pretending to be someone else, something you ain't. Wearing makeup and them appliances to look like somebody you not."

"That's acting. This is supposed to be reality."

"Supposed to be. You told me yourself it's all set up. Scripted. Cami don't know nothing about building houses.

It's fake. Actors playing parts. You think that fool playing president now actually fired nobody himself?"

"Brent's a builder. He's the real deal."

"I've seen the show, 5-0. Impossible for a man to do all that work himself, even a Paul Bunyan looking dude like him. People call them shows real estate porn, though Cami got too many clothes on for that to ring true to me."

We were pulling up to the site where Purdy's crew was working. It was a sunny afternoon, a bit on the cool side. They were taking advantage of the favorable light and temperature to work on the exterior of the project --- dressing up the windows with shutters, installing siding and decorative brackets under the eaves.

We got out of the car and walked around the house, looking for Bob Walsh or someone who could point us toward him. The first person who fit the bill was AD McLeish, who didn't look overjoyed to see me.

I said, "Nice morning. I'm looking for that PA, Bob Walsh. Any idea where he is?"

"Didn't show for work today. Tried calling him and got voicemail. Really put us in a bind and I'm doing some of his grunt work to take up the slack."

"We'll let you get to it then. Where's Brent?"

"In his trailer. Getting ready for his next scene. With Cami gone, he's got to carry more of the load. Don't suppose you know anything more about her, do you?"

"Working on it. See you later."

I headed for the trailer, Ginn beside me. He said, "You wanna split up? Got something I can do, other than be like Tonto when you talk to Purdy?"

"No, I think you'd be most useful saying things like, 'Him look like him hiding something, kemo sabe.'"

"You ain't all that funny, 5-0. Stereotypes is stereotypes, paleface."

"Seriously then, you could nose around and see if you can dig up something on Walsh. The fact he's incommunicado might mean something."

"I'll start with that Alison Reiger. I'd be interested in checking out her insights."

"You say Alex knows you're a man. Does she know you're also a dog? Happy hunting, Tonto."

"Ugh."

I knocked on the door to the trailer. Brent opened it and waved me in. "Whassup, Riley?"

He had a big smile on his face, as if last night had never happened. I expected him to be in a foul mood or at least a slight funk, but he was all grins and backslaps.

He offered coffee, I declined. I said, "The cops have the tracker."

His smile dropped. "Did you tell them it was mine?"

"No. I said I had a computer geek who tried to find out who bought it but couldn't. That was true. They didn't ask any further and I didn't lie. If it ever comes down to it, I won't perjure myself to protect you, but I won't volunteer anything either."

"Thanks for that."

"Look, I've got to ask you, point blank. I know a lot of lawyers say they don't want to know if their client is guilty, but I'm not a lawyer. I'm not even a licensed PI anymore. I'm doing this as a favor for Jaime because she believes in you. So tell me straight out, did you have anything to do with your wife's disappearance? Because right now, man, you're the main suspect.

I had to remember what Moses had said a few minutes before, that I was dealing with actors, whose main purpose is to make you believe something that isn't true.

He said, "I love Cam more than anything in the world. I just put up ten grand of my own money to get information on where she is. I'll make that a hundred if that's what it takes."

"I wish you'd talked to me about that first. Because of the reward, you're going to get bombarded with false leads that you don't have the resources to screen. And you've unleashed the media on this."

"Yeah, I know. They've been bugging me all morning. But I'm thinking this'll prove to this Montanez cop that I didn't have anything to do with Cami being missing. Why would I put out a reward if I did?"

"To a seasoned cop, it makes you look more guilty."

"How?"

"By muddying the water. They have a limited budget and not much manpower. If they waste time and money chasing down rabbit holes, they'll spend less time investigating the real suspect. You."

"I never thought like that, Riley, you gotta believe me. I'll take down the reward right now, if that helps."

"It'd be a good start. On the off chance there is a legit lead that someone's already sent in, I'm sure you'll have no trouble paying them. Now look, I got a little taste of your temper last night. I'll ask again. If you found Cami with another man, is that how you'd react?"

He shook his head slowly. "I won't lie. I'd be pissed but no, I think I've learned enough from my anger management sessions to control it.

There was a knock on the door. I got up and opened it. It was Ginn.

"Riles, a word?" he said.

"Can it wait? I'm in the middle of something."

"Jes' step out for a sec. Got something you ought to know."

I turned toward Purdy. "Hold on, Brent. I need to talk to my partner for a minute. Sorry."

I stepped down and Moses guided me a few feet away so that Brent couldn't hear.

"Don't know where you was at with that dude," Moses said. "But you should know, Alison didn't show up today neither. No answer on her cell."

36

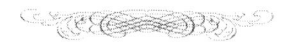

The circumstantial case was building against Brent. He had problems with Alison. Now she's MIA. He'd had a heated discussion with Cami the day she disappeared. The only piece that wasn't an easy fit was Walker, unless she had discovered something damning about Purdy and he'd killed her to keep it from surfacing.

After getting the news from Ginn, I went back into Brent's trailer.

"Everything okay?" he said. There was nothing in his wan smile that hinted he already knew about Reiger.

"I asked Moses to find Alison Reiger. She didn't report for her call this morning. Any idea on where she might be?"

"Nope. I didn't know she was on call to tell you the truth."

My understanding was that as a stand-in for Cami, Alison would mostly be used in scenes with Brent. I said, "Maybe they needed to show her working on a different project, shot over the shoulder. Was she still pissed at you?"

"I guess. Since I told her we needed to back off, she's been pretty cold when the camera's not on. But when we're shooting, she did her job. Faked it well."

"No harsh words off screen?"

"I see where you're going with this. Cam's missing and you think I had something to do with it. Now Alison. I suppose I'm some kind of serial killer after good looking blonde ladies, is that it?"

His voice rose.

I didn't need another demonstration of his anger management progress or lack thereof. He had no redneck goons for backup this time, and I'd take my chances with him, one on one. But this wasn't the time or place.

I said, "Brent, I'm the one holdout who doesn't think it's you. If the cops knew it was your tracker I found on her car, they'd probably run you in right now."

"And they'd look stupid when it comes out that I'm innocent." He sighed and rubbed his chunky fingers across his brow. "But I can't take that chance. The filing deadline for mayor is coming soon. I've got some influential folks supporting me, including the current mayor. If I get arrested, they'll run away faster than they did from Al Franken when that picture came out. You need to clear me and find the real bad guy."

"I'm not working for you. I'm working for Jaime Johansen. She believes in you. But if you did do this, I won't cover it up so you can win some election."

"There's nothing to cover up, I swear. I'm begging you --- find out who *is* responsible. I'm telling you the truth. Alison isn't my favorite person in the world right now, but I don't want anything bad to happen to her. Unless she had something to do with my wife vanishing."

"And if you were sure that she did, what then?"

"Oh, I see where you're going *now*. You think Alison admitted she killed Cami and I killed her in a fit of anger when I found out? That it?"

"That's what the police will think. You need a lawyer. If Alison doesn't turn up in the next few hours, I can guarantee you the cops come knocking on your door. They may already know you were intimate with her."

"They do know. 'Cause I told 'em."

"That's one reason you need a lawyer. You volunteered information they can use against you. There's one more thing we need to talk about."

"What's that?"

"You told me that you were prepared that Cami might have taken on a lover or two since the split. You said you wouldn't be happy about it but you could handle it."

"You're gonna tell me she did, right? You got a name?"

"I don't and if I did, I wouldn't tell you. Fact is, there might be a string of men she's been with since you broke up. If that's the case, would you divorce her? Assuming she's still alive."

"I got to believe that. It's all I can hold onto. If she's dead, I don't know what I'd do to myself. I sure wouldn't keep on with this stupid show. Probably not run for office either. Most likely, I'd cash in and go back to Texas."

"That's not what I asked. What if she is alive and doesn't want you back? And tells you she's had multiple lovers? Would you step aside then?"

"If there was any way she'd take me back, I'd forgive her for all her lovers. I'd do my best to start fresh with her. But *I'll* never file for divorce. If she does, I'd have to go along. But I'll never give up."

"We'll talk more," was all I said as I left.

I felt bad for the big hulk. He loves this woman so deeply that he'll forgive anything. That devotion might even be admirable on some crazy romantic level.

It's also dangerous. No matter how much you care about someone, there is a time when you need to let go. You can't force them to reciprocate. You can waste your whole life chasing that elusive butterfly, or you can accept the loss and move on. Obsession over lost love isn't healthy and Brent Purdy sure isn't healthy right now. People like that do things they normally wouldn't do. Like kill.

I could relate. I had murderous inclinations toward Jaime and Stone when I found out what they had done. They were a continent away. I'd like to think that if they were in the next town, I'd have enough control over my rage to leave them be. But the urge was there.

And now, I want Jaime back, to the point I am willing to disrupt my whole life in pursuit of her. She's given me signals she might be open to it, but that's my interpretation. If I was wrong, would I give up the chase as a lost cause and take solace elsewhere?

I shook off my self pity and set out to find Ginn. He was asking about Alison in the food tent, talking to a young intern.

When he was finished, I said, "Anything?"

"Nada. She didn't have a real busy day scheduled. Just a couple what they called 'pick-ups'. But people I talked to said this wasn't like her. She's dependable as the day is long, even if she wasn't feeling a hundred per cent."

"I guess it wouldn't be hard to find out where she lives and check on her there."

"Lives with her folks. Well, not *with* them exactly but on their property. They got some acreage, outskirts of Bluffton. Big lot with a bunch of outbuildings for their tractors and rigs and construction stuff. She got her own apartment over one of the garages."

"Do you know where Alex is?"

"Last we talked, she was on the island, keeping busy, nothing big. Why?"

"Much as I love riding shotgun in your Benz, we should probably split up. You could head to Alison's place and see what you can find out. I can chase down Walsh, our other MIA."

"So you needing Tomey to lend you her Honda again?"

"I'd rather she bring me the MDX. There's a spare set of keys in the kitchen. It'd be great if she could swing by the house, feed Bosco and take him out and then meet us somewhere in Bluffton with my car."

"You talking 'bout making a first grade detective your personal errand girl. Feed your dog and deliver your ride. You know she ain't gonna like that."

"Even if you ask and say *pretty ple*ase?"

"Burns a favor. I'd do it, but can't you come up with something better?"

"Okay. How about this? There's another missing person with the *Country Fixin's* show and we need to see if it's a police matter. If not and you two find Alison in her trundle down with the flu, you can treat Alex to a steak dinner. On me."

"Throw in a nice Cabernet and it's a deal."

37

Tomey came through with the car and took care of the dog's needs. She was even pleasant when she delivered the MDX, but had to get in a jibe.

She said, "I can see why Moses doesn't want to be seen with you in this piece of shit. When are you going to get that crack in the windshield fixed?"

The 'crack' in the windshield was caused by a sniper bullet, someone trying to scare me off a case. I had done an epoxy job on it from a kit. I didn't think it looked bad for a first time attempt, but it wasn't perfect. The leather seats were worn, there were a couple of dings in the body from grocery carts, but otherwise it looked good for a ten year old SUV. And mechanically, it was in great shape.

I said, "Long as it gets me where I want to go, I'm cool. The crack won't get any worse. You do know that the people who made your beloved Honda are the same people who made the MDX."

She said, "No, maybe their grandparents made your buggy."

Ginn added, "If you gonna drive an old car, leastways drive a classic like mine."

"Thank you Frick and Frack. Let me know what you find out about Alison. I'm sure you two crime stoppers will come through, if you can stop canoodling long enough, that is."

Tomey shot me a look. "Canoodle this," she said, extending her middle finger. Moses just grinned and they drove off.

Walsh's paystub gave his address as a modest home in a newer development of tract homes around a manmade lake in Hardeeville. A quick check showed that the house was listed in his parents' name, so I assumed that like Alison, he was living with them. It's a problem that more and more millennials face these days. Unable to find jobs or at least ones that pay a living wage, they're forced to mooch off their folks until they strike gold. Many never do, even if they're skilled at what they do. A good portion of them don't buy into the American Dream of a house with a white picket fence, preferring to live in an urban condo or rent free in the 'burbs with their elders.

I had just belted up when my cell chimed. Still in the parking lot where I'd traded cars, I turned the motor off and took the call.

It was Winona Sands.

"Hey Riley, how are ya?"

Her voice was deep and dusky, kind of Kathleen Turnerish. I liked it. She'd be great at phone sex. I could dream.

"Real good. Great to hear from you."

"Still working on that *Fixin's* case, I assume. The shit has hit the fan with that one."

"Yeah. Media's got hold of it. I haven't seen anything lately. What're they saying?"

"Well, like I texted, it's no longer a secret that Brent and Cami weren't together. Only a matter of time that whoever they both were screwing in the interim comes forward."

"I'm not one who kisses and tells but that's not the case anymore, is it?"

"That train left the station decades ago. The *New York Times* just had an op-ed piece about famous men's penises. Of course, they decried the trend, but it amounted to feminist porn in the old gray lady. Used to be only the tabloids wrote crap like that."

"It's a Brave New World. I kinda like the old one."

"Me, too, in some ways. Hey, reason I called was I just got a pitch I thought might interest you."

"Don't tell me. Someone wants to do a reality show about a grizzled old ex-PI."

"No, but if they did, I wouldn't be calling you. You're not old and far from grizzled, at least the parts I've seen so far."

I let her flirt sit without comment. "So what kind of show is it?"

"Interesting. There's already a show on HGTV where a mother and daughter rehab houses. And of course, you have the *Property Brothers*. But this idea was for two young women. Sisters, either real or imagined. Two hot blondes who fix old houses."

"They have *All Girls' Garage* on the *Motor Trend* network. Same idea I guess, only this is rehab porn for guys."

"That's the clever part. Car shows are mostly for men. In this case, guys would watch for the obvious reasons. The pitch said they'd sometimes be wearing outfits that wouldn't necessarily be what real builders would wear on the job. So there is that aspect. But they'd also be strong independent women. Ladies who wouldn't take any shit from subs, buyers or realtors. So modern women would relate and tune in, as well."

"Sounds like a winner. And I imagine they'll be holding auditions for the right two girls. Should be hard to find, I'd think. You interested in producing it?"

"Well, that's just it. It came from an agency I've never heard of. But they claim to have one of the biggest women in reality TV already committed."

I had been so taken with Winona's sexy voice that I'd missed the obvious. "And those two wouldn't happen to be Cami Purdy and Alison Reiger, would they?"

"The pitch didn't use names. Implied she was a star of an existing show. Contracts were expiring soon. It was strange, sort of semi-professional, asking if I'd be interested in producing such a show and that a demo reel would be coming soon."

"When did you get this proposal?"

"Just today. You're the first person I called. I tried to track down the agency that sent it, but can't find any online presence and like I say, I've never heard of them. Sounds to me like a little family operation."

I said, "Well, you know Cami is missing. Today, Alison didn't show up for work either."

"Could be they were polishing up their pitch. Or it could be it's two other women entirely. If Cami is dead, that'd kind of rule her out."

"Uh, yeah. But she may not be. I'm not telling you any big secrets but I'll trust that you not to tell anyone. There's no body so far and no ransom note. That could mean that she's still on the right side of the grass."

"Huh. Reminds me of an old show biz story. Agatha Christie went missing for a couple of weeks, back in the twenties I think. Came back in public with some bullshit story. She was already a big writer and the equivalent of a TV star today. People thought she was having an affair. Or that she wanted to escape her husband. I'm not sure the real story ever came out."

"I doubt someone like Cami would know about that."

"Maybe not, although a fictionalized account of it came out in a novel ten years ago. Best seller. Based on Agatha's story but modernized. Used different names and it was a movie star, not a writer. Set in present day Los Angeles. I forget who wrote it."

"Sounds like something John Petersen would do."

"Yeah, that's the guy. He did write it."

38

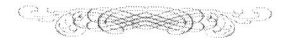

Sitting in the Walsh's living room, I felt like I was in a museum, or maybe a creepy teenager's fanboy den. Robert Walsh's parents were named Lindsey and Stephanie and it didn't take Cameron Crowe to figure out why.

Their living room was a tribute to one of the biggest bands of the seventies.

They had welcomed me in, no questions asked, when I told them I was Riley King from *Country Fixin's*, here to ask about their son. I found it odd that they'd offer an uncredentialed stranger entry to their home without asking more about the nature of the visit. There was a certain herbal aroma permeating the space, one I was quite familiar with as a former concert goer.

They were a little too young to be relics of the sixties; they were definitely rooted in the following decade. Before getting down to business, I commented on the unusual decor.

"Looks like you guys are big Fleetwood Mac fans," I said, stating the obvious.

Stephanie Walsh, who insisted I call her Stevie, said, "Big time. We met at one of their concerts. We love them so much that we changed our first names, legally. It's so sad that they're fighting with Lindsey now, but we're sure the prodigal son will return, after he gets past his health problems."

Stevie was short, a bit zaftig, and pretty. She dressed like her idol --- long flowing dress, a multi-colored shawl, and a necklace chock full of trinkets that only the most devoted follower could decode. Her straight, waist length dark blonde hair was nicely conditioned, which must be difficult without Stevie Nicks' coterie of assistants

I said, "Funny, When I met your son, I mentioned his name sounded like Bob Welch, who was with the band before Buckingham-Nicks."

Lindsey said, "That's why we named him Bob. We liked *Sentimental Lady* and *Hypnotized*, but the band didn't really take off till he left. Our son doesn't like the reference much but he hasn't changed it because most of his friends don't know from Bob Welch. You touched a sore point with him. He hates the Mac almost as much as we love them. I guess that's our fault for pushing it on him. He's into the crap that passes for music today. All rhythm, no melody."

He looked much more like Mick Fleetwood than Buckingham. He was tall, slim, and bald, but made up for his lack of hair on top with a ponytail with what he had left. He sported a bushy black beard and wore a loose fitting white shirt, black leather pants and vest.

I said, "You've certainly got some impressive memorabilia. Signed tour posters. How did you come by that guitar? Did Lindsey actually play that onstage?"

"Just in the studio. Won it at a charity auction. Came with a letter of authenticity so I know it's real."

I was tempted to point out that counterfeit items are prevalent in the memorabilia biz, and most come with fake provenance. Crain told me that the Walshs were retired, but didn't see a sustainable source of income. No pension or Social Security yet. They appeared to be living off dividends and interest from an investment portfolio. My computer wizard said that things didn't add up --- they must have a source of unreported income.

I'd made enough small talk about their favorite band to gain credibility, although in truth, they extended a warm welcome the moment I darkened their door. That didn't make me feel special --- they probably would have extended the same naïve courtesy if El Chapo had come knocking.

I said, "Just a few questions, if you don't mind. I don't want to take up any more of your time than necessary. I'm sure you have plans for the evening."

She said, "We were going to take in the November 11, 1979 Nassau Coliseum concert on You Tube. Audio right off the mixing board so the sound should be excellent."

Again, it was odd that they seemed more interested in a forty year old show than why someone was inquiring about their son.

I said, "The reason I'm here is that Bob didn't come to work today. We tried calling and got voicemail. I don't want to alarm you but there's been some weird stuff going on around the show and we want to make sure he's okay. Have you heard from him in the last twenty four hours?"

Lindsey said, "No, but that's not unusual. Generally we only see him Sundays. Family tradition. Roast beef dinner, mashed potatoes, peas and apple pie. My dad started it long as I can remember and we honor it to this day."

"I was under the impression that Bob lived here. This is the address he gave the HR department."

"Technically he does. His room's in the back. House came with a three car garage and we didn't need it so we had the builder convert one of the bays into a bedroom with a private entrance. Has a small bathroom, too. But he hasn't stayed here since your show starting shooting this season. Says they gave him accommodations closer to where they're shooting and it's much more convenient, given the long hours."

"Ever been there?"

"Oh no," Stevie said. "We've always encouraged Bobbie to be independent. Honestly, we don't even have a key to his room here. He's a good boy and we trust him."

"Well, I only met him a couple of times but he seems to have a good head on his shoulders."

He said, "I'd like to take credit for that, but we did have some bumps in the road when he was in his teens. But he found himself and it's been cool ever since."

Crain had unearthed a rap sheet on the younger Bob Walsh. Selling pot at school, nailed twice. That was eight years ago and the records had been expunged, but my computer geek accessed them as only he can.

I said, "I don't want to frighten you, but the show doesn't provide him accommodations. I'd assume he was living with someone, maybe someone working on the show. Do you know if he had anyone that might fit the bill?"

"Shacking up is all he wants to do," Lindsey said, quoting his namesake. "They always said it best, didn't they? But no, the only one he talked about was Cami Purdy, the star of the show. He was responsible for her, you know. It was Cami this, Cami that. He really took a shine to her, as much as a boy like him could."

"I'm not sure what you mean by that."

Stevie said, "Mr. King, I understand that you only met Bobby a few times, but he's not into the ladies. We're cool with that. He's never brought anyone home to meet us, male or female. We've actually never spoken to him about it. It's his business and he doesn't need our approval. He did have some little girlfriends as a boy, but I think it was because it was expected, rather than something he really was into."

She said this in a matter of fact manner, as if talking about someone else's son.

I said, "I don't need to pry into his preferences. I just want to be sure he's okay. Maybe he didn't return the AD's calls because he was afraid they'd be mad at him for not coming to work. Would you mind calling him now?"

Lindsey Walsh pulled a flip phone from his vest and made the call. He gave me a wincing look, which indicated that he had reached his son's voicemail.

"Bobby, it's your dad. Got a couple of things coming up I wanted to let you know about. Call me?"

He turned to his wife. "Knowing Bobby, he just forgot to charge his phone. Happens to me all the time."

I said, "Was he at your Sunday dinner last week?"

"No, not the last couple of Sundays. He said the show was running behind schedule and they were shooting seven days a week."

Another lie. There was no point telling them that. It was clear that even though Bob Walsh maintained a legal residence in his parents' former garage, they weren't close. Their son could be running a car dealership and they wouldn't know. Nothing I could say now would affect that relationship. I thought about asking to see his room, but if they didn't have a key, it would entail picking the lock. Even though I anticipated the answer, I asked anyway.

Lindsey's voice took on an edge. "Mr. King, that would be a violation of our son's privacy and I won't be a party to that. Now, I'm sure he's all right. Something important must have come up that he had to take care of. It's either that or now that it's come out that Ms. Purdy is missing, he feels bad that he didn't keep a tighter leash on her."

That was their story and they were sticking to it. It wasn't my place to criticize their parenting skills or lack thereof. If anything, they'd indulged him too much. The house in a gated community was sweet, surrounded by two acres of forest. Private and nicely maintained, a little large for empty nesters, but I couldn't criticize them on that score. Glass houses.

I blew it off. "Here's my card. Please call me if you hear from him. We just want to make sure he's all right."

"He's a big boy," his mother said. "I'm not worried in the least. We've always encouraged him to go his own way."

Fleetwood Mac to the end.

39

Back home, Ginn, Tomey, Bosco and I compared notes. The dog didn't add much, just that he'd caught up on some sleep while we were out. He'd barked at a couple of squirrels who had the temerity to run across the front yard. All in all, he'd accomplished very little, but his job wasn't all that demanding.

The three humans didn't fare much better. I told my cohorts what I had learned at Bob Walsh's house, which was that he lied to his parents about his whereabouts. If that was a crime, every teenager in America would be in jail.

Ginn said, "Was me, I'd say your Fleetwood Macking friends got another business on the side. Maybe not legit."

I said, "Scalping tickets for the Mac tour? Legal these days. Hard to believe the time I wasted with the feds busting scalping rings back in the day."

Tomey said, "You can never break the chain. Oh, well. What does interest me is that their son's been AWOL from their house since before Cami disappeared. Opens up the possibility that he killed her, doesn't it? If he's not really asexual as you put it, maybe they had a lover's quarrel."

"I'm not buying that." I told Tomey and Ginn about Winona's call and the proposed *Sisters* show. I said, "They could be in this together. If she gets her own show, he could be the showrunner or assistant director or whatever. It'd be a big step up from gopher. That could be his reward for helping her disappear."

"So you thinking if we find him, we find her?" Ginn said. "Not saying that Brent's off the hook here, but what you say makes some sense."

"What about Alison's folks? Did you learn anything there?"

Tomey looked over to Ginn and he gestured for her to take the lead. "They haven't seen her in two days but they're not worried. She's usually lets them know if she'll be away, but there've been times she hasn't."

"She must have been out all those nights she was with Brent."

"No. They said she'd been keeping late hours working on the show, but she always came home. They're early risers and she comes up to the main house for breakfast every day."

"So she didn't ever spend the whole night with Purdy. Interesting. Kind of old fashioned."

"The Reigers strike me as good people. Christians. They run a family construction business. They do six to ten custom houses a year. Kind of like Randy Lustgarden, the guy you two framed, who's rotting in jail in the Caymans."

Moses said, "Don't be changing the subject, Alex. You was on board with that, don't lie. You even thought he got off light. But she's right about the Reigers, 5-0. They ain't too pleased about their daughter going Hollywood. They wanted her to take over the family business. She was construction foreman on half their houses last year. Her pa did the other half. He getting ready to dial it back some and he ain't too thrilled she's more into this TV show than doing what he calls *honest work*."

"Do they know she was sleeping with Purdy?"

Alex said, "We didn't ask in so many words, but I think they had an idea. They're real religious and they implied their daughter had strayed off the path when it came to men. Said she'd been seeing a nice boy from Savannah but since she got caught up in the show, she hadn't had time for him."

I said, "Sounds like she's a girl who wants to make it on her own, rather than riding on her parents' work. She could probably make more money on TV and wouldn't have to get her hands dirty. Well, not the way she used to anyway."

Ginn said, "That whole thang went south once Brent dumped her, 5-0. She might've killed Cami like old Grizzly thinks. She figured once Cami was out of the picture, she could slide right in there. Once he put the ki-bosh on that, she goes to Sands and pitches her own show."

Tomey said, "I don't think so. Kids rebel against their folks all the time, but seems to me these people raised her right. Taught her how hard work pays off. She may have had her head turned by the glamorous life, but I don't think she'd do anything shady to get there. I got the feeling she'd want to earn whatever success she gets, not take shortcuts. Especially if it means something as drastic as murder."

Ginn disagreed. "Not so sure. She just happens to vanish once we start sniffing around? Ever think that she and Walsh hooked up to get rid of Cami? They come from the same place. Ain't happy some no talent bimbo from California getting all the goodies, when *they're* the real deal. But that didn't fly with Brent, so she comes up with this *Sisters* idea."

I said, "But then who does Alison know that could be her partner in a *Sisters* show? There's nobody affiliated with the show that I see fits the bill."

Tomey said, "Her *real* sister. She has a twenty one year old sibling, who looks a lot like her. Blonde, attractive, smart. Senior year at USC, Bluffton. Wants to be a TV reporter. She never had any interest being a builder. Her parents are really proud of her but early on, they knew she wasn't cut out to work in construction."

40

It's been a long time since I played basketball for Georgetown. Even though I continually get letters inviting me back for alumni functions and fundraisers, I haven't set foot on that campus since I graduated. It's not that I have bad memories about the place. I enjoyed my time there and I learned a lot, on and off the court. My education and minor basketball fame opened the door to my job with the FBI. Even though that didn't exactly work out, it gave me a leg up for my private practice.

Friends have jokingly said that my current financial status was achieved because I never married or had children. The cost of putting two kids through college today is daunting. And knowing my history with women, they speculate that there would have been one or more divorce settlements to contend with. I see their point. This ran through my brain as I drove to the University of South Carolina, Beaufort County, whose main campus is in Bluffton.

Ginn and I had split duties this morning. First, he was going to ask around the motel where we found Walker's body. He would show photos of Alison, Brent, Cami and Walsh to see if they had been there any time around the time of the murder. Then he'd go to the set of *Country Fixin's* to monitor Brent. He'd only encountered the man peripherally and I wanted to see if his impressions matched mine and if he saw a deadly side under the folksy veneer.

My task was to interview the younger Reiger sister. If I could quickly ascertain whether she was to be part of the *Sisters* TV proposal, it could clarify Alison's role in this.

I could have wasted time around the bursar's or registrar's office trying to obtain Dorothy Reiger's class schedule. I am out of touch with college administrative structures and it could take me the better part of the morning to locate her. The most efficient way was to ask Crain to hack in and tell me where she'd be when I got to the Fording Island Road campus.

As fortune would have it, Reiger was in a television workshop studio just off the main quad. I left the Beretta in the MDX, guessing correctly that there would be metal detectors and guards. The highly visible security presence was designed to as a deterrent to some fanatical shooter, bent on destroying lives for reasons known only to their own sick mind.

Once inside the building, I was struck by how well appointed the television facility was compared to some of the professional outfits I had seen. The equipment was state of the art, a far cry from the battered cameras and sound equipment that I saw on Purdy's set. When I was in school, the campus radio station employed hand-me-down gear, some of which was Army war surplus. The concept there would someday be a television curriculum was outlandish.

There was no obvious security around the TV studio, just a flashing red sign instructing visitors to remain silent while taping was going on. From what I gathered, there were only a handful of students in this particular class, and this was the day they were presenting their projects on camera.

It was easy to pick Dorothy Reiger from the group. She looked very much like her sister, just a bit shorter and not as curvy. With shoulder length blonde hair, she was clad like a local TV anchor. Although many of the women now look like they're dressed for a cocktail party. Hard to take them seriously as reporters, if there is such a thing, in this era of cell phone videos of dogs doing cute things passing as news.

Not that I'm an authority, but the younger Reiger struck me as telegenic eye candy, which is about all that is required. She read the teleprompter script without flubbing, and hit her marks without hesitation. Her voice was the singsongy nasal whine of most female anchors. But overall, it was a smooth performance, leaving little doubt she could get a small market job upon graduation. How far she could go in the business was another matter, one that Jaime is far more qualified to evaluate.

As the class broke up, I introduced myself and told her I was with *Country Fixin's* and I needed to ask her a few questions about her sister. Was there a quiet place we could go to talk?

She said, "Why? Is there some problem with Allie? Is she okay?"

"She hasn't reported for work in the last two days and it's very unlike her. She's very reliable. Have you spoken with her over that period?"

"Uh, no. I really don't see how I can help."

"Ms. Reiger, I'm sure it's nothing but if you could spare a few minutes, it would be helpful."

She was suspicious. I understood. Some tough looking older man approaches an attractive coed and wants to speak privately about her sister? If I had a daughter, I'd advise her to be wary in that situation.

I tried to allay her fears. "If there's some student union building or other place with people around where you'd feel comfortable, that'd be fine. It'll only take a few minutes."

She smacked her lips and hesitated. "There's a coffee shop across the quad. Meet me there in fifteen minutes."

She turned and walked away. I went to the bistro, took a corner booth and waited. I checked my phone for email and messages. As I had told Dorothy before confirming it, Alison hadn't shown up for work today either.

Twenty minutes later, Dotty did show up, but she wasn't alone. She was accompanied by one of the campus rent-a-cops. He was a fat man, short and sweaty but regaled in full uniform and armed with a service revolver. She pointed at me as if picking me out of a lineup and they both walked over to where I was sitting.

The guard said, "This lady tells me you've been harassing her. Can I see some ID?"

Elbows on the table, I raised my hands. "Excuse me, but I haven't been harassing her. I need to ask her some questions about her sister, who may be missing. I'm reaching for my wallet to give you my card."

He hadn't drawn his gun but I wasn't about to take any chances. The fact she had told him I was harassing her automatically made me the bad guy, possibly one who'd draw down on him. So much for my boyish charm.

I gave him one of my business cards that didn't indicate that my license had expired. I'm sure this is in violation of some statute, but Dan Logan, my FBI friend, had bailed me out of worse spots.

I didn't expect the security man's reaction. "Young lady, this is Riley King. Surprised you didn't recognize him. He's pretty well known 'round these parts. Let me shake your hand sir, and offer my assistance on anything you might need."

"Thanks for the offer, but I can handle this. It's really a minor matter."

The smile never left his face. "You're in good hands, Ms.?"

"Reiger," she said, without a hint of embarrassment.

He said, "Well, if that'll be all, I'll leave you to it." He almost saluted as he turned and strode off.

This was one of the few times when my reputation actually helped with a LEO. Normally they hate PIs, although Lieutenant Tragg showed Paul Drake respect when the script called for it. A shame I wasn't working for Perry Mason.

Dorothy sat across from me and gave me a blank look.

My move. "Hey, no hard feelings you got security involved. It's a shame that college campuses aren't safe places these days. Sorry if I scared you. I come in peace."

"Apology accepted."

There was a time when I would have challenged her as to who owed who an apology, but the years had taught me not to antagonize someone you were asking for help. So I swallowed the instinct to tell her to respect her elders and stay off my lawn.

I said, "I caught a little of your presentation. You're quite good. Talent runs in the family, I see."

"Campus security may be impressed with you Mr. whatever, but I'm not. I only came because I rang Allie and got her voicemail and my folks would give me hell if anything happened to her."

She was making this hard. "I don't want to scare you but you've probably heard that Cami Purdy is missing. Some strange stuff is going on around the show and we're taking precautions with everyone involved. The name is King, by the way, Riley King."

She grimaced. "I won't bore you with the details but you should know that Allie and I aren't very close. My folks always treated her like she was the chosen one. She was going to take over the family business, not me."

"Was that something you wanted? Not all women, or men for that matter, want to work in construction."

"You said you needed to ask me about Allie. I don't know what I can tell you. I'm renting a house with two other girls off campus, so I don't live at home and don't see her all that often."

I suspected there was more to it than her parents favoring the older sibling. Did Alison harbor the same kind of animosity toward Dorothy?

I said, "I'd imagine you had some mutual interests when she got involved with the show. You seem to have aspirations along those lines."

"You figured that out, did you? Sure, I wouldn't mind being on a successful cable show, even if I'm not Ms. Handy-person. The showrunner came to the campus to give a speech to our media department. Said there'd be opportunities for jobs. I was going to contact them but my sister grabbed it right from under my nose."

"Not very sisterly. She told me they approached her because she was working on one of their projects and bore a strong resemblance to Cami Purdy."

"If there was something I wanted and she could snatch it, she would."

"Still, her being on the show could help you. Maybe hook you up with some of the right people. Did she ever offer that?"

"Yeah, she invited me to the last wrap party. I met a few folks there but strictly on my own. Wasn't like Allie showed me off or anything. And now that she's gone Hollywood, my parents expect me to carry on with the business. I can tell you that ain't happening."

"I'm sure they're disappointed, but I get it."

"Again, I don't need to get into it. It has nothing to do with her not showing up for work. But if I had to guess, she met some good looking piece of shit and they're off screwing their brains out. It's happened before."

This made me think there was some good looking POS Dorothy set her sights on that Alison preempted. Maybe it was more than one, who preferred the curvier sister.

It wasn't worth pursuing. "I won't keep you then. One final thing. A producer friend of mine told me there's a pitch out there for a reality show involving two sisters who rehab houses. Seems like a natural for Alison. Did she ever mention this to you? Maybe wanting you to do it with her?"

"You're serious? I'm the last person she'd ask. She'd want all the glory to herself. And there's no way I would take crumbs off Allie's table. I have a class to go to. Goodbye."

41

Jaime was due in at five. I offered to pick her up at the Savannah/Hilton Head airport. She insisted that my time was better spent working the case as opposed to chauffeuring her around. I protested: It would be great to see her and we could get dinner on the way home. I could update her on our progress. Still on West Coast time, she said it would be too early to eat and that we should meet at the house and make plans from there.

It wasn't worth arguing about. I'm learning to pick my spots. If it's of minor consequence, I just go along rather than waste time trying to prove my point. Give in on the small things, be resolute on the big ones. Maybe someday, I'll give up and learn to compromise on those as well.

Besides, in this case, Jaime was right. Rush hour on I-95 isn't as severe as New York or Atlanta, but it can be exasperating and I hate getting stuck in traffic. Splitting concentration between battling the congestion and giving Jaime her deserved attention wasn't ideal. A late dinner at WiseGuys might be just the ticket.

Ginn called.

"Hey, Mo. What's up?"

"Lordy, got thrown a curve just now. That Reiger chick showed up. Late, but she's here. Your boy McLeish was freaking, trying to change the schedule on the fly, but now, everything's cool."

"Is Walsh there?"

"Nope. McLeish say he miss one more day and they fire him. Only keeping him on 'cause Brenda Showrunner likes him."

"Sounds like you're getting along well with Jaime's spy."

"Stinks like an old bourbon barrel, first thing in the morning. But I'm good at finding common ground with folks, even the likes of you."

"I'm headed your way. Anything at the motel?"

"Maid said Cami looked familiar. Asked her if she mighta seen her on TV. She said, yeah, that might be it. Take it for what it's worth. Couple of folks say they seen Walsh around a few times. Never stayed there that they could recollect, but they seen him around."

"Jaime's coming in tonight. I may take her out to dinner so if you're cooking, it'll just be you and Alex."

"Ain't no restaurant making something I can't make better, but if you need alone time with your lady, I'll abide."

"Gives you the house to yourself, too. A little private time with Tomey wouldn't be a bad thing."

"Oh, by the way, she put out a BOLO for Walsh. Almost forgot."

"Kind of extreme for not showing up for work, no? How'd she manage that?"

"With all the funky shit going on with this show, anything out of place is fair game. Media's swarming all over. Bunch of sleazebags, you ask me."

"Doing their job, Ginn. They probably don't think much of private eyes like us either. Spend any time with Brent yet?"

"Not one on one, but he said he'd hang with me between takes. Did see Mr. Hyde though."

"Talk about burying the lede. What happened?"

Ginn said, "Didn't bring it up first 'cause you saw it yourself. He was checking out taping sheetrock joints. Shines a bright light on the seam and sees a ripple in it. Takes out a big ole hammer and smashes the shit out of it. Yells 'this ain't the kind of work Brent Purdy puts his name on'. Scared the kid doing drywall half to death."

"Did anyone from the media see that?"

"No. And thing is, a second after he flips out, he puts his arm around the kid and says that he's sorry, but he has high standards. Offers to help repair the damage but the cameraman said he needed to move on."

"Did they get it on tape?"

"Believe so. I know what you're thinking. I'll see if I can get hold of it. Camera guy could make a classical buck selling it to one of the sleazes."

I said, "Exactly. Plus, we might need it ourselves later. Hey, got a call coming in. I'll see you soon."

The call was coming from an unfamiliar number in this area code. I'd passed my card out to a bunch of potential sources, so I couldn't afford to ignore it.

"Mr. King. It's Percy."

Percy. Who the hell was Percy?

I said, "I'm sorry, did you say Percy?"

"Yes sir. Percy Mayfield. Met you at Ribaut."

"Oh yes, Percy. What can I do for you?"

"Do nothing for me. You told me to call ya if anyone was holed up at the house. Well, that kid I told you about, one who gives me water. He's there."

"Percy, don't let him leave. I'm about fifteen minutes away. Stall him anyway you can and there'll be a nice reward coming your way. Chat him up, whatever it takes."

42

I called Tomey. She was closer to the house on Ribaut and could get there quicker. She said she'd park on the street in front to keep Walsh from leaving and then we could double team him. She had no grounds to arrest or even question him. When I got there, her Honda was blocking the driveway, under a palm tree, but she was nowhere in sight.

I stowed the MDX behind her car, fortifying our little blockade. As I got out, I heard her voice coming from the bushes behind the wall surrounding the property.

Tomey said, "Riley. I'm over here."

I owed Percy Mayfield big time. Past the gate, in the circular drive fronting the house, he was washing a truck I assumed to be Walsh's.

I said, "Alex, the man washing the truck is the caretaker who told me Walsh was in the building. I'll take the front and you go in through the garage. There's a way into the living space from there."

"Listen to you, giving *me* orders. So I suppose when I find this dude, I arrest him for unlawful entry. Then we sweat him to see if he'll tell us what's going on with Cami. That your plan?"

"Great minds. Yeah, that's the gist of it. Gives you probable cause to search the truck, in case he's stealing something. I don't think he's armed, but be careful. I'll cover the front door if he tries to go out that way."

Percy saw us advancing toward the house and started to greet me, but I shushed him. "Percy, the lady with me is a police officer. Good job stalling him."

"He was getting ready to leave but I told him that his truck was all muddy and I took it on my own to wash it. Wouldn't take but a few minutes. He told me to hurry up and went back in."

"Fast thinking. I appreciate it," I said, handing him two twenties. He stuffed them in his shirt pocket. I glanced into the truck's cab before walking up to the front door. The passenger seat was covered with women's clothes on plastic hangers. More justification for a search.

As I reached the entry, I heard shuffling noises inside. Tomey could hold her own in a fight with a gawky kid, but he might have surprised her and I couldn't take that chance. I was ready to kick the door open, but it was unlocked so I walked right in, Beretta at the ready.

My fears were unfounded. Alex was marching a handcuffed Walsh down the stairs.

She said, "It's all clear, King. Found this gentleman upstairs, going through drawers in the master bathroom."

Walsh was stone faced. A flicker of recognition passed his features as he saw me. He said, "King. Tell this chick I'm with the show. It's cool that I'm here. Tell her."

"This 'chick' is Detective First Grade Alex Tomey. You're not here on behalf of the show. I checked that on the way over. And why are there women's clothes in the truck?"

"The show needed them. For Cami's body double."

"No dice, kid. You weren't on assignment."

Tomey said, "Stealing women's clothes, eh? Next thing you'll tell us is that you're a cross dresser. Save your breath. These are size four. You couldn't have fit into them when you were ten."

They reached the bottom of the staircase. Tomey pushed him onto a bench in the foyer. "Now tell us why you were really here. Were you bringing these clothes to Cami? Where is she?"

"Okay, okay, you got me. I was stealing the clothes. I have no idea where Ms. Purdy is. I figured she's gone and has no use for them. I was going to donate them to a women's shelter."

I said, "You believe this guy? Robin Hood. Couldn't wait until we knew if Cami was still alive. Had to help those battered women right away. So noble."

"And so much bullshit," Alex said.

Walsh was vamping. "All right. I know about a place that sells used designer stuff on consignment. This stuff is worth a whole lotta money."

"On the off chance he's telling the truth, let me check out what's in the truck. Outside. Now!"

She jerked him upright and pushed him toward the door. I'd never seen Tomey manhandle a suspect before, but she worked out regularly and was strong. She'd also had martial arts training. Not someone you want to mess with, despite her height. It wasn't that she was short, but I'm used to women like Jaime and Charlene, who are pushing six feet in heels.

Percy Mayfield was drying the truck with a chamois but backed away when he saw us frog march Walsh from the house. I said, "It's okay, Percy. We caught this guy stealing. The truck looks fine. You can go back to work, doing whatever you were doing before."

Tomey said, "We may need a statement from you later. Just routine."

"I ain't looking for no trouble," Percy said.

I took him aside and said, "Probably no need for you to get involved. She's just trying to scare the kid. Stay cool." He walked toward the garage to gather up his landscaping tools.

Tomey made a show of donning gloves, then opened the passenger door of the truck and flipped through the items. She said, "No way is this stuff worth much. A lot of it is from TJ Maxx. Looks good on TV but hardly designer quality that anyone would pay a premium for."

Walsh opened his mouth again, digging himself in deeper. "I wasn't finished. I figured I'd take it all and let the store sort it out. I know there's some good stuff in the closet. Cami told me that."

"When did she tell you?" Maybe he'd stumbled into admitting she'd sent him.

"I don't remember when exactly but she said it when I was driving her around. She had some really nice stuff she got on Rodeo Drive that they wouldn't let her wear on the show. It was a mistake bringing it here to hick country."

His was improvising his ass off. These creative types are quick on their feet, even if their tale turns out to be full of holes later. Walsh had a future as a screenwriter. And if he spends time in jail, he'll probably be even more in demand.

Tomey said, "Let's see what else we find in this trove of stolen goods. King, keep an eye on this man."

She was giving the orders now and I was following her lead. What Walsh had done so far amounted to trespassing and petty theft. Unless they opened his Juvie records, he'd get off with a warning and probation.

"What have we here?" Alex said, holding up a large glassine bag containing something that looked a lot like marijuana.

Walsh screamed, "That's not mine. You planted it. Damn cops are all the same."

I said, "Show some respect, Walsh. Detective Tomey, you want me to help you get him into your car?"

"No. I'll send for some backup. They'll take him in and book him. If this is what I think it is, it's possession with intent to sell. Add that to the stolen goods and this boy's in for some serious time."

Walsh finally got wise, hearing the threat of charges. "I'm done talking. I want a lawyer."

"It's your right," Alex said. She placed him under arrest and Mirandized him. "King, you wait under that tree with Mr. Walsh until our backup arrives. I'm going to continue the search."

She was giving me an opening. Asking a civilian to guard a prisoner is not procedure.

I guided Walsh into the shade. "Look, Bobby, Detective Tomey won't like me telling you this, but you have some leverage here. I know you were bringing those clothes to Cami. We're closing in on her. Just tell us where she is and I bet all this can go away."

"I ain't saying nothing. I have no idea where Cam is. I just hope she ain't dead by the hand of that brute she married. That's all I have to say."

"Suit yourself. I hope she's as loyal to you as you are to her. The other day we found some hair on a pillow in the master and they're running DNA," I lied. "Sure looks like you were sleeping with her. If she is dead, you automatically become the lead suspect. Just saying."

"I'm not saying anything till I talk to a lawyer."

By early evening, Tomey, Ginn and I were back at the house, awaiting Jaime's arrival. Alex told us that Walsh was in a holding cell and had refused to say anything further. He called his parents and they sent him a lawyer. Walsh spoke with the attorney for ten minutes and was returned to his cell. The counselor said little on the way out, just a quick aside that the drugs had likely been planted.

This became laughable after a thorough search of the truck. Hidden compartments contained more weed.

Moses was busy in the kitchen and said that he'd wait for Jaime to get in before he shared details of his day with Brent. Didn't want to repeat himself and undergo two separate interrogations. Smart man. He also said that once Jaime caught a whiff of what he was preparing, our plans to go out to dinner would evaporate.

As usual, he was right. Jaime's rental pulled in shortly after seven. Tomey said, "No limo? She comes in a Toyota Camry? There's a girl with her feet firmly on the ground."

I went out to help Jaime with her luggage. Her frequent last minute trips had taught her how to pack light. All she brought was a medium sized suitcase and a laptop backpack.

I played the gracious host. "You know Moses, of course, and you've met Alex. I've got you set up in the front guest room. Fresh towels and bedding. Just ask if you need anything."

"Great. What's that wonderful smell? Moses, are you at it again?"

Ginn smiled. "Chicken breasts stuffed with crab. King here said you were fixin' on going out, but I made plenty 'case you're tired from your trip and just want to snuggle in."

She said, "Sounds like a terrific idea if you're sure it's no bother. Anything I can do to help? Set the table?"

"All taken care of. You just relax. King, offer the lady a drink."

I said, "Yes, dad. Got a nice Predator Zin open if that works for you," I said.

Jaime gave a weary smile. "Appropriate name under the circumstances. Sure, that'd be fine. Let me splash some water on my face and freshen up. I'll use the master if you don't mind."

"You know where it is." Anticipating her arrival, I made sure my main level master bedroom and bath were tidy. I wasn't going to presume that we'd share a bed. Our relationship was in limbo and now wasn't the time to push it.

When she was out of the room, Tomey said, "She looks tired. Works out better that you stay in tonight."

Ginn agreed, "Yeah, never seen her looking this ragged. Even when she brought Stone's ashes here, she seemed more put together."

"The stress builds up. Poor girl's been through a lot and she didn't need this crap with *Country Fixin's*. I hoped I could settle it quickly and she wouldn't need to get involved to the point of coming here."

"We can fill her in over dinner, 5-0," Ginn said.

"Let's not. Let her decompress from the trip. Just make small talk. We can get into it later."

After dinner and some Zin, Jaime had indeed decompressed. She said, "That was wonderful, Moses. I'm surprised Riley doesn't weigh three hundred pounds with cooking like that every night. You must be a personal trainer as well as a personal chef."

Ginn wouldn't appreciate the characterization as my manservant, but he rolled with it and smiled.

I said, "Small portions, my dear. Ginn doesn't skimp on the butter and rich sauces so I just stay away from seconds. I still run three times a week and he manages to stay ripped, well, I have no idea how."

Ginn said, "Dynamic tension." I was the only one who got the reference to the old Charles Atlas comic book ad.

We were on our second bottle of Zinfandel and were all pleasantly buzzed. At least, I was. Tomey was laughing louder than normal. Ginn could down a whole bottle of Scotch with no visible effect so I had no clue as to his condition. Jaime looked 'dappled and drowsy and ready to sleep'. *Feelin' Groovy.* I guess her presence reminded me of Stone's penchant for quoting song lyrics.

Jaime said, "So guys, it's pretty obvious you were trying to avoid telling me what's going on with the show while we ate. Thanks for that but I take it you're trying to spare me bad news."

The remaining three of us looked around at each other, deciding who should go first. I took the lead.

"Well, the good news is that more and more, we're getting the feeling that Cami is alive." I told her about

Walsh and the clothes and the Winona Sands proposal. "Apparently, Agatha Christie vanished a hundred years ago and your dad wrote a book about it, just updating the characters. Did Cami read his stuff?"

"She was a big fan of his later work so she probably did read the one you're talking about, called *Lady Ghostwriter*. He had a real ghost writer on that one, like most of his junk over the last decade. That's when he descended into pulp. Lots of gratuitous sex and violence, not much plot or character development."

"Why keep at it? With his dementia, I can't imagine he has much to offer."

"Money. He still throws it around like he always did. Buys stuff online or from TV and when it arrives, doesn't even remember ordering it. His name on a cover, no matter how lame the content is, sells books. He owes his publisher two books a year and he's out of original ideas. They just write the same tired formula, different names, same trite dialogue. It's a shame because he had so much more talent than that. Now his books have big margins, large print, blank pages between chapters. Takes every trick in the book to fill two hundred fifty pages."

"Sad. Well, let's focus on what brought you here. Cami's driver Bob Walsh is in custody but won't crack. Still insists he was stealing the clothes."

Tomey said, "King, you told me that the showrunner said they used to keep a pharma guy on the set in the old days to keep the cast and crew amped but they no longer do that. She's either lying or has blinders on. He had way more than anyone would need for personal use, plus there was quite a variety of shit. All those hidden compartments in the truck? This kid was dealing."

I said, "Yeah and Crain got hold of his Juvie records, Busted twice in high school for selling weed back then."

Ginn half-sang, *Moving on Up*, in that deep rumble of his.

Jaime said, "I'm disappointed but it doesn't surprise me that Cami's back into drugs. Coke was her drug of choice, though. I'm pretty sure she stayed clean for a year, which made me think she was ready for this job."

Tomey said, "You may have told King and I missed it, but were you aware that Iris Walker was into drugs and apparently did blow with Cami?"

"I didn't see it. If Iris was using, she never showed it at work, which makes me think it was strictly recreational and under control."

Tomey shrugged. "Could be. If she was just dabbling, she might not know how strong Fentanyl is. Many multiples of heroin. Tox tests said that the coke she did was laced with it. Question is, was it an accidental OD or did someone kill her?"

Jaime shuddered. "You think Walsh could have killed Cami the same way? Disposed of the body instead of leaving it for anyone to find because of her fame and ties to him."

I said, "Possible, but I don't think we're looking at some demented serial killer. Walsh really loved Cami. And really, would Cami sleep with someone for drugs?"

"I'd hoped that was behind her but I told you, she was a casting couch victim. Not a big step from that to using her assets to get high. But if he was just dealing weed, that doesn't add up."

Ginn said, "Before ya'll send this kid to the gas chamber, let's think a piece on your boy Brent. I saw his temper first hand today. Then hanging with him in his trailer, all he talked about was Cami. Man had a serious thing for her. I couldn't get him off it. Even got pissed at me for the way I talked about her. Lucky for him, he thought better of it."

I said, "It's been a long day for all of us. Let's get a good night's sleep. I'll take Bosco out and you guys turn in."

No objections from the tired group. I leashed my dog and took him for a short walk on the beach. Ten minutes later, we were back in the house. I gave him a cookie, washed up and got into bed, falling asleep almost immediately.

I don't know how long I slept. Bosco woke me with a whimper. He often has doggie nightmares and cries in his sleep. I don't know what scares him at night, because when he's awake, he has no fear. Thunder, German Shepherds, alligators --- nothing frightens him.

As I rolled over to comfort him, I felt a presence. Jaime tip-toed into the room and nestled in next to me under the covers. I didn't know what to say or what this meant, so I stayed quiet and held her. She felt good, like she belonged.

"Riles, I'm lost. Can we just snuggle and you tell me that everything's going to be all right? That's what I really need now."

43

When I awoke the next morning, Jaime and Bosco were gone. Even though all we did was literally sleep together, she probably didn't want Ginn and Tomey to think we were doing anything more. At heart, she's a very conventional girl.

When we were a couple, there were long periods when we were apart. She would have business on the Coast or I might have a case in the Northeast. I never worried that she'd be tempted by Hollywood types on the make. It was only after we broke up that she and Stone got together and she is guilt ridden about that. As much as it hurt me when it happened, I now understand and have accepted it.

I expected to find her in the kitchen and sure enough, she was sipping coffee and reading the trades online, Bosco at her feet. His bowl was full of untouched kibble. He was clever enough to wait for Ginn to come down and supplement the dry food with something tastier. If Jaime was here for any length of time, she'd try to break him of that habit. I was equally certain that Moses would find a way to surreptitiously slip him some goodies when she wasn't looking.

I said, "Sleep well?"

"Off and on. Time change plus I've got a lot on my mind. Thanks for understanding last night. It was just what I needed. I felt safe with you."

"I aim to please. I expect Ginn will be down soon. He whips up a hearty breakfast."

"I don't eat much in the morning these days. I'm trying to go vegetarian, but I'm not succeeding. I still love a nice steak, even a burger."

"It'll be hard to go Vegan with Moses around."

She smiled and waved her hand toward the main living space. "The place hasn't changed at all since I left. What are you thinking of doing with it?"

"That depends. Ted McCarver's renting now and he's not sure if his radio station is going to be viable. If he sells it, he may want to go back to a condo or move somewhere out of the area."

"Too bad. I know he dreamed about starting over with a small station and making great radio again. What about Ginn and Tomey?"

"It's actually working out well with them living upstairs. I don't even know they're there most of the time. They take care of Bosco if I'm out working. Something needs to be done around the house, Ginn's a great help. And his cooking speaks for itself."

"Sounds like a nice setup you got going. A mini-commune."

"It's missing one thing. You."

She drank some coffee. She reached down and petted Bosco. I'd made her uncomfortable. It was too soon.

I said, "I'm sorry. I know it's awkward. I shouldn't have brought it up."

"No, I understand. It's just that I'm re-evaluating everything now. Part of the reason I wanted to be in California was that dad's condition was getting worse. This isn't something I want out in public, but he had almost nothing to do with his last book."

"I read it. You know I'm not a big fan, but it was his best in quite a while, I thought."

"He doesn't even know it's out. I hired a really good ghostwriter. I gave him some ideas and he ran with them. He's going to be writing all of dad's books from here on in. It'll be like the Parker estate continuing with Spenser and Jesse Stone. That Reed Farrel Coleman dude did a great job developing Stone. Difference is, dad is still alive. Such as he is."

"He's that bad?"

"It breaks my heart to see him. There's a live-in who takes care of him 24/7. Truth be told, I don't visit him much. He has no idea who I am. It makes me feel awful to see what's happened to a once great mind."

"I'm sorry."

"That's the disease. People say I should see him more but it's no comfort to him. He just babbles and stares into space. The doctors say it could be years before it starts shutting his systems down. It's terrible. He's not my dad anymore. Just a shell that he once lived in."

"I don't blame you. If seeing him doesn't help him and makes you feel bad, what's the point? I know it sounds cold, but why torture yourself if it doesn't do him any good? How's the agency going, other than this issue with Cami?"

"The good news is that I've got a great second in command who handles all the day to day business. I trust her completely. If anything happens to me, I've got total faith that the company would be in good hands and not miss a beat."

"That's got to be a relief, but nothing's going to happen to you. You'll be around for at least another fifty years."

"Into my nineties, huh? Thank you, Doctor King. Any more predictions?"

It was my turn to stall. Everything she had just told me opened the door for a relationship, if we both wanted it. But she was going through an emotional crisis and that's not the time to make life altering decisions.

I said, "Just know I'll be here for you. I'll support whatever you need."

"Damn it, you're going to make me cry."

"Well, don't do that. Moses is on his way down and if he thinks I made you cry, he might hit me upside the head."

She laughed as she wiped a tiny tear away. Ginn was bopping down the stairs, fresh as the morning dew. Big smile on his face as he said, "Finally. Things back where they supposed to be. Hope y'all ain't had no breakfast yet, 'cause I feel like cooking."

"Jaime's thinking veggie. Maybe one of your special omelets?"

"I'll see what I got in the fridge. Any preference?"

"Surprise us. Where's Alex?"

"She got called out late last night. Some big bucks tourist got mugged on the beach. After taking care of that, she bedded down on the couch in her office. Lonely night for old Moses."

Jaime said, "Sorry to hear that. So what *are* you two exactly?"

I said, "Come on Jaime, that's between them."

Ginn said, "No, she got a right to ask, us living here and all. We're together. That's it. Ain't nothing in writing, no need. We free but far's I know, neither one thinking of straying. We appreciate King's hospitality long as he gives it. That changes, we work it out then."

Jaime said, "Good for you. Money not a problem?"

"We cool."

I would have been interested in knowing how Ginn makes ends meet since he never takes a penny from me. Whenever I ask him for a bill for his services, he says he'll get around to it. But he never does. If it was anyone else, I'd expect a whopper of an invoice someday, but with him, that day will never come.

My cell buzzed. Another local number I didn't recognize.

"Hello." I used a high pitched, nasal voice. With unwanted solicitations, I act crazy and waste their time to the point where they put me on *their* 'do not call' list.

"Is this Riley King?" A mellow sounding woman, not a polished telemarketer. I took a chance and said 'yes' in my normal voice.

"This is Cameron Wordsworth. I understand you're looking for me."

44

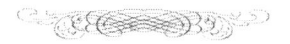

I said "Cami?" loud, so that Jaime and Ginn could hear. I'd never heard her voice other than on television, so I couldn't be sure if it was really her or some troll or prankster. I activated the speaker setting.

I said, "If this is someone other than Cami, you'd be wise to hang up now. There're big penalties for fraud. Impersonating a kidnap victim."

"I'm the real deal baby, you can be sure of that."

Jaime nodded, recognizing the voice as her half sister.

I said, "I'm going to put you on with someone you know well."

"Hey, Cami."

"Jaime. Where are you? Are you in South Carolina with King?"

"I am. Because of you. What's going on? We were all worried sick. We thought you'd been kidnapped or maybe even killed."

I laid the phone on the island counter and the three of us clustered around it. I let Jaime handle it.

Cami said, "It's complicated, sis. Too complicated to talk about on the phone."

I said, "Cami, why did you call me and not Jaime directly?"

"I didn't know she was back East. I figured you were working for her and you'd tell her what she needed to know."

Jaime said, "And what is that?"

"Can't say on the phone. Let's meet in person. And come alone."

I said, "No can do. Not that I don't trust you, but some strange things have been going on around your show. I can't take the chance that whoever's behind it isn't watching you. I'm sure you know the police are looking for you."

"I don't know that they aren't listening right now, do I? No police. Not now."

Jaime said, "Hold on, Cami. I'm going to put you on hold for a second."

Cami said, "I have a better idea. I'll call you back on *your* phone."

Before I could say anything, she hung up. "Can your computer guy trace that call, Riley?" Jaime asked.

"I doubt it. If she's smart, she's calling from a burner. Look, she wants to meet. Let me think of a safe place."

Jaime's phone buzzed. Cami. "Take me off speaker, sis."

"Riley's trying to come up with a place we can meet."

Cami said, "I have a place. Tell King we'll meet at Bob. He'll know what I mean. He's been there. One hour from now. Just you and him. I'll trust you this one time, sis."

She hung up.

Jaime was confused. "God, she's acting like somebody on the ten most wanted list. She's assuming all our phones are tapped."

"She's being careful. She may *be* a fugitive for all we know. And just because I didn't know if Crain can trace the location of her call, that doesn't mean he can't."

"You're starting to scare me, Riley."

"We have to be careful, too. If she's involved in something illegal, we could be accessories after the fact if we meet with her. Moses, I'll have to borrow the Benz. I doubt whoever's involved in this knows your car."

Ginn said, "That's a negative, 5-0. Not that I don't trust you with my baby, which I don't, but there's no way I let you two go out there alone without me giving you cover. This chick's got something up her sleeve."

"Appreciate the thought, but what are you worried about? You think I can't take care of Cami myself?"

"Play back what you just said. You wouldn't let Jaime go alone. What was *you* worried about?"

"It's crazy. I think Bob Walsh was helping her all along and he's still in stir. Unless she's got another ally, I can't see her hurting you by herself, Jaime."

Jaime almost spit up her coffee. "Hurt me? Why would she? I got her this gig. Helped her start what could be a nice career. Why would she want to hurt me?"

I wasn't sure I wanted to feed her mistrust with a theory out of left field, but I had to be honest. Something had been percolating in my mind since Jaime had told me about her father's illness.

"Jaime, have you seen your father's will?"

"There isn't one. I've been after him to do it for years but he's a stubborn man and never did. I've sent accountants and lawyers to talk to him about it, but he wouldn't budge. He said he planned on living forever and would always joke that so far, it was going well."

"Now that he's sick, I don't think anything he bequeaths would be valid. Not being of sound mind and body. Are you your father's heir as his closest living relative? No aunts, uncles or other kids?"

"I'm his only acknowledged child. No brothers and sisters. You can't be thinking.... no, there's no way."

"You're probably right. But just consider it. Your dad has Alzheimer's and you said he won't be around too much longer. There was a written agreement after Cami's mom died that your dad would provide for his illegitimate daughter until she was twenty one. Cami must have a copy of that."

Ginn said, "See where King's going, girl? Your dad's estate be worth millions. Her disappearing might have been a ruse to get you to come out here. With you out the way, Cami could say she got dibs on the estate, being his daughter and all. Just sayin'."

~~~~~

We were in the MDX, headed to Cami's retreat. Ginn said, "Why you turning toward Ribaut? She said Bob and that you'd been there. Those Fleetwood Macking hippies live in Bluffton."

"Ribaut used to be called Bobb Island. Still is on most maps. I think the plantation changed it because it sounds cooler. More exclusive. French."

"That be the old plantation way, 5-0. Just do things they want, don't ask no permission. Gather up slaves in Africa, bring 'em here to work for free."

Jaime nodded in sympathy but changed the subject. "Is Cami in trouble legally? I mean, could she get arrested for this?"

Ginn said, "Yeah, smart thing would be to call Alex. Have her meet us there."

I said, "We need to hear Cami's story first. I don't know what to do about Cami and I don't want to put Alex in a bad spot. I don't want her loyalty to you make her compromise her job. We've been there before and it was dicey for a while."

"Montanez is the one out to get you. This island is Alex's turf, not his." Ginn said. "But I guess what I don't know, I can't tell her. So you want me to stand lookout 'case there is something naughty 'bout to happen?"

"Yeah, that way you won't have to lie to Tomey if Jaime and I are stupid and have to do something borderline."

We pulled up to the Ribaut house. Percy Mayfield wasn't working on the landscape this morning --- one less obstacle. Jaime and I walked to the front door and rang the bell. Cami Purdy answered.

She looked great. Young enough not to need makeup to disguise anything, she still had it laid on thick. False eyelashes, violet eye shadow, ruby red lipstick. Her perfume was overbearing. To my ancient eyes, she looked like she preparing for a job interview with a pimp.

She was barefoot, wearing a Pearl Jam tee shirt and tight cut-off shorts that barely covered her lovely bottom. She grabbed Jaime and hugged her tight. Jaime stiffened at the embrace.

Cami said, "Thanks for coming, sis. I really need your help now. Can we talk, just the two of us?"

Jaime said, "No. Anything you have to say, Riley can hear. I'm happy you're okay but there's been a manhunt for you the several days. I need you to tell me the truth."

"Come inside. I wanted to talk in private for your sake. This whole thing started 'cause of you, sis."

"Stop calling me sis, please. Just Jaime will do."

Cami shot her a nasty look. "Have it your way. You haven't been much of a sister to me, that's for sure."

Jaime was about to blow up but I stepped in. "Ladies, let's sit down and talk. You two want to explore your sisterhood or lack thereof later, that's fine. But right now, we have a more immediate problem."

Cami walked to a wet bar in the great room and poured herself a drink. It was too early for Jaime and me, but it didn't matter, since Cami didn't offer. She took her glass and sat on a loveseat, opposite a larger sofa. An ornately carved cocktail table separated the overstuffed floral couches that had gone out of style twenty years ago.

Cami took a deep pull on her bourbon and crossed her arms. I said, "Why don't we start with the night you disappeared."

She said, "I need to go back further than that. The night I called you, sis. I told you I was terrified of Brent. You said you'd look into it and protect me. You didn't do a damn thing, did you?"

"That's not true. I called someone from the show and they told me that you were at a bar drinking, nowhere near Brent that night. I sent Iris Walker the next day. She stayed on the set for a week and saw no signs of him hurting you. You didn't call again, and Iris said she'd taken care of it. I would have come myself, but I had some personal issues and couldn't leave."

She was talking about Rick's fatal illness. His last days coincided with Cami's call but she didn't tell her half sister that.

"You could have hired someone to look out for me. You could have called *this* goon to keep watch over Brent."

I said, "No, she couldn't. Goon isn't what I do."

Cami smirked. "The only one I could turn to for help was Bob Walsh. And now he's in jail."

"That he is," I said. "For running a pharmacy out of his truck. Most jurisdictions frown on that."

"He's a sweet kid and he shouldn't be in jail for trying to make a little on the side."

Jaime said, "Was he selling to the cast and crew?"

"I don't know anything about that. I'm not into that stuff. You know that, sis."

We knew otherwise but would hold that card for later, if necessary. I said, "Okay, we're not here to talk about your drug use or non-use or Bob Walsh. We're here to talk about why you disappeared."

Cami took another pull. "I'd think that was obvious, dude. I had to get away from Brent Purdy before he killed me."

I said, "Cami, I get that you were scared of him. He can be a scary guy. But why didn't you go to the police? If you were that afraid, they could slap a restraining order on him. Or go to a lawyer. Jaime could have hooked you up with one."

"Why would I think she'd help when she didn't take me seriously? Matter of fact, she took Brent's side. Jaime, you said you sent Iris out to help me. That ain't true. Iris told me you were more worried about Brent and your precious show. It was all about the money, not me or my safety."

Jaime lowered her eyes. "Cami, I should have done more. I can see that now. But I did have someone keeping an eye on you. Ron McLeish, the AD. He said he talked to you and told you if there was anything you needed, he'd be there."

"That old drunk? He was a mercy hire. Nobody else would have him, he's such a pathetic sack of shit. I was supposed to rely on him to protect me?"

"Ron was a cop in LA before he started working in TV. He told me he was keeping a close eye on Brent and didn't see a problem."

"So you took the word of an old drunk over your sister. Thanks for nothing."

She got up to refill her glass. I stopped her. "Cami, no more. We need to figure some things out. For your sake. You need to be thinking clearly."

She threw the leftover ice from her glass in my face. The remaining tinge of bourbon burned, but I'm a big boy and can tolerate my liquor.

I took her arm as gently as I could and led her back to the loveseat. Even gentle for me left a mark.

She began sobbing. She was playing to the last row. Theatrical. It didn't work for the all seeing camera. Or my stinging eyes. Take two.

45

Jaime and I waited a respectable period for the crocodile tears to subside. The hysterical crying didn't mean she was lying about her fears, but Brent was a better actor and more convincing.

Jaime felt guilty over not supporting Cami in more tangible ways. She suspected her half sister of crying wolf, and took only token measures to ensure her safety. Her plate was full at the time, trying to comfort a dying man. Now with a firsthand look at Cami's concern, she wanted to make amends. I still didn't believe her.

Jaime turned to me. "Let's take this one step at a time. If we call the authorities and say we've found Cami, is she in danger of any legal trouble?"

"I doubt it. Technically, it might be fraud, forcing the cops to waste resources investigating a crime that doesn't exist. But that would open up a Pandora's box. They'd have to indict every woman who runs away from an abusive spouse. I can't see even the most Neanderthal DA supporting that."

Cami had stopped sobbing and looked up at me. "You see, that's it. I did what I had to do."

I said, "No. You should have gone for the restraining order."

Cami's contempt for me resurfaced. "You really were thinking of marrying this meathead, sis? I suppose you never heard of any men who ignored restraining orders and killed their wives?"

Jaime gestured to me with an upraised, open palm. "She's right about that, Riley."

"Brent terrorizes her and he can kiss his TV show goodbye. And any chance he has to run for office. He may really want you back Cami, but he'd be giving up his other dreams if he tried anything."

Cami said, "I'm not willing to bet my life on that. You may be, but I'm not. I can't tell you how many times I found him here after I left him, waiting for me to get home, late at night. How many times he terrorized me. I changed the locks. I had Bob stay with me. That didn't stop him. He's crazy."

I showed some cards. Brent's tracker had revealed her travels the week before she vanished. "Cami, you were staying at different motels because Brent knew you were renting here, didn't you?"

"Great detective work. I won't bore you with the details, but I've slept in a different bed every night for the last week or so. Worn disguises. Had Bob check me in under his name."

"Right. Well, he's got his own problems now and you can't count on him. We need to find a safe place for you. So let me make a few calls pack up some things. I want you to dress like you're going to Sunday Mass."

"Who do you think you are, telling me what to wear?"

"I think I'm the man your half sister hired to protect you. If you think you can avoid Brent without any help, you go right ahead. Otherwise, take a shower and change clothes. Take your time."

She sniffed and walked up the stairs to the master. I didn't think she'd try to bolt from another exit, but I was thankful that Ginn was standing guard at the gate, just in case.

Once I heard the door slam upstairs, I said to Jaime, "We need to let the cops know we found her. They'll be pissed about wasting manpower and drum up some charges on us if we don't."

"I don't care about me," Jaime said. "As long as she's safe, let them try to charge me with whatever. My personal attorney Jack Furlong will shut that down in a millisecond."

"I'm also thinking about Brent. I'm concerned for her but that doesn't mean I trust her."

"She's not playing some kind of scam. She's done it before, she's really street-wise. But this is for real. I know it."

"Okay, but once we tell the cops we found her, Brent'll want to know where she is."

"We're under no obligation to tell him. I'm thinking she stays with us at your house. You have extra bedrooms, and with Ginn and Tomey and us there, I don't think Brent would be crazy enough to come after her."

"It's the first place he'd look. He's got a posse of rednecks at that bar who I think would do just about anything for him, including try to abduct Cami. I don't want to turn the house into the Alamo if it comes to that."

"You really think he's capable of that?"

"No. I'm really just sketching out the worst case scenario. But I *have* seen his temper. So far, he backs off pretty quick, but every man has a boiling point where his emotions are so strong they can't be controlled."

I wasn't going tell Jaime, but I identified with Brent. When Rick first told me they had gotten together, I came close to booking a flight out to the coast to kick the shit out of him. Luckily, Ginn talked me down. And even if he hadn't, the cross country flight probably would have cooled me off enough to avoid doing something stupid. But I couldn't be sure of that, I was so enraged.

After that initial impulse, I did talk to Tomey to help me get through it. She made me realize how insane such an act of retribution would be. It wouldn't get Jaime back, in fact, it would drive her further away. Hurting Stone might give me a moment's satisfaction, followed by consequences that would follow me for the rest of my days.

I told Alex that I would never find someone like Jaime. I'd spend the rest of my days alone, save for the occasional drunken coupling with someone I couldn't wait to dispatch before the sun came up.

Tomey played shrink and traced my desperation back to childhood. Although my parents were never really warm and affectionate, with me or each other, they did the best they could. Something in my upbringing had made me feel I was unworthy of a good woman. I believed I'd have to trick one into loving me. If she eventually saw through my brilliant disguise, she'd leave and there would be no hope that I could fool another woman into accepting me, once so exposed.

I thought my childhood was pretty normal, no real dysfunction. But Brent had told me stories of *his* youth, how his ultra religious guardians had deliberately undermined his self image in service of their beliefs. How brutal football coaches made him feel like the fat boy who was merely an expendable cog, serving at the pleasure of the glamour boys at quarterback.

Once he became a semi-celebrity, marrying a hot little number like Cami was his temporary victory over his childhood. But the fat boy remained lurking under the surface, ready to emerge once Cami discovered the real Brent Purdy, who was not remotely in her league. He'd do anything, debase himself to any degree, to prove himself worthy of her love.

There were differences. I realized that roughing up Stone in front of Jaime to prove I was the better man would backfire. Brent still believed some grand heroic gesture on his part could win Cami back. He spent sleepless nights trying to imagine what that might be.

As much as I sympathized with Brent's plight, my immediate mission was to protect Cami.

46

I walked Cami over to the MDX, and faking a gentlemanly pose I did not feel, I opened the rear door for her. She wasn't impressed by my gallantry.

"I thought you were some big time private dick. I wouldn't be caught dead driving a shit heap like this."

I said, "Didn't you see the bumper sticker that says, 'my other car is a Porsche'?"

"Yeah, right next to your Hillary 2016 sticker."

"I thought I'd peeled that one off a while ago." Actually, the old Acura displayed no stickers, other than the one my community insisted on. You'd think the SUV was distinctive enough without additional signage, but there was frequent turnover in the development's security department and a newbie might not recognize a classic.

I said, "Luckily, Maggie's heard worse so she's not offended by you calling her a shit heap. But if you don't get in and shut up, her owner may take offense and you wouldn't want that."

She grumbled. "Cute. You have a name for this wreck, grandpa. I don't get why I have to sit in the back. I'm surprised a crate like this still doesn't have a bench seat in the front."

The 'grandpa' remark stung a little at first but the only way I could be Cami's grandfather is if I had relations with her mother when I was ten. That precocious I was not. I let it roll off. "Jaime called shotgun and frankly, I prefer her company to yours. Can't imagine why."

As she stepped into the SUV, her eyes grew wide. Ginn was sitting in the back seat, .38 in his lap.

He said, "Well, well missy, what have we here?" His eyes were canvassing every inch of her now smartly dressed physique.

Cami said, "No way am I sitting back here with Steppin Fetchit. Not happening."

I cringed as I awaited Ginn's reply. He was cool.

"I forgot that we'd been graced with the presence of television royalty. Is there anything I can do to make your journey more amenable? Champagne? Caviar? We colored folk is here to please."

I'd had enough. "It's a short ride Cami. Just get in and shut up."

Jaime watched the joust with an amused smile but so far, said nothing. She stretched out her long legs in the front passenger seat and tilted her head back. "He's right. Short ride. We're going to Riley's place. I think you'll find the accommodations there up to your standards."

Cami sneered. "Just tell your field hand to keep his hands to himself."

She was testing me and Ginn. I knew Moses wouldn't take the bait, but she couldn't know that. She was trying to see how far I'd go to protect her. I couldn't stop him from getting in a quick lick in before I intervened. Even if I wanted to.

As much as I didn't love the idea of taking Cami in, the only alternative I had wasn't a good one. WPHX station owner Ted McCarver had founded an asylum for abused women on the island. Under normal circumstances, it would be a great place to hide her. But I couldn't trust that he wouldn't mention it to someone. Ted has do-gooder instincts and would try to intervene in some way, even if I tell him not to. He had done that in the past, and almost got both of us killed.

Ten minutes later, we were at my place. Jaime took Cami upstairs to one of the guest rooms while I quieted Bosco, my enthusiastic greeter. He was trying to bolt upstairs with the ladies to see if he'd like the new girl's bed more than mine --- the insensitive, disloyal cad that he was.

While Jaime played innkeeper, Ginn poured us both an adult beverage. I said, "Early in the day, my friend, but your instincts are right on."

"Haven't used that expression since Barry White. Salud." He took a deep pull and smacked his lips. "Now what do we do with her?"

"First thing is, we call Tomey and tell her we have Cami and that she's safe. Then Jaime's going to have to come up with some kind of press release announcing it."

"And how you planning to explain where this chick was last week or so? Ain't like she went to some nunnery."

"They still have nunneries? Whatever. That's Jaime's bailiwick. She knows how to massage the media way better than I do."

Ginn plopped himself down on the great room sofa and sighed. "Alex ain't gonna be taking orders from Jaime on this. I'm not so sure what to tell her."

"Far as I know, Cami hasn't broken any laws. I'm just thinking we need to let Alex know. It's not like we're harboring a fugitive. She might be able to get Montanez to cool it. I sure as hell am not going to be the one to give him the news."

Jaime came down the stairs. "She's hanging up her clothes. Said she needs to lie down for a while. While she was using the john back on Ribaut, I took her phone. Didn't want her calling anybody. She hasn't noticed it's missing yet."

Ginn smiled. "Smart move. "Spect there'll be hell to pay once she finds out."

I agreed. "We're going to let Alex know that we have Cami. What are you going to say to the media, Jaime?"

"Let's see. We could go with the temporary amnesia scenario. But I think that's too mid 20th century."

"Like temporary insanity. Played well in *Anatomy of a Murder*, but I think Preminger ruined that defense for us."

Jaime said, "We could say Cami was worried she was getting hooked on pain killers. Got hurt swinging a hammer on the show and needed some help with the pain."

Ginn said, "Got straight with a little help from some friends. Pain killers be worse than H, but since they're legal when a doctor prescribes, folks don't look too unkindly on 'em."

"Friends like Bob Walsh?" I said. "I know we haven't talked about it but that's why she came out. Walsh must have told his lawyer how to get hold of her and told her to contact me. I told him that Cami was a bigger deal than the drug charges and if he told us where she was, Alex might make the weed charge go away."

Ginn said, "That's assuming a whole lot, 5-0. Alex ain't playing that game. She might lessen the charges, but no way does he skate with that much shit in his truck."

I said, "I'm sure you'll do your best to persuade her. Meanwhile, Jaime, did she let on anything about the real reason she disappeared?"

"No. She just said she was really scared of Brent and blamed me for not taking her seriously. She has a point."

"Don't take this on yourself. You sent Iris, you alerted McLeish. You didn't believe there was a clear and present danger. I'm still not sure there was. Are you going to try to get her to go back to the show?"

"I can't see her doing that unless you or Moses agree to be her full time bodyguard."

Ginn licked his lips at the thought, then shook his head to let Jaime know he was kidding. I said, "If Moses wants to volunteer, I'm okay with it."

Jaime looked longingly at our half empty glasses. "Any of that Scotch have my name on it?"

"If your name is Glenfiddich, it do," Ginn said. "Rocks or straight up?"

"With soda, please."

"Damn, King ain't got you trained right, lady. Now I'll abide it with the Glen, but you try that with Macallan and that's a sin that don't get forgiven."

There was a banshee shriek from upstairs. Cami materialized on the bridge overlooking the great room and screamed, "My phone is missing. Did one of you assholes steal it?"

47

Nature or nurture? Had something gone awry in the John Petersen gene pool? Or did being raised by a wastrel mother in a disadvantaged area versus highly educated parents Holmby Hills and Englewood, NJ make these two women as disparate as Lizzie Borden and Joan of Arc?

I pondered this while Jaime and Cami argued over the purloined phone. Jaime was calm, her voice modulated as she explained why she had taken it while her half sister used the facilities. Cami was hysterical, acting as if Jaime had ripped out her womb while she slept.

Cami said, "You don't trust me. You never have. That's what this is all about."

"Trust is a two way street. If your relationship had reached a tipping point and you were determined to leave Brent, you could have told me instead of bolting and starting a manhunt. I would have hired Riley or his like to protect you. Instead, you don't tell anyone and get involved with some drug dealing kid, which by the way, is gonna complicate things for you even further."

I didn't fancy Jaime saying 'Riley or his like'. There isn't anyone like me. The closest approximation, Moses Ginn, sat on the sofa, ignoring the bickering.

Cami said, "You don't know Bobby. He's a good guy."

"That remains to be seen. Right now, you have to stay away from him. What we need to do is put out a release saying that you're safe to keep the wolves at bay. We need a reason that you disappeared that'll play in the media."

"Tell the truth. I was scared for my life. Brent was going to kill me."

Jaime bit her lip and walked to the refrigerator, I assumed, for a bottle of water. I never touch the stuff and since we split, never keep it in stock. It makes no sense to buy bottled water originating in East Jabib in flimsy plastic bottles when I have expensive filters curating the stuff coming from the door of a ten thousand dollar appliance.

Moses did have a carton of store bought OJ tucked away and Jaime poured herself a glass. If this battle continued, she'd want another shot of Scotch to accompany it.

Cami was standing near the island, hands on hips. Jaime carried her juice to one of the stools nearby.

She spoke softly. "We're halfway through the season. We do that and the show is dead, except for reruns and I doubt the network will even want them. Some sins are unforgiveable in the Me-Too era."

"See what I mean. Thinking of your precious show instead of my safety."

I had to interject. "Cami, that precious show is your livelihood now, unless Bobby's splitting his drug money with you."

"Tell your goon to shut up, Jaime."

"I'm in the room. Tell me yourself." Jaime was trying to apply reason but I decided to cut through the bull. "Your sister's trying to help. She flew all the way across the country to be here. She hired me to find you and aid to spare no expense. And oh yeah, she got you this gig in the first place."

"Look how it turned out."

"She didn't make you marry Brent Purdy. It was your idea to hitch your wagon to his. You start in on him and he dishes it back at you and you'll both be finished on TV. Your *Sisters* show will never get off the ground."

"What do you know about that?"

If there was any doubt that Cami was involved in the proposal to Winona Sands, she had just erased it.

"I know enough. Listen, Jaime's been in this business a lot longer than you have. Work with her. And work with me. We have some leverage over Brent. We can get a restraining order. You might be able to wrap this season, get a divorce and go your separate ways."

Jaime put her hand on Cami's shoulder. "Listen to him. I could help you get on a show based in California. You'll be three thousand miles away from Brent. He's got strong ties here he won't want to leave behind."

Cami said, "You ever hear of airplanes? I'm telling you, he won't stop. He'll find me, wherever I am. And unless I go back to him, he'll kill me. He's said that in so many words. Fuck your leverage."

~~~~~

Ginn called Alex Tomey to tell her we had Cami at the house and that she was safe. Jaime was preparing an announcement for the media and might even do a press conference at some point.

When Alex got to the house, she was having none of it. She appeared a few minutes after the call, and although she wasn't exactly milk and honey to Ginn and me, she reserved her harshest treatment for Jaime. "I need to ask a few questions and I prefer it not in the presence of your handler," she said, giving Jaime a contemptuous look.

Jaime wasn't about to back down. "I'm not a *handler*. Ms. Purdy is represented by my agency. Cami, you don't have to answer any of her questions and I prefer to be present when she interrogates you. If you want, I can call a lawyer, that's up to you."

A *Clash of the Female Titans* was shaping up here and I wanted no part of it. The women had jobs to do and were determined to do them without any interference. Ginn and I would only step in if it came to blows.

Tomey said, "This isn't an interrogation, Ms. Johansen. Mrs. Purdy's situation has cost the county considerable manpower and resources at a time when our budgets are strained."

"Cami didn't know where to turn. She was alone and confused."

"I'd like to hear that from her. Mrs. Purdy, I need to ask you some questions. Like your mouthpiece says, you can refuse. As *she* says, it's your call."

Cami had been arrested in her previous life in L.A., so she knew the drill. If she had broken the law, Jaime would be supportive and enlist a top lawyer.

Allegations of spousal abuse could ruin Brent, whether they proved to be true or not. I'd seen a ruthless streak in Cami, and I had no doubts she'd lie to save her own skin.

Cami spoke up. "What the hell? I'll talk to you. And I don't need you sis, or your pals."

Jaime turned to me for help but all I said was, "The screen porch is the best place to close the door and talk in private. Just remember Cami, the truth shall set you free."

"Eat shit, gumshoe."

With that, she and Tomey walked through the French doors that led to the back porch. I felt like I'd been following Cami's latest dietary advice since this whole affair began, so I was fine with letting the chips fall where they may.

Jaime said, "You think this is a good idea? You never told me that Alex didn't like me. I thought we were sort of friends."

Ginn said, "That's her game face, James. Don't take nothing from it. She playing tough cop for Cami's sake. Don't expect no apology, but she *will* explain."

I said, "Yeah, honey, I've been on the receiving end of that act a number of times and now she's living in my house, so don't take it personally. She can be tougher with Cami than we were. She'll poke holes in her story if there're holes to be poked."

"So what do we do next?"

I said, "We'll wait till Tomey's done with her. Then I think you and I need to drive up to see Brent. We'll leave Cami here in the capable hands of Mr. Ginn. Unless Alex cuffs her and takes her away. Then it's a whole different ballgame. Think you can handle Cami for a few hours, Mo?"

"I'll do everything I can to keep her from tearing off her clothes and coming on to me. I'll admit, there be times when the flesh is weak but I'll stay strong."

48

Jaime and I were driving to Judy's Island to talk to Brent Purdy. I like to think that we're both reasonable people, but in this case, we see things differently. I tend to believe in Brent and she is now on Cami's side.

She said, "Are you sure we can trust Moses with Cami? She's pretty street smart."

"That may be, but in the dictionary under street smart, you'll find a picture of Moses Ginn."

"Tomey didn't say a word about her interview with Cami. And Cami blew us off when we asked her about it. We're flying blind."

Alex's silence wouldn't last. She was a stickler for procedure, but she'd tell Ginn and me what we needed to know in due time. The fact that she didn't arrest Cami was key. If Tomey felt she had grounds, Ms. Cameron Wordsworth Purdy would already have been booked.

I said, "Seems to me you need to come up with a game plan, Ms. Johansen. We need to let Brent know she's alive and safe, but that he can't contact her. That's going to take some doing."

"You remember Watergate? I was a child then but I read all about it later. Nixon wanted to do what he called a 'limited hang out.' Tell some of the story, based on the truth, but spin it in a direction that favors the narrative. Maybe that's what we do with Cami. Tell the public that they're splitting, but take blame off Brent. They did that on that *Flip or Flop* show. Even though they got divorced and she married some English mechanic, they're still doing the show and the ratings are better than ever."

"You can only hope."

"Right now, I can't see Cami going along with that. But if we can muddle through the rest of this season with just him, we can reposition the show next year with Alison as the female lead or Brent as solo act. He's got a high enough Q rating to carry it on his own now. Maybe a spin-off for Cami. We can take advantage of the publicity. As long as Brent's not perceived as a wife beater, we can make this a win/win."

"Far as we know, he wasn't. Terroristic threats are against the law, if he actually said he'd kill her. We've got to keep Cami from saying he did that."

Jaime nodded. "We'd have to buy her off. Even though I didn't want them to get a divorce at first, that's the way to go. Irreconcilable differences, leave it at that. She'll get a big settlement but he'll have enough to go forward and we'll recast the show."

"There's some more damage control you need to think about. If it turns out to be that Bob Walsh is a drug supplier for the cast and crew, that could hurt the show more than Brent and Cami splitting."

"Wrong. People assume TV shows and movies are rife with sex and drugs. Wouldn't surprise anyone. Music, too. How many of your favorite bands were full of druggies and wastrels and you still bought their records?"

I stopped the car and pulled onto the shoulder of William Hilton Parkway. Maybe I'd had a Saint Paul moment on the road, but my brain finally went into OVERLOAD.

"Jaime, what the hell are we doing here? You wanted me to find Cami. She found us. She's alive. They both can rot in hell far as I'm concerned."

"Riley, what're you saying?"

"I'm saying we've got our priorities backwards. Iris Walker is dead. You've barely mentioned her name since you got here. A woman who worked for you that you sent out to protect the show and your clients. She may have been murdered. And your focus has been on the show and how to salvage it."

Jaime sat in stunned silence.

I said, "Is this what Hollywood's done to you? I didn't much like Iris but she's a human being. Jaime, we're all turned around. Following your lead, I put Iris on the back burner and I don't feel good about it. God, you're making me think about that speech Holden gave to Dunaway in *Network* about how the television culture corrupts everything it touches. Remember? Then they killed Howard Beale for ratings. Is that where we're at?"

In a small voice, she said, "Who do you think I am? Of course I care about Iris. But she's dead and there's nothing we can do to bring her back. I'm trying to save a product that makes money for a whole lot of people. You even said it could turn the whole island around if Brent can get elected mayor and turn it into a destination."

"Listen to yourself. You're talking about money like it's the answer to everything. Protect a den of thieves and villains, as long as they're your thieves and villains. You've got lots of other clients. You can't be that hard up for money."

"That's easy for you to say. You're living in a big house on the ocean. You don't need to earn a living and fight every day for every dollar. Sure, I'll live if I lose

Country Fixin's. But I owe it to the agency to do everything I can to keep it earning."

"Even if Brent turns out to be a monster and Cami a grifter? These are the kind of people you want to work for?"

"It's the life we've chosen. Money always wins."

"No, it's the life *you've* chosen. I thought after Rick died and we talked, you said that you were reassessing everything. Maybe winning wasn't the only thing, that people you care about matter more than dollars."

"I did reevaluate my life. And I realized what makes me get up in the morning is winning. Making deals. I can't be like you. Waking up when you feel like it, doing whatever you want every day. Taking on a case if it amuses you or appeals to your sense of justice. That's not the way the world works, Riley. You're lucky you've never had to deal with the sharks in the business world."

"I worked for the FBI for ten years. I saw every form of despicable human behavior back when your biggest concern was who was going to be your prom date. I try to make the world a little better for me being in it, not just to die with the most toys."

"I think you need to drop me off at the nearest car rental place. I'll do this on my own. I'll send someone for my things at your house and you can tell Ginn to let Cami leave. I'll do things my way from here on in."

49

"He's coming to. Riley, are you okay?" Jaime said. The small towel on my forehead was damp and cool. Where was I?

"Must've dozed off," I mumbled.

"You passed out, 5-0," Ginn said. "Can't hold your liquor."

Jaime said, "Not funny, Moses. We were about to call an ambulance. I'm going to dial 911."

I was rejoining the real world. I remembered sitting down on the sofa after a sip of Scotch, then blinking a couple of times and….

I fainted? That happens to frail ladies in drawing room mysteries, not red blooded he-men like me. Was Ginn right? My body isn't conditioned for whisky this early?

"I'm okay, Jaime. What happened to Tomey and Cami?"

"They're still on the screen porch. They didn't see you pass out. We need to get you to a doctor."

"No, really, I'm fine. Just got dizzy for a second, is all."

Jaime must be having flashbacks to her last days with Rick. She hadn't told me what it was like. She *had* told me that Rick had shown no symptoms. The disease was discovered during a routine physical that the studio insisted upon for insurance purposes. From the diagnosis to his death was a matter of weeks.

No one should ever have to go through that. If it happened a second time to another loved one, even the strongest of us would suffer emotional devastation from which there could be no recovery. I was confident I was in fine fettle, but what had happened to Stone was on my mind as well.

Fate, the luck of the draw, the randomness of life? Who decides these things? Didn't John Lennon write that *God is a concept, by which we measure our pain*?

Ginn said, "You know, you had a hard shot to the head a couple nights back. If it was the NFL, you'd be in concussion protocol. I bet you just had an aftershock."

"What hard shot to the head?" Jaime wanted to know.

I hadn't told her about my fisticuffs with Brent's goon squad, just that he had riled easily in my presence a couple of times. I made light of the punch.

She wasn't convinced. "I'm making an appointment for you right now."

"Wait. I'm fine. Tell you what. You've a doctor on the *Fixin's* set. When we go to see Brent, I'll let her look me over. If she thinks it's something serious, I'll do whatever you say. Okay?"

"She's a med student who can sew up a finger if someone gets cut with a saw or a foot if they step on a nail. Give a tetanus booster. She's not a brain specialist. But I can see other than knocking you out and dragging you in to the hospital, this is the best I can hope for."

Ginn said, "You get involved with us tough dudes, that's what you get, honey. You still want me to babysit Cami when you go to see Purdy?"

I said, "Yeah, let's stick to the plan."

It struck me --- I hadn't been in the car with Jaime, arguing about Iris Walker. I must have dreamed that little sequence while I was out cold. But now, as the details of that imagined conversation filtered back to me, it made me think.

I wondered whether the real Jaime's reaction would be the same as the phantom Jaime, who by this time had already rented a car and lit off on her own to confront Purdy.

Ginn went upstairs to change, giving Jaime and me the room. Tomey and Cami were still on the screen porch --- talking quietly, it seemed.

"Jaime, let me ask you something. What's your end game? You sent me out to find Cami and we have her. What's the mission now?"

"We tell Brent that Cami is safe and that she'll get a restraining order if he comes near her. I'll advise her to file for divorce, but that's up to her."

"Is his Q rating or whatever you call it high enough so the show can stay on the air?"

"Probably. Brent's built his own following and if that's not enough, Alison or someone like her can fill Cami's role. Hey, if the show dies, it dies. There'll always be another."

"That's it?"

"No. I really want to know what happened to Iris Walker. If her death was accidental or if someone killed her. She was my responsibility. I sent her out here. I owe it to her family and to my other workers. They need to know I have their back. I know you didn't like her much, but I'd appreciate your help."

This is the real Jaime. Her Faye Dunaway phantom can go back to hell.

50

Ginn was driving his vintage Mercedes with me in the passenger's seat. There had been a change in plans that I had gone along with, trusting that Ginn had a reason for the move.

I said, "You were going to explain why it's you and me headed to talk to Purdy instead of Jaime, who I'd much rather be looking at right now. Alex sure was no help. Blew us off when she got through with Cami, like we weren't even there."

"That's right, 5-0. She be a sworn officer of the law. She can't be leaking shit to you. Now, if she tells me and *I* spill the beans to you, well, you get it."

"She knows her way around politics, I'll give her that. But what's the harm in telling us about what Cami said?"

"You had a fight with Iris Walker, she turns up dead. Jaime sent her out there in the first place. Somebody with a mind for conspiracy might say she sent her East so's you could kill her."

"What motive would she have for killing Iris? And who'd be stupid enough to buy into that theory?"

"Fellow by the name of Montanez."

"The guy is certifiable if he thinks that. But the question was, why are you coming with me to see Purdy, instead of Jaime? Is Tomey afraid to let Jaime and me talk alone?"

Ginn shook his head in exasperation. "Alex is on our side. It's just she hates lying and if she gets asked if she told you anything, she can say no and her conscience is clear. Not saying she wouldn't cover for you if it came down to it, but she'd rather tell the truth. She's in line to be the next chief here on the island and she got to keep her nose clean. Someday she might even be up for county sheriff if these rubes here be woke enough to elect a chick."

"Not many would use 'woke' and 'chick' in the same sentence. Wait till the electorate finds out she's hanging with the likes of you."

"We can handle that. Now, main reason it's me and you seeing Purdy is the vibe she got from Cami. Something needs to get worked out between the two sisters. They gotta to air it all out. 'Sides, Brent'll get the message to stay away better if you got me backing up your weak fainting ass. You okay now?"

"I'll never live that down, will I?"

When we got to the house Brent was supposedly working on, he was nowhere to be found. In fact, nobody seemed to be working. For a minute we thought we'd come to the wrong place, but when we saw a large group clustered around a food truck, we realized they were all on a break.

"S'pose I could grab a couple of them dogs?" Ginn said. "My eatin's all disrupted these days, thanks to you."

I spotted Alison Reiger apart from the group, working with a piece of wood. "You grab a dog, I'm going to talk to Reiger."

Ginn said, "Why should you have all the fun? I'll wolf down a couple of dogs and let you soften her up. Then, I'll be by to close the deal."

"I'd like to visit your world someday, Mo. Enjoy your tube steak."

Alison was dressed for work. A sleeveless tee that showed off her lean, muscular arms. Tight cut-off jeans, heavy socks, DeWalt work boots. I'm sure that if it wasn't television the jeans would have been longer and looser, but the camera loved those long tanned gams. The camera wasn't the only one.

I gave her my brightest smile and said, "Hey stranger, where've you been?"

She didn't look particularly happy to see me. My rakish charm wasn't working with the Reiger sisters.

I said, "Good news. We found Cami. She's alive and well."

She didn't seem overly excited to hear that. "Great. Where was she?"

"Long story but she's fine. But my question was where were you? Not like you to go AWOL."

"Had some personal business. This ain't my full time job, you know."

"Sure. Your parents were worried, that's all. I met your sister, by the way. Sweet kid."

"Glad *you* think so." She peered at me, suspicion radiating from every pore. "How'd you happen to meet her?"

She was sanding a piece of trim, scraping off the remainder of some white enamel to get down to bare wood.

"Worried about you. I thought your sister might know where you were when you didn't show for work."

She sanded harder, concentrating on a small indentation in the wood. It looked fine to me --- the touch of color in the crevice gave it a nice patina. I guess she was planning to stain it and the white would show through.

"I don't much care for my sister much, but stay away from her. She's got nothing to do with any of this."

"You're right. I was just giving you the benefit of the doubt. Thinking that the *Sisters* show that's being shopped around might have been something you were doing with your *real* sister. Not Cami."

"I have no idea what you're talking about."

"But I know all about your proposal. Your stairway to stardom."

"Well, whatever it is *you* know, I hope you'll enlighten me. Because it's news to me."

I told her about the pitch that Winona had told me about.

When I finished, she said, "Here's what I know. After Brent and I cooled it, Cami saw me looking down and asked me out for drinks. She knew I'd been with Brent but she didn't care. We drank and talked that night, more than we ever had. She said she wanted out of the show and had an idea for another show. She didn't get into details but said there'd be a place for me on it if I wanted it."

"And what did you say to that?"

"I said that I'd think about it."

"So *Sisters* was something you'd do?"

"I forget who came up with it first, but the idea made sense. Two young women, rehabbing houses. I have the expertise, she has the star power. But that's where it ended. Cami went missing couple days after that."

She stopped sanding and looked up at me with those clear blue eyes. I liked Alison. She was smart, independent, self-sufficient, tough, resourceful, clever and as the pitch said, a hot young chick.

"So you had nothing to do with the pitch that got sent around."

"No. Cami did talk about finding someone who could put a pilot together. I said, why not use Ms. Johansen but Cami didn't want her part of it for some reason. She did say something about Iris Walker being someone she liked."

"You think she figured she could lure her out here on Jaime's dime by disappearing?"

"That sounds like something Cami would do. She did say Iris was thinking of starting her own agency. Okay, I've told you everything I know. Now you tell me: what happened to Iris? I've got a hunch you know something about that."

Ginn was sauntering over to us, but I looked him away. I didn't want to break the flow.

"I don't know. That fact she was planning to leave Jaime is interesting. It's possible Cami did use her to put together that proposal."

"And my name was on it?"

"No. Cami's wasn't either. Just said two stars from reality shows."

"I'd hardly call me a star. I bet she had someone else in mind. After that night of drinking with her, I still didn't trust her. She wanted to screw Brent so bad and I wanted no part of that. This morning, I straight out asked him if he was fixing to get me fired. He said it crossed his mind but that it would be a shitty thing to do and he decided against it. The man is honest as the day is long. I really like him a lot, in spite of everything that's gone down."

"I think deep down he really likes you, too. You guys are cut from the same cloth. Take care, Alison."

As I walked over to retrieve Ginn, the conspiracy theory he'd espoused on the way over took on some credibility.

If Iris quit the agency and took a popular star with her, undermining *Country Fixin's* and Brent Purdy in the process, Jaime *would* have a reason to do something about it. And I'd have incentive --- to win back my woman.

Killing Iris would do the trick --- punishment for her disloyalty.

It made sense if you didn't know Jaime. And it goes without saying that desperate as I might be to get her back, murdering a potential rival was way past where I'd draw the line. Maybe the phantom Jaime with her rental car would stoop to such a thing, but the real one --- no way.

The problem was that Marty Montanez didn't like me, and he didn't know Jaime. It was all bogus, but people have been busted on less.

51

Ginn and I were hunkering down in Purdy's trailer to deliver the goods on Cami and explain his options, which were essentially non-existent. I had the honors.

"Good news, bad news, Brent. The good news is we found Cami and she's alive and unharmed."

He swallowed hard and raised his eyes to the heavens. "Hallelujah. That's great."

"The bad news is that she did this to get away from you. Cami doesn't want to ever see you again."

Brent wasn't going to let that little tidbit spoil his joy. "Oh, she'll change her mind. Typical woman. We've had our ups and downs. She'll get over it."

Ginn stuck his tongue in his cheek, as if trying to dislodge a shard of his lunch.

I said, "Look, fella, Cami's going to file for divorce. She wants no more contact. If you try to see her, she'll get a restraining order."

Brent smiled. "Cami wouldn't do that. She'll wanna clear the air one on one, just like I do."

"Brent, she says she disappeared because she's deathly afraid of you. This isn't some minor misunderstanding over a credit card bill. It's been going on for months and it's reached critical mass. Don't go on kidding yourself, it's over."

"My bad. I let it get to that point. I'm just so over the moon you found her. I'll apologize and we'll work it out."

"I'm afraid it's too late for that. Hey, you've got a nice career going and plans to get into politics. Don't blow it all over a battle you can't win."

The smile never left his face. "I ever tell you about the Colorado game, my senior year? We were down by three touchdowns, fourth quarter. They were playing at home, light air, heavy favorites. But we never gave up. Forced a fumble in their end zone. Onside kick. Long pass. Suddenly it was seven points. Nobody ever thought we could do an onside kick twice in a row and it'd work, but it did. We scored, no time left, and coach said, let's go for two. No ties. You can guess the rest."

Ginn said, "If that's the year I'm thinking, you only won three games and they fired your coach at the end of the season. That game was early in the season, made the AD think the team was better than they really was, so they canned his ass. Won the battle, lost the war."

I'm not a big college football fan, so I had to trust Moses' recollection. The look on Brent's face told me my friend's memory was accurate.

He said, "More to that story than ever got out. Turns out coach was sleeping with the president's wife. They kept the scandal quiet, but we all knew. Different times."

"My point exactly," I said. You guys wage a public divorce and the tabloids will eat it up. Cami'll say you abused her physically, true or not. She'll pull out all the stops, if you don't go along. She said as much to Jaime. When she's finished, you won't be able to get elected dog catcher, if they still have those."

"I never hit her. Never would."

"That's great but it won't matter. The press and the public will side with the woman. They always do these days. Much bigger names than you will never work in the business again. No respectable media outlet will touch you. Your reputation will be ruined and you still won't get her back."

"According to you. I believe the Lord intended me and Cam to be together, rain or shine. But what I ain't getting is, you're supposed to be on my side. Why are you so negative?"

Ginn said, "He *is* on your side, you dumb rube. He telling you the best thing to do for yourself and you ain't listening."

"Hey, no need for name calling, man. Was a time I'd be in your face for that, but see, I'm cool. Tell me, where's Cam now?"

I said, "Somewhere safe. That's all you need to know. What I'm asking you to do isn't easy, believe me I know. I've been through it. There's no such thing as an amicable divorce. Even if you agree to go along, it'll hurt like hell. But trust me, it's the best way."

He was still calm. But I'd seen him explode from a dead stop so I was glad to have Ginn around. To hold me back, of course.

He was like Bosco with an old chew toy. Cami belonged to him and he wouldn't let go. I needed to make it clear that the decision had already been made and he had no say in the matter.

I said, "She's off the show. They're working on a press release that you two have split for the old 'irreconcilable differences' excuse. You'll finish this season on your own. Jaime'll talk to you about going forward on your own or maybe getting a new co-host."

Brent rubbed his hands together. "Listen up, boys. I appreciate your concern and that you found Cam. That's all to the good."

"Cami found us. She trusts us to protect her from you. Purdy, this isn't some little lover's spat that can be fixed with flowers and candy. It's over. Move on with your life. You're a big strapping hunk of man. You got money and fame. You won't have any problem finding somebody else once you set your mind on it."

"Don't want nobody else."

Ginn was becoming impatient. His tolerance level for recalcitrant clients was far shorter than mine. "Purdy, the cops already got it in for you. You go against a restraining order and they'll put you away, man."

Brent stood and turned his back on us, walking to his sink and turning on the water. He soaped up his hands and acted like we weren't there. He'd tuned us out, so I tried another approach --- giving him false hope.

I said, "Brent, look at it this way. I'm not saying you're right about Cami, but *if* you are, let her go for now. If you're really meant to be together, she'll come around someday. Play the long game. Divorced people re-marry all the time. But it's got to be her call and it's got to come in *her* time, not yours."

"I need to get ready for the next set up. Then I need to find some people who really *are* on my side. Somebody who can find Cami and reason with her. I can see it ain't either of you two."

Ginn rose suddenly like he was about to knock some sense into the man, but instead, he turned toward the door. He said, "No use arguing no more with this pig-headed loser, King. He gonna do what he gonna do. Adios, Purdy."

Nothing more for me to say either. I followed Ginn out the door.

52

"Move over little dog, the big old dog is coming in," Ginn said.

"See, I thought you were the big dog, not Jaime. Whatever happened to you closing the deal?"

"Worry not, 5-0. I got this under control."

We were waiting for Jaime to descend from upstairs. When Moses and I came back from Judy's Island, reporting that Brent wasn't buying what we were selling, she decided to take matters into her own hands. She called Purdy and told him meet her at WiseGuys at 6 p. m. --- no excuses and dress nice.

The house is ten minutes away from WiseGuys, but it was already past six and Jaime had yet to grace us with her presence after retreating to her room to shower and change. Normally she is a bug for punctuality, arriving ten minutes early for most appointments. This evening, she was in no hurry. At quarter after, she came down.

It was worth the wait.

She was dressed all in black and Johnny Cash never looked as intimidating as she. In three inch stilettos, she reached my height. She was dressed to kill, although there was no place to hide a gun or anything else in her form fitting outfit.

I said, "You look ravishing. You sure you don't want me to come with you?"

"Moses will suffice."

"Hear that, big guy? I got a mind to print up some business cards for you with that slogan."

"Me sufficing means you ain't. Don't worry, James, I'll melt into the background. Purdy won't even know I'm there," Ginn said.

I kissed Jaime on the cheek and said, "If you need anything, I'm ten minutes away."

She said, "Don't worry. You just keep an eye on Cami. She taking a nap now, but I imagine she'll be up and hungry in a bit. I'll leave her phone with you. Don't give it back to her."

Ginn said, "Alex won't be back till later and she's grabbing dinner out. If Cami's hungry, there's enough left over from last night for both of you. Just zap it for two minutes in the microwave, fifty per cent power and let it cool for a minute after you take it out. Might even be better second day."

"Yes, Emeril. Take good care of my baby."

"Gotta a feeling she be taking care of us. Let's ride."

Jaime said, "I had a long talk with Cami while you guys were gone and we came to terms with a lot of stuff. Got a lot of poison out of the way and we're in a good place now. I don't have time to tell you about the deal, but she will when she gets up. I think you'll find her a lot more respectful to you now."

The sweet, sensitive vulnerable Jaime Johansen had morphed into the take-no-prisoners businesswoman who just got things done. It made me feel that if instead of asking me to investigate, she had flown here immediately when Cami disappeared, things would have worked out better. Iris Walker might still be alive. She was surprised to learn that Iris was unhappy working for her and planned to leave the agency. She took it calmly and said she wasn't the first and wouldn't be the last.

After they left for the restaurant, I watched SportsCenter and waited for Cami to wake up. I wasn't all that hungry.

The plan was for Moses to drive Jaime to the meeting with Purdy and hang at the bar, out of Purdy's sightline. I understood why the girl was in no hurry to get there. Power tactic. Make your opponent wait for you. Show him who's boss, whose time is more valuable.

Jaime would set her phone on the table during the meeting so I could listen in. At six thirty, her number showed up on my phone. I answered without saying hello. The ambient noise in the restaurant made it hard to pick up the conversation, even though they were at one of the quieter back tables. I clicked on my tiny digital recorder to document the meeting.

The man who seated them asked if they wanted a cocktail. Jaime said, "Two double scotches. Glenfiddich, if you have it."

Brent said, "Actually, I prefer bourbon."

Jaime brushed his objection aside. "Like I said, two scotches. Neat. And whatever bourbon my friend is into."

"Yes, ma'am."

As the server shuffled away, she said, "Riley told me about your conversation this afternoon. I sent him to relay the message but apparently it didn't get through."

"He said you had Cam safe and sound. I got the message."

"Don't bullshit me, Brent. The message was that you and Cami are through. I was with her all afternoon. We spoke to an attorney and you'll be served with papers in the next forty eight hours."

"But..."

"No buts. Even though she's entitled to half of everything you own including residuals for the show and royalties from ancillary projects, she's agreed to accept thirty three per cent of the revenue accrued to date and waives the right to future earnings. It's the best deal you could ever hope for and I'm telling you to take it."

"I'm not agreeing to no divorce. It ain't about the money. That doesn't matter."

"Great. I'm glad you don't care about money because by the time this is over, you won't have any. You'll never have another TV show and I doubt too many people will even want to hire you for construction work. Most you could hope for would be a handyman or a super at some low income project."

He laughed. Even over the phone, it sounded nervous. "That's the best you could do as my agent?"

I heard a bustle as she pulled something from her purse. "Here are my termination papers as your agent. I represent Cami and since you're now in an adversarial position, it would be a conflict of interest to keep working with you."

"Why are you doing this?"

"Why are *you*? Riley tried to explain the facts of life. I thought it might sink in if it came from another man. But now *I'm* telling you, Cami will get her divorce whether you agree or not. You don't own her. We can drag this out and she'll dirty up your name something wicked. I can't stop her."

"Even if it's all lies?"

"Are they lies? I wasn't in your bedroom. She says she can produce witnesses to your abuse. That's for a judge to decide legally, but the public won't be so tolerant."

"Ms. Johansen, you know me. You know I'm a good man. I'd never hurt Cam. Anyone tells you otherwise is lying."

Jaime had to be touched by this man's devotion to his marriage. "Brent, we've been through a lot together. I really didn't want it to come to this. I do think you're a good man. And you have talent. The viewers really like you. You've done a lot of good for your little island. You could be the new Pat Conroy of the Lowcountry. But you've got to let go."

"I can't. I love Cam."

"I never told you this. Cami is my half sister. I helped her get this job with you."

"So that's why you're on her side? Blood over gold?"

"We never knew each other growing up. She was the result of one of my father's many affairs. I felt bad for her. She had a rough early life. Did a lot of things I'm sure she never told you about. She was damaged goods. I never in a million years thought you two would get married. That wasn't something I anticipated."

"We fell in love."

"*You* fell in love. Cami was a scared child, looking for security and here was this big uncomplicated man who had money and was a star in the making. She gravitated to that. She's very insecure and you represented stability. But once she started feeling her oats, she wanted more and unfortunately, you couldn't give it to her."

"If I knew what it was, I would have given it to her. I'd do anything for her."

"Anything she wants?"

"Yes, anything."

"What she wants now is for you to let her go. You'll still have *Country Fixin's*. You'll be able to run for mayor like Riley told me you wanted to. You'll be the loyal, heartbroken, hard working, blue collar gentleman and people will love you even more."

"Yeah, that all sounds great. But it doesn't mean a thing without Cam."

The waiter arrived with their drinks and Jaime said to give them a few minutes, they'd look at menus later.

Jaime said, "It makes me sad to think of you as an enemy. I really like you. You have a big heart and I'm sorry it's broken. And I'm sorry it's because of something I did and someone who's related to me. I shouldn't say this but she's not worth it. There are so many more appropriate women for you. I'm telling you as a friend as well as someone who *could* still be your agent. Please, take the deal. In time, you'll thank me for it."

All I could hear was chatter from the room for a minute as Brent drank and thought. It felt like I was listening to a radio version of *Jeopardy*, waiting for the final answer.

He spoke slowly. "I'll agree on one condition. I want her to tell me to my face that this is what she wants. King told me. You told me. I need to hear it from Cam. She tells me and I'll sign anything you want. Them's my terms."

I heard a chair slide out and I assumed Brent had stood up to leave. Jaime confirmed that.

"Riley. He left. Stuck me with the check. How rude. Just kidding."

"You okay with his terms? And do you think you can convince Cami to see him one last time?"

"Yeah. We'll have to make sure it's somewhere where she can be safe, but I'll leave that to you. God, you should have seen his face. I feel so sorry for the big lug."

"I can imagine. Poor guy had never been in love before and he's taking it real hard."

"It's gone way beyond love with him. It's obsession and it's not healthy. I'll be home soon. I'm going to wave Moses over, wherever he is. No sense letting good scotch go to waste."

53

Text messages are a mixed blessing. It's a great way to send a quick note to someone that you're running late. To tell someone you haven't forgotten a request or appointment. When only a line or two is necessary, it's a great timesaver.

Yet it also pre-empts conversation on deeper matters that require more detail than you are comfortable typing with your thumbs, or in my case, my hunt-and-peck index fingers. All I typed was 'K' when Jaime texted that she and Ginn were going to stay at WiseGuys for dinner since they were already there and the food smelled divine.

Ginn's crabmeat stuffed chicken breasts from last night could be consumed alone or in the company of Cameron Wordsworth Purdy. I'd rather dine solo but something in my chivalrous nature made me knock gently on the door to Cami's room to ask if she wanted to join me.

"Cami, it's King. Are you decent?"

"As I'll ever be. Come in."

The definition of decent must be generational. I expected her to be dressed in something that could be loosely categorized as outerwear. The lacy thong she wore was more than decent, but not the way I meant it.

She sat cross legged on the queen bed, the flat screen opposite beaming a *Real Housewives* show. The room smelled of weed. Jaime and I didn't go through her travel bag when we left Ribaut, trusting that she'd only bring along essentials. Maybe she had, if we defined essential as differently as we did decent.

She wasn't hiding her high or anything else for that matter. "Just did half a joint. Got the rest if you want to share."

"Not my choice of toxin. Thanks, anyway."

I was familiar with the heady aroma from my days of accompanying Rick Stone to rock concerts, but I've never been a fan. Catholic school upbringing, college athlete, ten years in the FBI --- it wasn't my thing. I was having a hard enough time concentrating anyway with Cami's breasts on display in all their glory.

She said, "Suit yourself. What'd ya need?"

"Jaime and Ginn are dining out. But Mo did leave some good stuff for us to heat up. I was checking to see if you were hungry."

"Ravenous. I don't do much cooking. Can you get it together by yourself?"

"Mike Ro-ave and I are good friends. It'll be ready in five minutes."

"Give me ten. I want to see if Darlene leaves her husband. I know it's fake, but it's fun. Am I okay or do you dress for dinner here?"

If I didn't know better, I'd say she was flirting with me. Did the weed make her ravenous for more than food?

"You do need to put something more on. Jaime would insist that the only breasts I see at dinner are from a dead chicken."

"James Bond you're not. I'll be down in a shake." She shook her boobs to underline the point.

I closed the door and said goodbye to the glorious sight. Was it the grass or had Jaime really softened her toward me? Slow as I am on the uptake, I got the feeling that if I suggested we skip dinner and I move onto her as the main course, she wouldn't object. That was a far cry from her calling me Jaime's goon.

I was not at all tempted by her curvaceous come-on. (I'd seen that term from Playboy as a kid and it stuck). Sleeping with Jaime's half sister would put a serious crimp in my hopes for reconciling with her. I hadn't seen Charlene Jones in months, yet the mention of her name turns Jaime's face red. There *were* lots of jealous bones in her body.

I heated up dinner. Since I expected her 'ten minutes' to be more like twenty, I opted to warm it up in the convection oven rather than the microwave. Makes for a nicer texture. Besides, Ginn would kill me if I made his creation chewy by nuking it too long.

My timing was off. Cami came down in fifteen minutes, wearing a thin white tee, no bra. Black nylon running shorts covering the throng and little else. Decent, but just barely.

I said, "I'm having Scotch. Would you like a drink, hard or soft?"

"Oh, I like it hard, big boy." She laughed as I blushed. "Oh, come on, King. I'm sure that Jaime told you I did some skin flicks in my misspent youth. That was my go-to line."

"Scotch, bourbon, a cocktail or soda?" I ignored the unrequested CV.

"Scotch is fine."

"Cami, I hate to spoil the mood, but you seem a lot friendlier than you did when we first met."

"You don't find me attractive?"

I could lie, but there were parts of me that might betray that upon close observation. "Who wouldn't? But I think you can see how it wouldn't be a good idea on many levels."

"I'd never tell. It's been a while for me and there's no one around."

"You're forgetting Bosco. He can't be trusted to keep secrets. One MilkBone and he'd sing like a bird."

She found that funnier than it was. Bosco had sniffed Cami when she first came down, then went back to one of his dog beds. He wanted no part of this human nonsense until the chicken came out of the oven.

I said, "Let's stop this silliness. Why the turnaround? I'm aware of my obvious charms, but I had them going full force earlier today and you were oblivious."

"I had a long talk with my sister while you were rousting my soon-to-be ex. Among a lot of other shit, she told me a lot about you. It was the kind of talk I wish we'd had years ago. When it was over, she made me some promises. Some really nice things are coming my way."

"And you want to repay her by trying to seduce her boyfriend?"

"She said you two were not attached now and that you were just good friends. She didn't exactly say it was open season, but she could have gone to meet my ex with you and not Morgan Freeman there."

"I think Ginn would rather be compared to Woody Strode." I could tell she had no idea who that was.

There was no way Jaime was setting Cami and me up for some frolic. Cami wasn't stupid enough to believe that. Was I giving her too much credit for having a strategic reason to seduce me? Or was she just a free spirit who lived in the moment, was feeling horny, and I was her only available option?

I said, "So what did you and Jaime decide to do about your ex?"

"You first. What did he-who-shall-not-be-named say?"

"I'm not sure I should be the one to tell you."

"Come on man, I'm dying to know. Does oral sex count as cheating? I'm real good at it."

"Stop. No sex please, we're British." I have no idea where *that* came from. Maybe inhaling the smoke from her room gave me some kind of contact high. "Okay. Brent might accept letting go but he needs you to tell him face to face that you're out."

"That's not happening. I never want to see him again."

"That's a negotiation and that's where I get off. Jaime said you've talked to a lawyer. That's what they do."

I walked over to the wet bar and poured us both a strong one. I went for Johnny Walker Red rather than Glenfiddich. The marijuana had clouded my brain, just as those high school health class films predicted.

Cami called across the room. "So that's not your strong suit, eh? But just for the hell of it, what would you do if you were me?"

"Depends. What did Jaime offer you?"

"She said I could get a third of the earnings Brent had made on the show till the end of this season, plus syndication royalties on past shows. Well over a million bucks, maybe two. No alimony going forward. But she'd represent me for a new show, based on the West Coast."

"Sounds pretty good. Ten minutes with Brent for all that dough? A no brainer."

"You don't understand, you're not a woman. I was afraid he was going to kill me. He grabbed a knife during one argument. A hammer another time. He owns guns. You haven't seen his temper."

"Oh, but I have. He always stopped short though, didn't he?"

"So far. But I ain't willing to risk that the next time he won't."

"All I can tell you is that if we did arrange some sort of face to face meeting, me or Ginn or even a cop could be there. We'd make sure he couldn't hurt you."

"You don't think he could kill me with his bare hands. You've been with him. He's scary."

"He can be, I'll grant you that. We'd stay close enough to stop him. If he agrees in writing to give you a divorce on those terms if you meet with him for a few minutes, wouldn't it be worth it?"

"And what if he still won't quit? What makes you think he won't find me on the Coast and try to kill me? He's said many times, if he can't have me nobody will."

I took a nip of the scotch. Not Glen, but not bad. "Cami, there're no guarantees, whatever you do. You fight him on the divorce, if he's of a mind to come after you, he will and he'll be more pissed off. Then all we can do is give you a 24/7 bodyguard and you'll always be looking over your shoulder. I do believe as time goes on, he'll get wrapped up in his work as mayor or maybe he'll meet someone, and leave you alone."

"So, take the money and run? Jaime said we could leave in a day or two. She even has a place for me to stay in L.A. she swears will be safe. Already guarded day and night. Twenty four hour protection, like you said."

"Oh, where is that?"

"In Holmby Hills. My father's place."

54

Brent was still the one I identified with. He loved her and wanted to shelter her from the cruelty of the world. He thought her a beautiful cherub --- an innocent, sweet child who was worthy of all his devotion and fealty. He saw only Dulcinea and was blind to Aldonza.

I tried to put myself in Cami's place. A tough childhood with a negligent hooker for a mother and an absentee, albeit rich father. Using her looks and her wits in any way she could to survive.

Maybe Jaime's dad is the lucky one. What world does his mind inhabit now? Is it all golden memories of his youth, innocent frolic, free love distributed freely? Might he live in an idyllic setting, taking pleasure from the glorious days of yesteryear?

I could also imagine that his existence is constant torture, what hell really is, where he can't escape a prison of his own construct.

Bosco was lying on the bed at my feet, his gentle, steady breathing interrupted occasionally by a muted yelp. *You have bad dreams too, pal.* What reward or punishment awaited him after his time on this sphere? Someone once said heaven was the place where you'll be reunited with all the dogs you had owned.

I hope so.

My spiritual musings were interrupted by the soft creak of the bedroom door opening. Jaime, clad in silk pajamas. She carefully moved Bosco aside, trying not to disturb him.

"Are you awake?" she whispered.

"Yeah. I turned in around ten. Cami went up to her room. High as a kite. Apparently, she brought her stash with her."

"I looked in on her before I came down. She's out cold. Snoring like a chainsaw."

"Grounds for divorce. I'll tell Brent next time I see him. Are Tomey and Ginn upstairs?"

She slid a little closer as Bosco stirred and gave her more space. "Ginn drove me here and he's up in his room. Tomey is staying at her place for the time being. Keeping some distance between us and the case. If there is a case."

"Well, I heard what Brent said to you. I told Cami about his terms. You think it's a good idea to stash her with your dad?"

"There's so much room in that empty mansion. Walls around the whole compound. Round the clock security. And it wouldn't hurt her to talk to him in his more cogent moments. Get to know her father."

"Maybe bring some light into his darkness? As long as she doesn't connive him into changing his will, although you seem to have that covered. But back to Brent, I think she'll agree to give him a one-on-one."

"You're good with that?"

I said, "Beats the alternative. We'd have to make sure that she's safe if he really is capable of hurting her. Find a way to give them some privacy but stay close enough to protect her if he tries anything."

"You think he will?"

"I don't think so. If she handles him delicately, I think he'll back off. But your semi-sib isn't the most diplomatic person in the world. She could set him off if she isn't careful. You need to coach her up."

Jaime sniffed. "I'll try."

"You're the master negotiator. You know how to make deals that leave both sides thinking they've won. And you know Cami and Brent. Actually, if they'd agree, you could be in on their talk, sort of a marriage counselor. Although you'd actually be brokering their divorce."

Dealmaker that she was, this was a negotiation she didn't look forward to. Both sides would lose something important. She said, "I started this ball rolling. Another of my colossal fuck-ups."

I reached across the sleeping dog to pull her closer. "Not your fault. You were trying to save a damaged soul. Two of them, as it turns out. And for a while, it worked out. They were married, had a hit show, fame and fortune. Life was good until it wasn't."

"I just hope I'm capable of fixing what I broke. Brent's a desperate, unhappy man. Cami is a, well, I don't know what Cami is. We had a great heart to heart talk this afternoon, one we should have had a long time ago. She said I was the big sister she always wanted and never knew she had. Iris was a surrogate for a while, but I was the real thing."

"Poor Iris. You heard about the tox report. ODed on a bad mix of coke and Fentanyl. Tomey's got a meeting tomorrow with her DEA contacts. See if they can help figure where she got it. Won't help Iris but might save some others."

"I really hope Cami had nothing to do with it. She seemed so innocent today. Like a little girl caught up in an adult game. She just wants people to like her. She needs the acclaim after growing up thinking the most she could ever be was a rich man's whore."

"You've given her a positive role model. Same genetics."

"Only half our genes were the same and I had my dad growing up and my mom after I went out into the business world. I lived in gated communities and she was out on the street at twelve, doing whatever it took to survive. But she wasn't bitter about that. Just said I was lucky to have a man like you in my life. She said you were like Sir Lancelot, the perfect romantic warrior. She hoped she could find somebody like that someday."

The warning bells went off, but I kept them inside my head. Cami had tried to seduce me and I didn't fall for it. That made it clear she was playing Jaime and was trying to find what buttons to push with me. I couldn't be sure what her end game was, if she thought that far ahead.

I didn't tell Jaime what Cami had done while she was at dinner. That would hurt her and if confronted, Cami would probably say I was the aggressor. She might try that anyway --- to undermine Jaime and me. But why? Sibling rivalry? Revenge for the advantages Jaime had that she didn't? Cami didn't think I was the perfect man for Jaime. She was trying to wound her sister, sensing that I was her easiest vulnerability.

Now I was the one who needed comfort. Nothing more.

55

Alex Tomey called me at seven the next morning. Jaime had already gone back to her room upstairs. I felt like we were a couple of unmarried college kids staying over at her parents' house. We had to sneak around at midnight to sleep together. The analogy fell apart because no actual hanky-panky had gone on. Neither one of us was ready.

I took Tomey's call in the kitchen while I drank coffee. Bosco was nowhere to be found but I wasn't worried. Ginn often arose before me and took the dog out for his morning walk before breakfast. The prospect of bacon trumped Bosco's desire to burrow deeper into my warm bed.

Tomey said, "I'll make this quick. I shouldn't be talking to you at all."

"I didn't recognize the number. I thought it was a telemarketer and almost didn't answer."

"Burner phone. I know you think I'm paranoid but I can't be caught feeding you evidence. Montanez is trying to make a case to arrest you and Jaime for Iris."

"You can't be serious."

"I wish I wasn't. Apparently, Iris was about to leave the agency and take Cami with her."

"I found that out yesterday. Moses didn't tell you?"

"He didn't. I don't know how Montanez found that out."

"Probably the same place I did. From Reiger. I don't think she'd volunteer that to a cop but she wouldn't lie if he asked."

"I don't think he has enough to arrest you but he's working it. Hard. He thinks you and Brent are in cahoots."

I told her about Cami and Brent and how they'd be meeting to talk about a divorce. If it went well, Cami and Jaime would be headed West soon.

Alex said, "Montanez won't want Jaime to leave the area."

"Meaning he'd arrest her to keep her from fleeing? Crazy. He does seem to like me for Iris though. Any idea how I'd slip her Fentanyl? Not like I can call my local CVS. Wow. The way you're laying out this ring of circumstances, I'm surprised *you* aren't arresting me. Of course, you were at my house that night so you're an alibi."

"That's it King, I can't be definitive about that if I ever had to testify and Montanez knows it. Your damn house is so big, you could have slipped out. From upstairs on the opposite side of the house, I wouldn't have heard a thing. I'd try to protect you, but any competent DA would shoot holes in my alibi."

I mouthed 'Tomey' as Ginn came back in with my panting dog. He went about preparing Bosco's breakfast while I talked to his woman.

"Ginn's a light sleeper," I said, loud enough for him to hear. "Unless Montanez thinks *he's* involved. Say it ain't so."

"I've already talked to Moses this morning and he knows. When do you think this meeting with Brent and Cami will happen?"

"As soon as possible. There's legal paperwork involved. I don't know how long it'll take to get that ready."

"Just expect Montanez to be around when the meeting happens. He has an inside source but damned if I can figure who it is."

"I just don't get why he has such a bug up his ass about me and Walker. Well, thanks for the heads-up. Stay clear of me unless you need to. Last thing I want is for you and Moses to get burned by this."

"Don't worry about Moses and me. We'll be fine. Just know: whatever happens, I've got your back. But that may not be enough."

~~~~~

Jaime gets things done. It's quite remarkable how efficient she is when dealing with an obstacle that would have others stymied for days. Shortly after I'd hung up with Tomey, she came down for breakfast and asked, "Is your network password the same or have you changed it? And can I use the printer?"

"Same as it ever was and of course you can. Just check to make sure there's paper in it."

"Thanks. I need to print up the preliminary legal agreement for the divorce."

"When did you do that?"

"Last night, before I went up to bed. Called a lawyer we have on retainer in California and gave him the bullet points. It's quick and dirty and may not hold up but it's something we'll have in writing. Now we can schedule that meeting and get Cami out of here."

Ginn said, "Don't be doing all that on an empty stomach. Getting my world famous Huevos Rancheros ready for the frying pan."

I said, "Yum. Sleeping Beauty up yet?"

Jaime said, "Don't think so. I wish I could stay in bed till ten but I'm up before six whether I have to be or not."

I told her and Ginn about what Tomey and I had discussed. If Jaime flew back with Cami, Montanez might see that as an indication of guilt. I said, "Is there someone you trust who can handle her in L.A. if you don't go back with her?"

She said, "There is, but does this guy really think we killed Iris to keep her from stealing a client? And add that to the fact we had no idea until yesterday that she was planning that."

Ginn was busy with his creation, but taking it all in. He was chopping tomatoes, onions and cheese, sprinkling them with olive oil, pepper, cilantro, sea salt, cumin, lime juice and a dozen other ingredients. The only reaction he had to what Jaime and I were talking about was an occasional 'hmm' and bob of the head.

Jaime said, "Iris always was independent. I suppose I could see her branching out on her own someday. But no one at the shop would imply to a cop that I'd kill her over it. I really can't believe anyone there would have such a low opinion of me."

We ate and Ginn's huevos lived up to their billing. I suggested that Brent and Cami to meet at Shelter Cove Park that evening around five, well before dark. There was a pergola where they could talk in private, and a space nearby for us to observe if things began to go south. Jaime agreed to prep Cami and assigned me the task of cooling Brent down.

I got to Brent at just past three thirty. He had finished work for the day, showered and donned his best duds. His hair was slicked back and he'd drenched himself in aftershave. He cleaned up presentably with a jacket and string tie that were only a few years out of style. No fashion plate he, it was the best he could come up with on short notice.

We sat outside his trailer under a towering willow oak, its branches splayed awkwardly in every direction. Draped in Spanish moss, it looked like a third grader's crayon rendering of a Halloween tree inhabited by witches.

I said, "Brent, the best advice I can give you is to think about the long game and lower your expectations for this meeting."

"So you've said."

"Look, believe it or not, I *am* on your side. I just went through what you're going through. With Jaime. She left me for my best friend. We still aren't back where we were, even though it's what I want more than anything. But I have to let it happen when she's ready, and I have no guarantee she ever will be."

He crunched up his face. "You ain't just sayin' that? You wouldn't spin me that sad sack yarn to convince me to back off?"

"Not in my playbook, big guy. On the way over here I argued with myself about telling you that. Part of me wants to tell you that Cami isn't worthy of you, but the heart wants what it wants. Maybe I'm wrong about her, only just met her. I *can* tell you she won't go along if you try to force things."

He nodded slowly, digesting my words, which weren't going down easy. "Why's she so afraid of me? I get mad, I know, and I'm working on it. But I never hit her or nothing and I never would."

"You know that but she doesn't. You've got well over a hundred pounds on her. She's seen your rage. So have I, by the way. I didn't know for sure that you'd stop things in the bar the other night or if you'd rough me up good. You don't scare me but if I was a woman, I'd be terrified."

"That's just it. I thought Cam knew me. Knew what's in my heart. Yeah, I fly off the handle too easy, but then I say I'm sorry and buy her nice things to make up for it. She wearing that pearl necklace I got her last time we argued? Set me back a pretty penny."

The breeze off the water was welcome, making the humidity a bit more bearable. It did arrive with a sour smell of decay that even Brent's cologne couldn't overcome.

I said, "Textbook men who abuse women can be a terror one minute, sweet and loving the next. That's why some women don't leave, not knowing which is which, hoping it's the good guy who buys her stuff. I don't know you that well but I've seen it, man. Take it from one who's been there, you need to fix yourself first."

He scoffed. "You got a temper?"

"The worst. And as I get older there's more things that piss me off. Small stuff that doesn't matter in the scheme of things. I'm not a big drinker but alcohol does tend to bring that out more."

"Come on, I ain't no alkie. That ain't my problem."

"Not saying it is. What it all comes down to is that you and Cami need time apart and I mean really apart, not where you only see each other at work but time where you don't see each other at all."

"I can't imagine living like that. I need her. Don't you see that?"

"My friend used to quote rock lyrics all the time and it bugged the hell out of me. There's a song by Sting. *If you love somebody, set them free.* That's your only shot with her now. Let her go and if it's meant to be, she'll come back."

"Back at ya with the songs. Meatloaf. *I would do anything for love, but I won't do that.*"

"I know that song. But he never said what *that* was. Okay, man, I tried. I guarantee if you push this thing and don't sign that agreement, you're in for a world of hurt. Telling you I told you so won't make me feel any better. You've got the talent and ambition to do some great things. I'll be sad that you wrecked your future over this, but it's your life and you do what you want."

56

I drove Brent to the meeting. Whatever happened, he would need support afterwards, unless he and Cami kissed and made up and rode off into the sunset together. I give better odds for the Jets winning the Super Bowl.

As I pulled into the Shelter Cove parking lot, I drove past a Chevy Caprice containing my nemesis, Detective Marty Montanez. He was sipping coffee along with another man dressed in business attire. On quick glance, the other was dressed a cut above what I assumed a detective's subordinate would be sporting. Was he a higher up, here to supervise?

I dropped Brent off and told him I'd meet him at the pergola after I parked the MDX. The others hadn't arrived yet.

Rather than let Montanez dictate the timing of whatever he had in mind, I walked directly toward his car and tapped on the window. He appeared to be surprised to see me, but rolled it down nonetheless.

He said, "Here for the big pow-wow, King?"

The man in the passenger seat looked away. I said, "What big pow-wow? Isn't the French Bakery's coffee a bit upscale for a public servant?"

"A connoisseur of fine coffee?" he said. "I should have known from what you served at your house the other day."

"So what brings you to Shelter Cove on this fine evening? What a coincidence, seeing you here in your shiny cop car."

"Play dumb all you want, King. It can't be too hard for you. Comes naturally, I bet. We both know that the Purdys are meeting here in a few minutes."

"How did you come by that little tidbit?"

"That's not your concern. I'm here in the interest of safety. I think we can acknowledge that their marriage is on the rocks. Wouldn't want anything bad to happen in case things get out of hand."

I quickly sorted through all the people who were aware of this meeting and couldn't come up with a definitive source for his information.

"So you're here to provide security. You didn't think I'd have that covered? That I'd just let Cami wade into a dangerous situation?"

He rolled up the window and got out of the car. His passenger was still looking away, as if fascinated by the collection of shore birds that had congregated across the way. He wanted no part of my confrontation with Montanez, trying to stay above it all and keep his hands clean.

Montanez got in my face. "King, I'm gonna lay my cards out. I think Brent Purdy had something to do with Iris Walker's OD. Maybe you helped. You have a flimsy alibi, Purdy doesn't have one at all."

"Most single people living alone don't have alibis at one in the morning on a school night."

"I want to help you. I know you're on his side, and a lot of people I talk to vouch for you, that you wouldn't be involved in anything that shady. I'm just saying, this is your chance to tell me what you know."

"Or what?"

"Normally I'd talk about obstruction, accessory to murder, shit like that. But you've been around the block enough so I'll save my breath. This guy showed up at the motel less than twenty minutes after you found the body. Right after we got there. If you didn't call him, how did he know unless he did it and was keeping an eye on the place, waiting for the cops to show?"

"He was working on a house that morning so he couldn't have been keeping an eye on the place. There's time-stamped video to prove it."

I hoped.

"Come on, treat me with a little respect. He's got a posse at that dive bar he hangs out at. Any one of them could have kept a lookout for him."

"Why don't you question them?"

"I did. They won't snitch. They're like a cult with this guy. They think he's bullet proof because he's on TV. If we get too close, I wouldn't be surprised if one of them takes the rap to protect him."

Montanez had the tracking device Brent had used. I assumed he hadn't traced it back to its owner. It would explain how Purdy got to the scene so quickly, but it might open another can of worms. I'd hold off letting him know that unless it became necessary.

I said, "Detective, why would Brent Purdy want to hurt Iris Walker? I'm sure when you asked around the set, people told you they got along."

"Until he found out she was working with Cami to get her own show and get away from him. Classic betrayal."

"Which goes against your theory. She overdosed, for God's sake. That's not an act of spontaneous violence. That takes planning. Poison is a woman's tool. I'm sure you learned that in detective school. Men tend to be more direct when they kill."

"Right. That's why I thought you might be involved. Maybe even your girlfriend. Iris betrayed her and Brent. She was a known user. Got that from a few of her colleagues in Hollywood. Spike her load and boom! Problem solved."

"Trust me. Jaime's agency reps actors who make more on one film than this TV show makes in a year. It's small potatoes. Iris might've gotten the drugs from someone she didn't know very well and it was more potent than what she was used to."

"You really believe this was accidental?"

"Regardless of what I think, I don't know why you're here now. You think Brent will confess to Cami that he killed Iris?"

"Who knows what he'll tell her?" He shrugged.

I said, "So you think Brent found out that Iris was part of a conspiracy against him. And he just happened to have a stash of tainted cocaine handy to force up Walker's nose? You'll need a better DA than Hamilton Burger to make that case."

"Who?"

"Just letting you know. I'm going to be monitoring the meeting, just out of earshot but close enough to act if things get crazy. These are two married people, having a discussion about their future, whether it'll be as a couple or separately. It's not police business."

"You don't think he poses a threat to her? We have witnesses who say Brent Purdy threatened her. We could arrest him for making terroristic threats. We may just do that."

57

It started out peacefully. Jaime and Ginn delivered Cami, who was dressed all in white. She looked like an angel. Any man would have a hard time letting go of such a goddess.

Neither Brent nor Cami wanted Jaime to mediate. Neither trusted that she would be impartial. I tried the old argument Stone had taught me in his sportscaster days. *If fans of both teams think you have unfairly favored the other, you know you have done your job and been completely neutral.* It didn't play with Boomer and despite Jaime's efforts, Cami wasn't buying it either. So much for the sisterly trust they'd established.

Before Cami walked across the lawn to meet Brent, Montanez approached her. He flashed a badge and I could hear him say that he wanted to be sure that she was meeting this man under her own volition and that she wasn't coerced in any way. I couldn't make out what she said, but her body language indicated she agreed. Montanez drew her close and whispered something, probably that he'd be there to protect her and that she should walk away at the first hint of trouble.

As she approached the pergola, Brent made an attempt to kiss her but she turned away, stiff and unreceptive. They slowly circled each other like gladiators, sizing up their opponent. Constant motion in a ten foot square. Nerves.

From our vantage point thirty yards away, we couldn't hear what was being said, save for the occasional shift in the wind that carried voices in our direction. Bits of phrases and muffled fragments of sentences were all we could hear.

That was by design. This was a private conversation between husband and wife.

I stood with Ginn and Jaime, at the ready for the first sign of trouble. Montanez was waiting an equal distance from the proceedings on the opposite side. His friend in the suit was nowhere in sight.

After they stopped moving, Brent was pleading, supplicant. Cami stood resolute, arms folded. It made me sad to see this mountain of a man reduced to a quivering mass, begging for a chance to reclaim his beloved. We were too far away to see tears, but they were there.

He was doing almost all of the talking, her responses were generally one sentence. He was petitioning --- he'd do anything she asked. She shook her head at each entreaty, staying firm.

Finally, she'd had enough. She rolled her eyes and began to walk away. That's when he made a fatal mistake. He moved toward her and placed his right hand on her shoulder, trying to turn her around to face him.

Ginn and I started toward them. If he was of a mind to, Purdy might be able to land a blow before we got there. But he didn't look threatening, his touch was gentle. I thought he just wanted her to hear a final desperate appeal, but my opinion didn't count.

A shot rang out, and Brent Purdy crumbled to the ground.

Montanez got there first. He ran to Brent, running his hands over his torso, searching him for weapons. Cami stood back, in shock. Her gun was still trained on Brent and she looked ready to fire again.

Ginn and I got there a split second later. While Montanez frisked Brent, I wrested the gun from Cami. I said, "Cami, he was just trying to talk to you."

"Oh, yeah," Montanez said. "Look."

He pointed to the grass next to Brent where a silver utility knife lay, blade exposed.

"He was going to slash her with that. A peashooter like she had versus a brute with a razor knife? You two clowns would have been too late to stop him. Now back off. Don't touch anything. This is a crime scene and a police matter," he said.

~~~~~

Alex Tomey led the Hilton Head force that arrived at the scene within ten minutes of the shooting. When we told her what had happened, she said that the presence of the razor knife would make it a clear case of self defense, a righteous kill. We were witnesses.

Luckily, Brent wasn't dead, which he might have been if Cami had fired again. He was bleeding heavily and we did what we could to stanch the flow until the medics arrived. We were fortunate that Hilton Head Medical Center was less than ten minutes away and the EMS did their job, whisking him away over Montanez's objections.

After the police took our statements, Jaime and Ginn went home. I went to the hospital to see Purdy. I stayed in the waiting room for a couple of hours until one of the docs came out to tell me that the surgery had gone well and that he was in no danger. They'd sedated him and he'd be out for the night, but he might even be released the next day. The man was tough.

That evening was a somber one. Cami had taken some sort of benzodiazepine and was up in her room, asleep. Tomey arrived shortly after we finished eating our take out pizza, and turned down the two slices Ginn had saved for her. Bosco got some crust under the table, which ranked with pancakes, bacon and doughnuts as his favorite snack.

Jaime said, "I don't understand why she didn't just aim for the legs. That would have slowed him down enough so that you and Moses could have gotten there to subdue him."

Alex answered. "We're trained to shoot for center mass. Biggest target. It's too easy to miss if you shoot for the legs. Brent was lucky that she stopped at one shot. We keep firing until we're sure the perp is down."

I said, "You have the utility knife. I could see it was brand new, not like one that had been used on the job. I patted Boomer down before we left. He didn't have a knife on him. And Ginn and I didn't see it in his hand when he touched Cami."

"He could have planted it under the pergola or somebody left it there for him. And the reason you didn't see it is simple. He grabbed her shoulder with his right hand, so the knife must have been in his left, which you wouldn't have seen from your angle."

Ginn frowned. "Purdy's a righty. Swings a hammer that side. If he was gonna take a knife to somebody, why use his left hand? He's big enough to spin her around with his left and use the other to do the damage. Other thing is, if he was looking to kill her, he could've slit her throat from behind."

"Montanez thinks that he wasn't out to kill her. He wanted to go for the face. Scar her up so she wouldn't have a TV career anymore."

"Good to have a mind reader on the force," I said.

Alex exhaled in frustration. "So, what are you saying? Montanez planted it? Did you see him do it?"

"No, but he had time when he was kneeling over the body. Easily could have dropped it there without us seeing. Pressed it into Brent's hand for prints."

"Cami would have seen it if he did that."

Ginn said, "Maybe she did. You got nothing out of her at the scene. She was all catatonic like. Maybe in the morning she be able to tell you something."

Tomey said, "Maybe. We can't hold her on anything. We have a cop and you guys as witnesses that he grabbed her by the shoulders. You guys all said you couldn't hear if things got heated. Just that she threw up her hands and started to walk away. He followed with a lethal weapon. Self defense."

Ginn said, "Except he brought a knife to a gun fight."

I wasn't convinced. "I know you're going to think this is a crazy conspiracy theory, but what if she planned to shoot Purdy all along?"

"Why would she? And how could she anticipate that she'd have the chance to do that?"

I said, "She kept saying that even if he agreed to the divorce and she moved out West, that he might come after her. She might've been just looking for an excuse."

"And you never checked to see if she had a gun in her purse?"

"I was with Brent."

Ginn said, "I drove Jaime and Cami over. Never thought to go through her purse. My bad. But I did hold it for a second. Passed it back to her when she got out of the car and it didn't feel that heavy like a gun was in it."

I said, "Nobody's blaming you. Who would have thought she'd be carrying? But Alex, why was Montanez there? Did you tell him about the meeting."

She shook her head. "No, I didn't."

That had us all quiet for a minute. Jaime said, "None of us told him. It had to come from someone on Brent's side. But I specifically told him not to tell anyone connected with the show. With the media buzzing around, that'd be a juicy tip and it wouldn't serve him well."

I said, "Did you give Cami back her phone?"

Jaime said, "I did. But I told her to keep it quiet too. What would be the point of her telling anybody?"

Ginn said, "Loose lips. One way to find out. She's out like a light. One of us could go upstairs and lift the phone outta her purse. I'd volunteer, but she might be sleeping nekkid and someone present might object to me catching a gander at that, even though it be in the line of duty."

I said, "Me too. Alex can't do it because she's a cop and that could be considered an unlawful search."

We all looked at Jaime. She headed up the stairs.

58

The voice on the other end was familiar. Bob Walsh. I had dialed the last number Cami had called and he picked up. After he said, "Cami" a couple of times, I knew who it was and hung up. He tried calling back and I ignored it.

"It all fits," I said. "You can stop worrying about someone at work betraying you, Jaime. Walsh had access to the proposal and since she called him this afternoon, we can assume she told him about the meeting too. How long has he been out of jail, Alex?"

"Lawyer posted bail this morning. So he's Montanez's source."

I said, "That'd be my guess. Marty makes him a CI, with the promise to get him off on the drug charges in exchange for dirt on Purdy."

Ginn said, "Trading dope for dope on a dope. We know how but we don't know why."

Tomey said, "We know that Walsh adores Cami. She tells Walsh she doesn't trust us to protect her and he contacts Montanez to pitch in. She knows I'm on your side, so she tells Walsh to call the guy who was tasked with finding her."

Jaime paced the room. "Cami still doesn't believe in us? We talked for hours yesterday and I thought we'd established trust in one another. How could she doubt I was looking out for her?"

I started to say something but Ginn interrupted. "Pardon me for saying so, she told you she was scared of him months ago. Seems she still got doubts about whose side you on, no matter what she told you."

Jaime said, "So Brent's the bad guy here? You think they'll charge him with attempted murder? Assault with a deadly weapon?"

Alex took a deep breath. "That's what I'd do. Sorry to say, given the evidence."

Jaime said, "How about telling him you know Brent put the tracker on Cami's car? If he really was bent on hurting her, he knew where she was."

I said, "That's actually a strike against him. Underlines how obsessed he was with Cami. The only way we leak that is if they try to pin Iris' murder on him. Then we go for the lesser of two evils."

"Of course," Jaime said. "I should leave this to the pros. I'm sorry. What can I do that'll help, instead of just getting in the way?"

Jaime had fostered Brent and Cami's careers, taken two nobodies and made them stars. She had deep affection for one; the other was a blood relative.

I said, "You take care of Cami. She called Walsh. Maybe she'll tell you why."

Ginn said, "Just don't say you *know* she called. Slip that phone back where you got it after we take down some more numbers. Say somehow Montanez knew about the meet and does she have any idea how that happened? Did she tell anyone? You confront about you having her phone as proof, she surely won't trust you a lick. I'm betting she'll shut down even more than she already has."

Alex said, "Moses is right. I'll try to hook up a meeting with Montanez. I think you and Moses should be with me. Tag team him. I'll play like I'm on his side. Anything else?"

I said, "Actually, there is. When I first saw Montanez parked at Shelter Cove, he was in the car with a man in a suit. Nice threads. Late thirties, I'd say, dark hair, clean cut, good looking. But later, the man was nowhere to be seen. Had the smell of a cop, but not an underling. FBI maybe, or DEA if our drug theory is right. If we can identify him, maybe we can use it to pressure Montanez."

"Shelter Cove has tons of security cameras. You tell me exactly where the car was parked and I'll put someone on it."

I said. "Jaime, stay with Cami and try to keep her from calling anybody. Or if she insists, let her, but listen in if you can. I'm going to run some of the other calls she made by my man Crain. Maybe he can find some other links that'll help, like Walker's drug connection."

~~~~

I envisioned meeting Montanez in a dark room somewhere, a place where I could strangle him, cut up the body and feed it to the alligators. He must have anticipated my fantasy because he insisted we meet at the bar in the HarbourTown clubhouse. I'd played the seaside course a number of times and Rick Stone's ashes were scattered in the marsh in front of the eighteenth green. The place had bittersweet memories.

Montanez was waiting in a corner booth, drinking coffee. Late morning, the place was devoid of patrons, just a few custodial types and bartenders preparing for the day.

"I thought that it was just you and King, Tomey. What's he doing here?" he said, in lieu of a greeting, pointing at Ginn.

"He's like American Express. I never leave home without him," I said. "Alex, you told Mr. Marty that Moses was coming, no?"

"Thought I did. Makes it an even game, me and detective Montanez on the side of the good guys and you and Mr. Ginn on the other," Alex said.

Montanez wasn't buying it. "Don't take me for a fool, Tomey. I know you and this man have been bumping nasties. Three to one a fair fight? Shit, I say bring it on."

I said, "That's where you're wrong. I see this as a coming together, finding common ground. We all want to see justice served."

I could have used a glass of water to keep from choking on my words.

This building was only a few years old. When the Heritage Classic threatened to pull out because the facilities weren't up to par for a big golf tourney, they razed the old clubhouse and built this new, grander one in the space of a year. The taproom was particularly elegant, dark paneling, crimson oriental carpet over distressed hardwood floors. A swell place to light up a stogie and lie to your well-off friends about how you tamed the monster layout. For me, as long as the beer is cold and they stock single malt, the setting doesn't matter much.

Montanez said, "I agreed to meet with you as a professional courtesy. You said you had something for me. What do you have?"

I said, "A question first. How long has Bob Walsh been a CI for you?"

"Who?"

"Walsh told you about the meeting yesterday. He also told you about Cami and him working on a show with Iris Walker. He's the only one who knew about both things so don't deny it."

Alex fell into her role as Montanez's public defender. "No law against informants, King. We all do it when there's important information to be had. Don't tell me you never use them. Especially back when you were with the FBI."

"That's right, detective Tomey," I said. I was addressing her formally, trying to keep up the pretense that she was on the opposing side. Montanez didn't know that she had been very busy this morning. The probes she had launched had yielded the fruit that I planned to use to trip him up.

I flashed him some bogus respect. "Smart cop that you are, detective Montanez, you know you have to verify everything a snitch tells you. They have a habit of pushing their own crooked agenda. Walsh has been in bed with Cami Purdy all along, quite literally. And he sells drugs."

Montanez scoffed. "I don't know this Walsh character. He's no informant of mine."

"Okay, be that way. Let's move on. Why was Devin Hardy with you in the car yesterday? You know, the town manager of Judy's Island."

"That has nothing to do with anything."

"Why did he vanish when the heat came down? He grabbed a cab back to Judy's. We *do* have proof of that."

"He's a friend of mine. We met up for coffee and he hung out with me for a spell. Once the action started, he split. Not his turf, nothing he could do to help."

Ginn was looking for 'tells' on the detective's face. He was good at it.

"Coffee? Come on. Why was he with you in the first place?"

"I told you, he's a friend."

"I didn't see on the calendar that it's *bring a politician to work day*. I guess I'll have to ask him myself."

I didn't need Ginn to tell me that we'd struck a chord with Montanez. He said, "I wouldn't do that. He's a powerful dude and won't appreciate having his name associated with this."

"We'll see about that. Now, an interesting factoid. Did you know that *Country Fixin's* has a deal with Stanley, that calls for exclusive use of their tools? Product placement, they call it. The utility knife you planted was a Craftsman."

Again, his face betrayed him and his voice rose in indignation. "I planted? Eat shit, King."

"Craftsman is sold at Sears and Lowe's. A few hours before the shooting, you bought a Craftsman razor knife at Lowe's. You should have paid cash, not credit. How you anticipated that, I'll never know. Brilliant idea, but it backfired. That same knife just happened to surface at Shelter Cove."

I expected Montanez to be a tough nut to crack. He had talked a good game up to this point, but he could see it slipping away. He might continue to stonewall and thwart our attempts to build the case against him. Or he could play ball with us now and make the best deal he could.

He tried one last gambit. "You can't prove it's the same knife."

I said, "Okay. Show us the one you bought."

"Don't recall what I did with it."

Alex snorted. "Run that by the review board and see what they think."

Ginn said, "You planted evidence, man I'm a pretty good magician but it be hard to make that go away."

"He was going to hurt her. Even without the knife, a big guy like him could have snapped her neck like a twig."

I said, "You're right that he didn't need a weapon if he wanted to hurt her. You thought the knife would seal the deal, that he posed a deadly threat and she was justified shooting him. You were too smart for your own good."

Tomey said, "We all know how this works. I can't offer immunity on my own. But you didn't do this on your own. Someone's pulling your strings and if you give that person up, I'm pretty sure the DA will cut you a deal."

"You can't prove anything. You got nothing."

Tomey said, "I have to warn you, this offer has an expiration date. If I have to find out things on my own, I'm not known for advocating mercy."

He turned to me. "Again, you can't prove that was the same knife."

Ginn said, "You do know the Hilton Head folks have the gun and are tracing it? When Cami left the house, there was nothing like that in her purse. Wonder how she got it when the only other person she had contact with was you. Bet she snitches to save her own ass."

He had no answer for that, choosing to remain silent.

Alex went in for the kill-shot. I couldn't tell if she was stretching the truth or not. "You don't think big box stores keep serial numbers on their merchandise? We have the knife in our evidence locker. Might take a while, but I bet we can trace it all the way back to the Stanley factory."

"You come after me, I can do likewise to you and your pals, Tomey."

I looked at Tomey. She extended her palms outward, tossing the gauntlet back to me. I said, "Ooh, that sounds like a threat. I'm duly warned. Good luck making your case to the review board."

With that, we left.

~~~~~

Tomey, Ginn and I went to Dunkin' after our talk with Montanez. I limited myself to one old fashioned. Tomey had coffee and watched with amusement as Ginn munched on some gooey chocolate crème confection.

Ginn said. "This doughnut's on the stale side. I think I'm gonna go up and ask 'em for another one."

"You'd have a better case if you hadn't eaten the whole thing," I said.

While he went back to the counter on his quest for carbs, Tomey said, "Why do you think she had to shoot Purdy? If he didn't have a box-cutter, what was she so afraid of? She knew Montanez was there to protect her. You too, for what it's worth. They must have planned this on the fly, but what was in it for Montanez?"

"I think the mayor of Judy's Island might have that answer. After you told me about Devin Hardy, I asked my man Crain to get some info on him. Good job by you, getting his face on those security cameras at the mall. I don't know anything about politics on Judy's Island, but apparently Montanez wasn't lying. Hardy's a pretty powerful dude. I don't think he was there by coincidence."

Tomey sipped her coffee. "I'm not really a political animal either. All I know is that the mayor's been in office for fifteen years or so. Harmless old fellow. He likes me. His wife died last year and I got the feeling he wanted to ask me out but he was embarrassed because of the age difference."

I resisted making a quip about the mileage on her pastry eating consort. "I've heard he's kind of a figurehead who rubber stamps what the planning board puts on his desk. You think I could go see him later this afternoon?"

"God, you act like I'm your appointments secretary, King. Yeah, I could probably set that up. Mayor's only a part time job, he plays golf more than you do. Why later? Where are you headed?"

I said, "I'm going to see how Brent's doing. He might have some answers."

Moses came back with another coffee and two more chocolate doughnuts. "Got to maintain my size," he said.

59

Peter Morrison was eighty years old and he looked like a mayor --- the mayor of Oz. Short of stature, a slight Irish brogue, his mane of long white hair swept back. A Bob Hope arched nose veined with evidence of drink.

Alex had no problem arranging the interview at his modest office, although he expressed disappointment that she wasn't able to join us. She told me that Morrison was aware of me and had favorable things to say.

"Welcome Mr. King," he said, a big smile revealing perfect dentures. "I can't imagine why you'd want to chat with a grizzled old pol like me, but I'm happy to meet you."

"Same here, Your Honor."

"Pete. Let's drop the formalities. Mayor Pete's already taken it seems, so just Pete is fine. I wouldn't want anyone to confuse me with that young fellow."

"You don't approve of his uh, orientation?"

"I could care less about that. He's a Democrat."

I couldn't suppress a chuckle. "Well, to each his own. Thanks for taking time out of your busy day to meet me."

"Not that busy, believe me. Things here aren't the same as they are up North. You're a Jersey boy, I'm from Boston. I decided to retire down where terrorists aren't targeting our buildings or Patriot's Day races."

I looked around at his sparsely furnished office. The décor was what they used to call Danish Modern, now Ikea was the one-size-fits-all description. No papers cluttered his desk. The red chairs surrounding it were ugly and worn, but comfortable.

He said, "I'll offer you a drink if you like, but I won't be joining you. Gave it up years ago. Doctor's orders. I keep bourbon and Scotch around for special guests, and you sir, qualify."

"Thanks, but I don't want to take up too much of your time."

"Time is one thing I have plenty of, although I suppose at my age I shouldn't jinx myself. Mayor here is a part time job. No money in it. Just gives me something to do."

"You weren't involved in politics in Massachusetts?"

"The only contact I had with politicians was when they thanked me for giving them money."

"So what led you to get into it down here?"

"When Jess and I moved here, we were building our dream house. I saw how inefficient the building process was and in turn how sloppy the government was. Delays, lost paperwork, bureaucratic nonsense. Badly in need of deregulation. The Dems had been in power for a long time and fouled things up. The mayor was in office for twenty years. Old money, family had a big name in the county, otherwise there'd be no way a Dem would get elected. When he died there was a power vacuum, so I figured, what the hell, let me step in and damned if I didn't win."

"I imagine you've gotten it to the point where the county practically runs itself."

"Oh, I wouldn't go that far. It's not like I get involved in the day to day stuff anymore. I did when I first got in, but now the town manager handles everything. Of course, I appoint him so I technically have control, but I trust my man. Gent by the name of Devin Hardy."

My mission was to find out why Hardy was with Montanez yesterday. Just coincidence or did he have a stake in the Brent Purdy affair? Was he acting on orders from Mayor Pete?

I said, "So you intend to be mayor for life?"

"Au contraire. My term is up this year and the election is in November. I'm not running again. My wife Jess and I want to travel, see the world in the time we have left. We're both in good health and we want to take advantage of that while we can."

That was strange. Tomey had told me his wife had died last year. Had he remarried that soon? Tomey rarely gets her facts wrong.

I said, "Any thoughts on a successor?"

"Funny you should mention it. It was Brent Purdy until yesterday. You know, the TV fellow on that home fix-it show? I'm afraid the fact he tried to kill his wife disqualifies him. Shame. Nice young man, would never have suspected he'd do something like that."

The fact that Mayor Pete had no idea that I was working with Purdy showed how detached he'd become. He took an appointment with me without asking why, just knew me by reputation.

I said, "Well, that's actually the reason I wanted to talk with you. When Brent's wife went missing, I was hired to find her. Long story short, I did locate her. She wanted a divorce but Brent wanted to meet with her to try to fix it. Politics had nothing to do with it. He really loves her."

"That was in the paper this morning. But then he tried to kill her and she shot him. I haven't seen a police report yet."

"I was there, sir. I don't believe he was trying to harm her in any way."

"The paper seemed to indicate otherwise. I'm not sure why you wanted to talk to me. It happened on Hilton Head. I can't help him. I know the mayor there but he wouldn't get involved in a criminal matter if that's what you're asking." he said.

"I'd never ask you to do that, sir. I'm just curious about why you thought Purdy could be a good successor. He's registered as an independent, not GOP. Why would you support him and not someone from your own party?"

"He's a real go-getter. Lots of great ideas to bring business in. Very impressive fellow and very popular. With the name recognition and all, he could have won easily. Selfishly, I didn't want to go out backing a loser. Ironically, it seems that I have."

"Well, don't believe everything you read in the papers."

"Say that again. This last term has been hell for me. There's this reporter who's scrutinizing my every expense. I get paid twenty five thousand a year for this job, which I donate back to charity. My portfolio is worth many multiples of that. But if I take a potential investor out to dinner and expense it, they publish everything we eat and drink. Make it look like I'm living off the public teat."

"I don't blame you for being fed up with it all. Mister Mayor, I'm with you on Brent Purdy. I like the man and I think he'd be good for the island. I don't think he was trying to harm his wife. And I'm not saying the detective involved did anything wrong, just misinterpreted what was going on. If we can spin this as an honest mistake by both parties, Brent's reputation can be restored and your endorsement will look justifiable."

"You sure you're not a politician, young man?"

Morrison wasn't trying to bring Purdy down. It was quite the opposite --- it was in his interest to promote the man and his agenda.

I said, "Never wanted to be involved in that game for the reasons you just talked about. Brent Purdy still wants to be mayor, he can't very well run for office if he's on trial for killing his wife. Not the best path to getting elected."

It was Morrison's turn to take a breath. "If you manage to turn this around, I'll reiterate my support for Purdy. There's a lot of good will towards him in this area and folks'll give him the benefit of the doubt. But if he *is* guilty, there's no way I can support a wife beater. Jess would kill me."

"I'm going to visit him in the hospital now and start working on it."

"I'll get with Devin and let him know what you're up to."

"Sir, please don't tell Hardy or anyone else about this just yet. They may not see the big picture like you do. Let's just keep this to ourselves for now. No leaks."

"I trust Devin's discretion but I'll go along. You stay in touch. Brent Purdy was voted the most popular man in the county last fall. It's amazing how people watch these reality shows and think the man can leap tall buildings in a single bound."

"And people assume he could be a great mayor, even though he has no experience and he's never even run for office."

He smiled again, showing those expensive choppers. "Well, even though he's my guy and I support him a hundred per cent to this day, look who we elected president."

~~~~

There was a big surprise waiting for me in Brent Purdy's hospital room. In a chair next to the bed, Alison Reiger was reading something on a tablet. Purdy was asleep, unconscious, in a coma, or all three. I'm not sure of those gradations.

I said, "Alison. Fancy meeting you here."

"Not too loud. He's asleep."

"Haven't talked to any docs yet. How is he?"

"He's doing great, considering. Bullet didn't hit anything vital. No nerve damage. Lost a lot of blood, but he'll be okay. I talked to him an hour ago."

"Was he cogent?"

"He's fine mentally. We've talked a lot since I been here. He's just resting up before his lawyer gets here in an hour. Lucky, so far no charges have been filed so when he's physically able, we think he can go home."

"I expected to see him handcuffed to the bed. How long have *you* been here?"

"Since yesterday when I heard he was shot."

"Have to admit, I'm a little surprised. I thought you and he were on the outs."

"Strange how that works. I guess it took something like this to make me realize how much I care for the big guy. Works both ways."

"Meaning?"

"Meaning, when he came to and saw me here, he got religion."

There was a stir in the bed. Purdy said, "I been awake all this time. Just wanted to see if it was worth opening my eyes for."

I said, "Alison is drop dead gorgeous. How're you feeling?"

"Ain't gonna be blocking no middle linebackers for a spell but I'm okay. I don't know what I'm gonna do actually. That's why I'm seeing a lawyer. What happened? You were there."

I told him what I saw. When I was finished he said, "So she shot me because I touched her on the shoulder?"

"No. She shot you to keep you from being mayor."

Alison and Brent both said, "Whaaaa?"

I said, "Do you know a man named Devin Hardy?"

Brent wasn't sure why I brought the name up but answered anyway. "Met him a few times. A real asshole. I know his boss pretty well. Mayor Morrison."

"You may have those boss roles reversed. Tell me why you say that about Hardy."

He started to sit up. It was painful, but he struggled through it, refusing Alison's attempt at assistance. "After one of my meetings with the mayor, Hardy took me aside and tried to convince me not to run. Said that politics in this county is really complicated and I'd best stay out of it."

"Did he threaten you?"

"Not that time, leastways I didn't take it that way. Just kinda came off as friendly advice. Next time I saw him he told me that if my mind was all made up about running that he should explain some things to me. Implied I could make a lot of money off the books if I played my cards right."

"And what did you say to that?"

"Told him that was the problem all along. Folks was thinking of lining their pockets instead of what's good for the island."

"Did he say that the mayor was involved?"

"No sir. Morrison trusted him and just signed off on anything he put in front of him. Said that I could keep my hands clean by just looking the other way. Wouldn't have to do anything illegal myself. I told him I'd be much more hands-on than Mayor Morrison."

"How did he respond to that?"

"Just seemed to take it in stride. Shook my hand and said he hoped we could work together. I didn't say at the time, but I decided if I did get elected, Devin Hardy'd be the last guy I'd appoint as town manager. You know the manager's salary is six times what the mayor makes. And that doesn't include what he was implying he got under the table."

The last words were a little breathy. I could see he was getting tired.

I said, "I need to tell you some things. Alison, can you give us the room?"

Brent put his arm up, the one not tied to all the tubes and hoses. "No. Alison's cool. She can hear anything you have to say."

"Some of it's personal. Has to do with Cami."

"Allie, you tell him. You were startin' to when I interrupted before."

"You sure he needs to know all this?" she asked.

He nodded.

"Brent and I are back together. We're thinking of getting married, soon as his divorce comes through."

"Wow." That was all I could think to say.

60

Gobsmacked is a word I'd never heard until a few years ago. It sounded British and pretentious, but it was the first one I could come up with to describe my reaction to the Brent/Alison announcement. I actually used the word aloud for the first time to Ginn. He took the news calmly, as he did all things.

He gave me his best old sage smile and said, "Fallback position. Can't get the gold, settle for the silver."

We were deep into cocktail hour, nursing single malts. Jaime was upstairs on her computer, putting out West Coast fires at the agency. Tomey had taken Cami to the impound lot to bail out the red Mustang. They were due back within the hour, at which time we'd make dinner plans. Chinese take-out was the current polesitter.

I said, "That's what you'd think, but they both swore that the shooting opened their eyes to what was there all along. Purdy woke up and there was Alison. And for her part, Alison realized how much she cared for him when she heard he'd been shot."

"There's an old record called, *Don't get above your Raisin'*. That's what's happening here. Purdy's a country boy at heart and so's Alison. Though with a frame like that, she ain't no boy."

I nodded. "Something we saw from the beginning and I'm not talking about her physique. Brent was captivated by the whole Hollywood thing about Cami. It wasn't real, it was the agency's creation. Regardless, it made him blind to who she really was. What surprises me is how quickly he saw the light after being so obstinate all these months. He actually said Alison has more class in her little finger than in Cami's whole body."

"Ain't nothing wrong with that body neither."

"I just hope my libido's as strong as yours when I get to your stage in life."

"Ain't seen no purple pills around here, but you got a ways to go to catch up to Black Moses himself."

"Thank you, Isaac Hayes."

"He ain't around so I just naturally assumed the title. Anyway, seems it all come down to politics. This Devin Hardy dude getting some Benjamins on the side. He's seeing the honey train getting derailed if Brent gets elected, so he makes a preemptive strike. That how you see it?"

"I'm not saying that Hardy wanted Purdy dead. Just unelectable. These days, a divorce is no big deal. Hardy needed something more toxic. Domestic violence fits."

Moses got up to fix himself another drink, mine was still half full. "We still ain't sure who killed Walker. Smart money'd be on the Walsh kid, but he don't really seem like the killer type to me."

"One thing I learned with the FBI is that there *is* no killer type. Profilers try to narrow it down, but it's all percentages. Like baseball with analytics. They say you have a better chance of scoring if you don't bunt with a runner on first and no outs, but that's no guarantee you'll score if you swing away or that you won't if you bunt."

"Gimme an old fashioned manager any day, who sees what's in front of him 'stead of going on the computer."

I could hear Jaime's muffled voice coming from her room upstairs. She sounded perturbed, as if some producer had the temerity to suggest one of her clients wasn't worth what she was asking. It was good she had something to take her mind off her problems here.

"Mo, my gut tells me you're right --- this Walsh boy isn't a killer. I've never met Devin Hardy, just saw him sitting in the car with Montanez. From what Crain found out, he's a sleaze, a greedy opportunist, but not a killer. Making a lot of money as a public official, most of it off the books."

Moses rubbed his eyes. "Only reason I can think Walsh would kill Walker is if she was going to cut him out of the deal. He wants to be a producer or a show boater or whatever, and she decides he ain't got the chops and sells him out, so he feeds her a hot load."

"Could be, although if he found out that she betrayed him, he'd kill her in anger with a knife or gun. The kid dealt with grass, mostly. He might've hooked her up with something outside his area of expertise and she overdosed."

My phone buzzed that an email was coming. It was Crain. I'd asked him to look into Mayor Morrison and Devin Hardy. I'd also given him a list of calls on Cami's phone to see if we could establish any links.

I read the message aloud for Moses to hear. "Two recent calls to Walsh. Holy shit. Here's a call to Montanez. More than one. This puts things in a new light. Dating back months. And a couple during the time period she was missing. The bastard knew all along her disappearing was a scam."

"So Cami was working with Montanez? She planned the whole thing?"

"They probably planned it together. Call Alex and tell her what we know. Make sure she follows Cami back here. Her Honda's no competition for that Mustang, but we can't let Cami bolt. Not now."

"Damn straight. When she gets back, she be in for a little session that'll make the Spanish Inquisition look like a walk with old Bosco here."

The dog's ears twitched at the mention of his name and the word 'walk.' If only our lives were so simple.

~~~~~

Alex and Cami breezed in, no drama. Alex had a 'what's for dinner' look on her face that was soon erased when she caught the serious vibe that Ginn threw at her. I wanted to keep Jaime out of this until we could tie it up with a nice bow.

I said, "Cami, we have a problem. You've got to tell us the absolute truth. No lies or all bets are off. We just need to sort something out."

The girl was trying to play it cool, but she couldn't hide the look of dread on her face."

I said, "Sit down, Cami. Want something to eat or drink?"

"Prisoner's last meal?"

"That's up to you."

She sat on the loveseat. I said, "I'll get right down to it. We have phone records that indicate you've had a bunch of conversations with Detective Montanez."

"Not true."

Alex said, "I can start throwing subpoenas around and the shit will hit the fan. Even if you're innocent, there'll be an investigation and it could get nasty."

"Do I need a lawyer?"

Ginn was indignant, "Damn it woman, the man's trying to help you. He be giving you benefit of the doubt. You play ball with us and you got a chance to save your pretty little ass."

"I'm offended by that."

"Sorry, snowflake," I said. "You're going to hear a lot worse than that if this gets out of hand."

"All right. But I get the feeling you're fucking with me, I'll scream."

"That's okay. We lost the high end of our hearing years ago. Let's get down to it. You never volunteered that you knew Montanez. Never acted like you had the faintest clue as to who he was."

"I didn't think it was relevant."

Ginn said, "Really? I know this reality TV shit ain't the real world, but ain't no parallel universe going on here."

"We need you to start at the beginning," I said. "How did you meet Montanez?"

Her knees were locked together. Arms tight to her side. A little curl and she'd be full fetal position.

A baby voice completed the picture. "I met him at a bar. A few months back. He tried to pick me up. He knew who I was. I didn't know he was a cop till later."

Ginn said, "You say he *tried* to pick you up."

"We just had a few drinks. He got me talking. He was real interested about my troubles with Brent. I told him how scared I was. That's when he said he was a cop and he could protect me. Did the whole restraining order pitch."

"Why didn't you do that?"

"I was worried it would hurt the show, maybe kill it. I thought I could handle it myself back then. That was before Brent got really bad."

"So what did Montanez say then?"

"Said that Brent sounded like a bad guy and that I should keep a record of anything he did that was bad. In case it came down to his word against mine in the divorce. And that'd be a good idea to give him the records so's he could back me up."

"And did you?"

"No. I thought he was coming on too strong. Made me think he was more looking to get shit on Brent, instead of looking out for me. He kept calling. I called him back a few times but I never gave him anything."

"But you called him the day of the meeting with Brent. Right after we set the time and place."

"I did do that. Look guys, I know you said you'd cover me, but I still wasn't sure you weren't on Brent's side and were setting me up for something. And I had a tough cop who'd been offering me protection. So I told Montanez about it. I knew he didn't like Boomer and he'd be on my side, no matter what."

She knew we suspected that she was the architect of this whole scheme to kill Brent and she was deflecting the blame onto Montanez.

"Cami, did you have any idea that Montanez wanted you to shoot Brent? He said you did."

"That's a lie. All I wanted was for him to keep Brent from hurting me if he had a mind to. I never dreamed I'd have to shoot him."

Ginn said, "And did you? Did you *have* to shoot him? Was Purdy about to put a hurtin' on you?"

"I thought he did at the time."

I said, "So in your mind right then, Brent Purdy posed a clear and present danger?"

"Yes."

"Where did you get the gun? Cops couldn't trace it."

"Marty said that I should have it in case Brent got out of hand. I never dreamed I'd actually have to use it but when he grabbed me from behind and he had that knife, I shot him."

She started to cry.

Tomey said, "You actually saw the knife in his hand?"

"I thought I did. I'm not sure. It all happened so fast."

I said, "What did Montanez say to you before you met Brent. He whispered something we couldn't hear."

"He said not to worry. One false move and he'd take care of Brent. For good."

61

We were drinking coffee at Brent's house. No alcohol in deference to the pain medication that Purdy was on.

"So the women are doing all the heavy lifting today, is that what you're telling me?" he said.

"That's about it, amigo. Tomey is pushing Montanez to roll on Hardy, and Jaime is working the media. She said if I wanted to be useful, I could petition some bishop to put you up for sainthood, but I thought that was a little premature, being that you're not dead yet."

"Why would Montanez roll on Hardy?"

Late morning on a cool overcast day, Alison Reiger was nowhere to be found. Brent had insisted she go to work and that he'd be fine. And he was.

The man was a modern marvel. He'd been released from the hospital the day before and it was hard to believe the day before that, he was bleeding out under a pergola.

I said, "Marty Montanez could be charged with all kinds of crimes. Conspiracy to commit murder, attempted murder, falsifying evidence, to name a few. We have proof through Cami's phone records that he knew all along she hadn't been killed or kidnapped. Tomey's got the DA involved, who's also a female, by the way. They put together a plan and they're ready to make a deal."

"So, I get shot and the guy who engineered it skates? That don't seem right."

"He won't skate. He'll never work as a cop again. Might serve some time and get a lot of probation, plus community service, stuff like that. Hardy's the big prize and he'd be hard to nail without Montanez."

"He was really so afraid I'd get elected mayor that he'd tell Montanez to kill me?"

"I don't think he wanted to kill you. He wanted to disgrace you with spousal abuse which would ruin your chances. Montanez coached her to provoke you but your anger management courses paid off. But the second he saw you touch her, with us as witnesses, he saw his chance. He either planned on planting the knife or just had it with him after he bought it at Lowe's. He could claim you were going to kill or mutilate Cami."

"Would he have shot me himself if Cami hadn't?"

"I don't think he'd have gone that far. I don't think he was too upset that she shot you but he swears he didn't give her the gun and we can't prove he did. He planted the blade to seal the deal, figuring it would justify the shooting. Made it look like you were planning to use a deadly weapon. That was one step too many and that brought him down."

"Wow. Shooting someone to keep them from winning a local election. I ain't exactly Bobby Kennedy. This is all about money?"

"My computer guy hacked into Hardy's finances. He's got money hidden all over the place. Way more than a town manager could ever squirrel away, even though they get paid a nice salary. He was taking in God knows how much more under the table."

"The mayor makes something like thirty grand. But that ain't why I'm in it."

"Good for you. With it looking like you're the victim of a dirty plot to skew the election, you'll be more popular than ever, even with the divorce."

"Well, Jaime did talk to me about the divorce on the phone last night. She says we just tell the truth. Cami and I are splitting. No blame, just grew apart. I'll finish the season solo."

"I don't think she really was afraid of you. That was just a pretext to break away and put together her own show with Iris."

"Seems like a roundabout way, you ask me."

"That's how she grew up, not trusting anybody. Coming up with scams to get what she wanted, instead of just being honest. She was used to dealing with sleazebags so when she met someone who really cared about her, she couldn't accept it. If she wanted her own spin-off show, I'm sure you would have encouraged her, maybe even bankrolled it."

"Fool that I was, you're probably right. So I s'pose she'll be headed back to L.A. once this is sorted out. More coffee?"

He got up before I could tell him that I'd get it. I caught a slight grimace as he rose, but otherwise, he moved as if nothing had happened.

When he returned, I said, "Cami *is* going back to California to lay low for a bit. That *Sisters* pilot won't get made with Alison, but maybe she can find another lady who fits the bill. Or she'll do some acting on a sitcom or drama series. Home improvement was never her bag anyway."

"Tell me this, King. And be honest. Did she want me to get shot? Was she in on it the whole time?"

Even though I had anticipated the question, I stumbled to answer. "She said she had no idea. She says that

Montanez got her so paranoid, she actually believed you'd hurt her if she rejected you. I don't know that we'll ever know the truth."

"She did seem like she wanted me to hit her that day. She said some really nasty things. Took all my anger management training to stay calm and not haul off on her."

"That is possible. It would certainly open the door for Montanez to jump in and arrest you for domestic violence. That'd be enough to derail your chances for mayor and would have served his purpose. If you'd have hauled off and hit her in front of witnesses and she didn't have a gun, you never would have gotten shot. Your restraint might've worked against you, ironically. Would have saved Montanez, too. The box cutter would never have come into play."

He sighed. "You've been right all along about Cami. I wish I'd a listened. Would've saved myself a lot of pain."

"Yeah, well, when you love somebody, you're vulnerable. They have power over you, power you've given them. The good ones pay it back in kind. The selfish ones use it to get what they want, regardless of what the cost is to you. In matters of the heart, sometimes it's hard to know the difference."

"True that. One thing I'm wondering about. The utility knife. If Montanez planted it, how does he get off so light?"

"Good question. It'll be part of the deal. He won't be nailed for planting evidence if he rolls on Hardy."

"But you saw Montanez buy it."

"I got Montanez's credit card record from my hacker source, not the cops. It could get ruled inadmissible and the serial number trace could get ruled fruit of the poison tree.

Montanez obviously doesn't want to take that chance. He'll get off with a resignation and a reprimand. Pretty light."

"And you're convinced that Mayor Pete had nothing to do with all of this?"

"Yes. I saw him this morning. He didn't remember me. The man's wife died last year and he kept telling me about their plans to travel the world. Apparently he goes in and out, some good days, some bad. He trusted Hardy, just went along with everything he suggested. Hardy couldn't risk him staying in office for another term because of how he was deteriorating, and he had a hand-picked successor lined up who'd play the game with him. You threw a monkey wrench into that plan."

"Mayor Pete with dementia. Damn, I never saw it. Guess I only caught him on his good days."

"Me, too. I thought he was fine, but the part about his wife should have clued me in. I thought Tomey got it wrong, but she never does. This morning he wasn't up for my visit and I just saw a pitiful old man."

I looked around Purdy's living room. For a man with money, he could afford grander digs. The place was clean, everything in its place, nothing pretentious about it. Like the man himself.

He said, "Jaime figured we wrap this season, then maybe re-invent the show as the mayor of Judy's Island, depending on how things go. On the way to the hospital when I was bleeding out, I thought of the perfect way to end the show. I die, then we could say, 'Twas beauty killed the beast'"

"Snappy ending. What about Alison? You really thinking of marriage?"

"Even here in the Bible Belt, politicians get away with living in sin. I learned my lesson. I think I'll take a long test drive before I make a formal commitment. I told Jaime I'm not even sure if I want to do another show. We'll see."

"Jaime said she'd go along with whatever you decide. Hurts her pocketbook to let a hit show slip away, but she'll be okay."

"She's more than okay. My advice --- don't let that one get away, chief. Big old bruiser like you ain't never gonna do any better, I can tell you that."

"Back at you with Alison. You know, Brent, look at the two of us. We're dinosaurs. We're sitting here drinking coffee and philosophizing and the women are doing all the work. Jaime'll write a script for you to read into the camera about the divorce and how the shooting went down and you'll win the mayoralty in a walk, she'll make you look so good. Tomey'll navigate the politics of indicting Hardy and busting Montanez. Justice'll get done, probably better than you or I could do on our own."

"You got some years on me, bro. I ain't ready to concede I'm just an impotent old white guy just yet. I've got bridges to build, an island to fix, plenty on my agenda. I was you, I'd just let Jaime call the shots and you learn to say 'yes, ma'am' on command."

I took a sip of coffee. There was one small detail I picked up on that made me think he was sincere about moving on. Everyone called his wife 'Cami', but he always referred to her as 'Cam'. That was his pet name for her. Until today.

Brent Purdy had the makings of an excellent mayor. There'd be some speed bumps. He'd need to learn to navigate the rough waters of politics, but he was determined to make it work and he wasn't a quitter.

But he was wrong about me. Even though I could see the Exxon pump coming for me, this dinosaur had a few more roars left in him.

62

Ginn had tracked down Bob Walsh while I was lamenting my fate with Boomer. He gave me an address and I said I'd meet him there in a half hour.

Walsh was ensconced in a cheap motel off 278, playing video games and watching reality shows on the 50 channels plus HBO that the joint offered.

He showed no resistance or surprise when we knocked at the door. The room reeked of pot. There was a queen sized bed, a white lacquered dresser, a cluttered nightstand and a couple of Thomas Kinkade reproductions on the walls. A stained upholstered chair was plopped in front of the flat screen, wires from his game controller scattered loosely across the threadbare carpet.

Walsh focused solely on me, as if Ginn was part of the decor. "So what do you want, King? You got Cami under your thumb. I saw the paper this morning. All bullshit. Your boy Purdy's coming off like a hero."

Ginn said, "I'm in the room, too, kid. Don't act like I'm invisible."

He tossed it off casually but with his deep voice and scowl, the threat was implicit. Men shivered and women grew weak in the knees at the sight of him.

I said, "Did Montanez promise you a free ride on the possession charge?"

"Montanez? Who's that? Oh, right, the cop Cami was tight with. Never met the man but I'd like to shake his hand. Nah, I got a good lawyer. I'm looking at a warning and a fine maybe. No problemo."

Ginn said, "I don't think they'll let you off so easy for killing Iris Walker."

"Whoa, whoa, wait. I didn't kill Iris Walker. What gave you that idea? Iris was a friend."

I said, "A friend who was going to cut you out of the *Sisters* project?"

"Iris would never do that. She and I had a lot in common. Shitty parents. Even though we grew up on opposite sides of the country, we were like brother and sister. There's no way I'd hurt her."

"So her overdose was an accident? The problem for you is that it doesn't matter. If someone dies from drugs you provide, you're considered a conduit. Can be second degree murder, reckless homicide, manslaughter. Take your pick. Serious jail time."

"I didn't give her drugs. Yeah, we did some weed together but that's it."

Ginn moved closer to him, menace in his eyes. "You were the connection for the *Country Fixin's* folks. You might be thinking this marijuana thing ain't no big deal, but the po-lice are thinking you done a whole lot more than that."

"I never heard of this conduit thing. My lawyer'll have that covered."

I said, "Bobby, let me give you some free advice, that won't cost you five hundred an hour. If you were just selling pot and somebody wanted more and all you did was point them toward a place they could get it, the cops will be inclined to take your cooperation into consideration. But they find out on their own, they'll take the whole organization down, root and twig. And you might be the first twig they prune."

"You got someone saying I did that?"

"We do."

Ginn gave me a sly look that Walsh didn't see. He knew I was bluffing.

Walsh was shaken. I could imagine how his mind was working. Hollywood didn't penalize A-listers with drug problems; in fact, they lionized those who had 'conquered' their addictions, even when they knew they hadn't. It made for a better story arc when someone has fallen and risen above it, as opposed to those who never fell in the first place.

"If I tell you what I know," Walsh said. "Can you promise me no one'll know it came from me?"

"I can promise to try. That's all."

"Trying ain't good enough. Man, I can't do it. I'll take whatever's coming, but I won't snitch."

Ginn said, "Afraid whoever sold her the drugs will kill you to keep you from testifying? Depending on who it is, that'd be in play for sure. Be smart to clam up, I was you."

Walsh was stunned by his honesty, as was I. If it was anyone other than Moses, I would have reamed him out for blowing it with our main lead. But I knew he must have something else in mind, so I stayed silent.

Ginn said, "You protecting Cami, ain't ya? She did coke with Walker, that's a fact. And just so ya know, Cami ain't got no guardian angel in the business no more. *Country Fixin's* ain't coming back, *Sisters* is DOA, and no one in Hollywood got any use for some blonde bimbo can't swing a hammer."

"Not true. Cami told me *Sisters* is still happening."

Ginn gave him a knowing smile. "You were right about Walker. She didn't throw you under the bus. Cami did."

~~~~~

Right after we finished with Walsh, Winona Sands called. She had a piece of information that she hoped would help. It did, making a lot of things clear. I thanked her and said I owed her dinner, a promise she said she would hold me to.

There were suitcases in the foyer when Ginn and I got back to the house. There was a commotion coming from an upstairs bedroom, Jaime and Cami having words.

Moses stayed downstairs while I went up to see what all the noise was about. Jaime was saying, "We can send for the rest of your things later. Just take what you need for now. You still have things in L.A. you can make do with until we ship the rest back."

Cami looked flustered. "Why can't we stop at Ribaut on the way?"

"We don't have time. Check-in is easy at Savannah, but there's always traffic on 95."

I pushed the door open wider and said, "What's going on? Where're you going?"

She said, "Let's talk outside. Cami, get your shit together. I'll be downstairs."

Cami stuck her tongue out at Jaime and turned it toward me for good measure. She looked like a twelve year old whose mom had told her to clean up her room.

Jaime ran down the stairs with me trailing. Ginn had already poured himself a drink and was perched on the sofa, scanning the flat screen for sports news.

Jaime pointed toward the back of the house and said, "Screen porch."

My back porch was turning into an interrogation chamber. I shrugged at Ginn and followed her out.

"I owe you an explanation," she said.

"Damn right you do. You're shipping Cami out. We didn't talk about this. What about this heartfelt confession she was going to tape?"

"She can do that from Los Angeles. We actually have cameras and sound equipment out there, hard as that is to believe."

"Sarcasm noted. And you're going with her?"

"I need to get her installed at dad's place. Then I have to clean up some things at the agency. I've already scripted Brent's mea culpa. Brenda has it and he can film it as soon as he's up to it."

"Jaime, you can't just do things like this without talking to me. Ginn thinks Cami knows who supplied Iris with the drugs. She has some culpability here."

"Exactly. I talked to my lawyer. That's why we're leaving town."

"What? I thought you cared about Iris. Cami might be the key to who killed her."

"Done and done. I wrote you an email with all the information you need. I was going to wait until we were in California to send it, but now that you're here, I can give you the condensed version."

I wanted to wring her neck, just for a second. Impulse control.

"I'll listen, but this better be good."

"Don't threaten me, Riley."

This wasn't working. I understood that my blueprint for justice to all involved wasn't all going to fall into place overnight. *Country Fixin's* would go on this season. Or not. I couldn't care less. Hardy would be ousted, Montanez punished. Tomey would do her job.

Down the road, Boomer might be elected mayor and live happily ever after with Alison.

But still unresolved was the fact Iris Walker was dead and someone was responsible. Even though she wasn't the nicest person I've ever encountered, her life mattered. More than some stupid reality show.

I took a breath and said, "I'm not threatening you. I thought we were on the same page and you go off making flight plans without talking to me first. You're leaving me hanging."

"First off, I don't need your permission to do what has to be done. I have to protect my interests which very often coincide with yours. But sometimes they don't."

Her words had just slapped me in the face. I thought we had the same goals. Same values. When I was talking to Brent about being vulnerable, I was thinking about Jaime and how much I believed in her. But now, I was speechless at this callous disregard. Faye Dunaway was back and I wasn't dreaming this time.

She said, "Riley, she's blood. My sister. Do I like her? No, not really. But she's family and I have to protect her."

"What's in the email?"

"The upshot is Cami did drugs with Iris. But Bob Walsh didn't get them. His parents did. His parents are drug dealers. They got him involved in high school. It was their entrée to kids. But Bob somehow managed to develop a conscience, no thanks to them. He didn't think it was big deal moving some marijuana. But he drew the line at harder stuff. His folks had no such compunctions."

Now it was clear what the supreme motivation was for not turning in his supplier. Not fear of retribution, but that he couldn't bring himself to hand over his parents. That pesky blood thing again.

I said, "So they've been using the kid all along. Bringing him up as heir to their little family business. God, they seemed like such harmless hippies. Lax parents for sure, but not evil ones. They had me fooled."

"There's another reason Bob won't turn them in. He feels guilty."

"Sure he does. If he hooked Iris up with his folks and she accidentally overdosed...."

"That's just it. It wasn't accidental. *Sisters* was going to be shot on the West Coast. Iris wasn't about to move to Hooterville, South Carolina to run the show. She was going to take the Walsh's little boy away. They wanted him close by. Bob would be their Hollywood drug connection in the Lowcountry with the *two* shows. Add to that, *Mr. Mercedes* shooting in Charleston, they saw all kinds of opportunities to expand their empire. They figured with Iris out of the way, if *Sisters* happened, Cami would be fine with it being shot here."

"So what did they feed Walker? Fentanyl?"

"Yep. Fifty times more potent than heroin and cheap."

"Why did Cami tell you all this? Are you sure she's not covering for her friend Bobby?"

"She liked the kid and she knew he wouldn't turn on them. He'd take it on himself and she couldn't let him do that."

"How noble of her."

"Well, when you hear the rest you won't think she's so noble. She was in on this from day one."

"In on what?"

"She and Montanez were in bed together. In more ways than one. I caught her talking to him on the phone. I confronted her. She said they met at a bar like she told you. What she didn't tell you was that Montanez was out to get Brent and their interests coincided. She wanted Brent out of her life, Marty wanted to make sure he couldn't ever be mayor. Apparently this Hardy fellow promised to make him chief of detectives if he could ruin Brent. They came up with the plan to set Brent up at the meeting on the fly. Cami didn't plan on the shooting. She was just going to provoke Brent into hitting her."

"So Montanez is the bad guy and poor Cami just went along. That sounds like more of Cami's bullshit. You fell for it once. Don't fall for it again. He swears he didn't give her the gun and I'm beginning to believe him."

"I'm her sister. I don't want Cami involved any deeper. She'll do what I ask. Part ways with her husband. Do a nice on air mea culpa and stay quiet. I'll find something for her to do out West. But if she gets wrapped up this whole plot, it's baggage she doesn't need."

"So she gets away with it. You're enabling her, don't you see? Brent got shot, could've been killed. And what about Iris Walker?"

"The email I sent you gives Alex a roadmap to trap the Walshs. I don't want Cami to get involved any further. She tried to get Bobby to turn on them and he wouldn't, at least not yet. Worse comes to worse and Tomey pressures him, he might just do that. That'd be the cleanest way out and Cami doesn't get implicated. She says that Montanez promised to lay all the blame on Hardy and keep her out of it. He's hoping they'll get together out West when everything dies down."

"Let's hope Marty's not as determined as Brent was to never let her go. Although it'd serve her right. Trading one obsessed man for another."

"My dad's security guards will shoot him on sight if he tries. The bottom line is ---- she's my sister, like it or not. She's had a tough life so far but now she's got a future in television, if I can keep her clean. I owe her that chance."

Time to tell Jaime what I'd just learned from Winona. "She's already a step ahead of you. You know why she really disappeared? Not because she was scared to death of Brent. She was shooting a demo for *Sisters*. But not with Alison. She hooked up with Alison's sister, Dorothy. The kid recruited cameras and equipment from her school, and they shot it ostensibly as a project for her class. In reality, it was an audition reel for *Sisters*. Iris put it together and she was going to leave your agency to rep it herself."

"I kind of figured that. Doesn't change anything."

She was doing her job --- acting in her client's best interest. But the Jaime I loved was the woman who always managed to do the right thing, whose loyalty was to the truth. Cami had blood on her hands and Jaime was protecting her. I couldn't punish Cami without hurting Jaime and I couldn't do that. But our relationship had changed.

I said, "Are you coming back here after you get Cami settled in with your father?"

"*Country Fixin's* doesn't need me. They're fully capable of wrapping the season with a cliffhanger. There's no need for me here. Help me get the rest of Cami's things downstairs. We have a plane to catch."

63

I know better than to try to stand in Jaime's way when she has her mind made up. There was a lot unsaid, but she left me standing on the back porch as soon as she saw Cami emerge from upstairs.

I helped them load their luggage into the rental. Cami didn't give me a second look, which was just as well. I hope her acting career will crash and burn. After closing the trunk, I walked to the driver's side, and Jaime rolled down the window.

"Goodbye, Riley," she said. "Thanks for all your help. Look on your nightstand. I left something for you."

"No mint on my pillow?"

"You could use help with your one-liners. I'm sure I'm not the first to tell you that. I'll call you when we land."

"Just don't call collect. My phone bill is astronomical."

"Better. Archaic reference, but I get it. Good bye, sweet prince."

Literate to the end. Ginn had made his goodbyes inside. Cami was the only one who heard us and she was uninterested. Was this the same little vixen who tried to seduce me just a couple of nights ago? Had I aged that much in such a short time?

They drove off and I watched the tail lights disappear around the bend. When I got back inside, Ginn said, "I heard from Alex. She's still working on Montanez, but it's going good. Between what your dude Crain came up with and she's getting from Marty, Hardy is toast."

"Good to hear. I'm sure she'll find a way to get Crain's stuff admissible."

"So you wanna tell me what's going on with Jaime? We hadn't come back when we did, house'd be empty, I'm figuring."

"Got that right." I gave him the rundown.

He said, "Without Cami to back it up, I don't see what we can prove about his folks unless Bobby-boy flips. Alex is good, but I'm not sure she be that good."

"Might be an Al Capone situation. Now we know what they do to support their Fleetwood Mac habit, she can keep an eye on them and bust them for dealing. You making dinner?"

"Thinking on it. Alex said don't wait for her, so we can go out or eat in. Up to you."

"Let's go to WiseGuys. Give me a half hour or so. Got some stuff to attend to."

"No problem. At your age, hair and makeup takes time. See you in a few."

I could have gone back and forth with him with aging jokes, but I wasn't in a *Kominsky Method* mood.

I went into the bedroom and there was an envelope propped up on the nightstand. The outside just said *Riley* in Jaime's handwriting. The letter it contained was computer generated. Nice font.

It was obviously written and placed in the bedroom before she knew Ginn and I were coming back early. We had gotten so involved with Cami's issues that we hadn't talked about "us", if there was such a thing now.

Dearest Riley,

I'm sorry I had to leave so suddenly. I'll explain some of the practical reasons for that later.

There is one reason I'm leaving that isn't practical. It's emotional. I had hoped to build up the courage to say these things in person. But like we say in show biz, timing is everything. Maybe if you're willing to talk about it later, we can. I wouldn't blame you if you aren't.

Spending time with you over the last several days, it became clear to me that you could never be a 'kept' man in Malibu. You'd hate it and eventually hate me for it. I tolerate all the plastic people and artificiality because my business demands it. I know you can't suffer fools as gladly. It would get to you. You told me that you already started a business in different places three times and don't have the energy to do it again. I don't know what you would do out West. You've said you can only play so much golf before you go crazy.

Then there's me and my situation. When Rick died, I told you my priorities had changed. I no longer wanted to be a dragon lady in business. I wanted to explore my spiritual side, for lack of a better term. But I can't just suddenly discard everything. I have people who depend on me. If I leave, it will have to be a gradual transition and that could take a while.

And there is dad to consider. I can't leave California while he's still with us. The doctors can't say how long that will be.

I guess what I'm trying to say is that we can't be together now. But there is one thing I realized in the short time we were with each other lately. I love you more than ever. I want to be with you. But now isn't the time.

I can't ask you to wait for me. I don't know how long it will be and the brutal truth is, you're not getting any younger and you're in a dangerous profession. To postpone your happiness and put your life on hold for me isn't fair.

So I'm setting you free. If someone else comes along and you find love, I'll accept it as my loss. But if you haven't found that someone by the time I get my affairs in order, well, we might have some good years ahead of us in that big house by the sea.

I've got to protect my sister and I know you'll go after justice for Iris. Don't think I don't care about what happened to her because I do, very much. I know you'll do the right thing by Iris Walker. You always do.

I understand that this will hurt but trust me, it's for the best.

All my love,
Jaime

God damn it, Jaime. My temper rose as I read each paragraph. Like a hit and run driver, she didn't wait around to access the damage she caused. Didn't show me enough respect to tell me to my face, or let me propose alternatives. Just like she had done by spiriting Cami out of state, she'd preempted any reaction I might have.

I ran to the garage. I'd chase her down, run her off the road if necessary, and demand to be heard. Screw it if they missed their flight. I could get arrested for what I was about to do but I didn't give a damn.

Upon reaching the garage, an irresistible impulse struck me. Sitting next to my MDX and Ginn's Mercedes, was Cami's shiny red Shelby Mustang. They probably planned to have it shipped to California.

I can send a message ,too, Jaime. It works both ways.

I grabbed an aluminum baseball bat from my sports locker and got to work. I started with the rear window. It was immensely satisfying to see the glass shatter into thousands of tiny shards.

Take that Cami, bitch. You're the reason this happened.

I worked my way around the car, breathing raggedly like a snorting bull. The side windows gave way easily, but the windshield was another matter. It took several blows to crack it even slightly.

My heart was racing, blood pounding in my ears. The damn safety glass wouldn't yield. I was running out of adrenaline aided strength. I girded myself for one final blow to shatter the offending object.

As I wound up to apply all my might to the task, a pair of massive arms grabbed me from behind and dragged me to the ground. In my exhausted and enraged state, I couldn't break free.

"Damn it, let me go, Ginn."

"Ain't gonna happen, 5-0. Ain't never letting you go."

I was a crumpled heap as he stood up over me. Tears of frustration filled my eyes, blinding me. When I was finally able to wobble to my feet, I got my first head on look at the big man. For the first time since I'd known him, his eyes were moist.

64

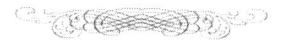

A week later. What had happened in the garage stayed in the garage. When I finally mustered up the courage to venture down there, the Mustang was gone and the remnants of glass swept up. I hadn't been ready to talk about it, except to Bosco and my bottled friend Glen, with whom I spent most of my time.

Moses and I were sitting on the screened porch and the sun had long since crossed the yardarm. I was on the wicker sofa, stroking Bosco's ears as he dozed next to me.

Ginn eased into the conversation by saying, "Whatever happened to us he-men making things happen, 5-0? These younger women be putting us out to pasture and taking over. Ain't the world I grew up in."

Aided by the Scotch, I was ready to talk about the situation dispassionately, or so I thought. "I had the same conversation with Boomer Purdy. We're sitting here drinking and the women are out shaking up the world. The one big holdout is the Catholic Church. No women priests. Period. How's that working out?"

"Got to admit, us manly men have messed up pretty bad. Wars, poverty, pollution, racial shit. I could go on, but you take my point."

"That I do. Got to give her credit, your woman's getting it done. She ordered surveillance on the Walshs and caught them moving heroin and Fentanyl. Good first step to busting up their ring. So far she can't pin Walker's murder on them, but they'll be going away for a long time."

"Could be for life at their age. Good riddance. Never been a big Fleetwood Mac fan, anyway."

"Your loss. They were great."

"Gimme the O'Jays any day and I ain't talking OJ Simpson. Anyway, maybe Bobby will flip on his folks. Alex is working on it."

"Tough call. I don't think Bobby Walsh is all bad. With his parents grooming him to be a drug dealer since grade school, you wonder how he came out of it with any kind of moral compass. Taking the Walshs down was big, no question, but I'm pretty impressed Alex got the DA to post a grand jury indictment on Hardy."

"Only problem is, Hardy got wind of it and split. Son of a bitch got all his money in offshore accounts. He probably living large somewhere in the Caribbean without a care in the world."

"Weird thing is, I never met the man, only saw him for a minute in the car with Montanez. I suppose Crain could find out where he went. Wouldn't it be great if he was the Caymans? Then we could go down and plant a gun on him and he'd be cooling his heels in jail with our builder friend, Randy Lustgarden."

Last year, we had framed Lustgarden for illegal gun possession in the Caymans, an infraction they take a lot more seriously than we do. He is serving major prison time, up to twenty years. He killed a man. For that reason, we didn't feel the least bit sorry for setting him up for a different crime that he didn't commit.

Moses said, "I know the police down there ain't exactly the FBI, but you don't think they be suspicious if we tried that trick two years in a row?"

"I was only half serious. But on the bright side, I saw the piece that Brent taped about his marriage. The man almost had me in tears. He threw Jaime's script away and just spoke from the heart. He's a shoo-in for mayor."

"But the dude who set up shooting him only got booted from the force and lost his pension. That's small change for gunning down an innocent man and planting evidence. Vexes me something wicked he got off so easy, just 'cause he rolled on the man pulling his strings."

"Bigger fish. But it's interesting. Someone from the FBI made a call to the State Board of Investigations. They're going to be taking over the case and the deal's going bye-bye. Montanez has no leverage with them."

"Wouldn't be a fed name of Dan Logan, would it?"

"Could be."

It was early evening and we'd cracked open a fresh bottle of Glenfiddich. Ginn held his glass up to the dying sunlight, savoring the sight, taste and smell of the amber liquid. "This ain't Macallan but it'll do."

Sitting in this great comfortable space, gently buzzed, gazing out at the ocean, I wish I could say all was right with the world, but for me, it wasn't. Not yet, maybe not ever.

My friend knew why. "You talk to Jaime yet?"

"Been putting it off. She texted me that Cami's hunkered down at her dad's place. I didn't write back."

"Serve Cami right if Alex extradites her to testify against the Walshs. Walker was supposed to be her friend but she didn't say a word about how she died until it got forced out of her. Take a team of shrinks to fix that girl. Speaking of folks needing a shrink, how you doing?"

Nice segue. "I've been better. Crazy thing is, I give great advice to others and I don't heed it myself. I kept telling Purdy he needed to move on from Cami and he wouldn't listen. Then he gets shot, has an epiphany and now he's with Alison Reiger, someone so much more suited to him. That was obvious all along to everybody but him."

"Hope it don't take a bullet to seal the deal with you. You moving on from Jaime? That what I'm hearing you say?"

"She told me to in that damn letter. I should have listened to Alex. She said it wouldn't work. Your woman *is* a lot wiser than we are."

"Ain't about to concede that about a female who don't appreciate fine Scotch whisky. That's a big hole in her game."

"There is that."

"So whatcha gonna do about it? For the kind of company I can't give ya. And don't say take up with Charlene Jones. That babe is a passel of headaches."

"I learned my lesson with her, thank you very much. Our country music star's out on tour now. We haven't spoken in months. The short term answer for me might be on an island twenty miles southwest of here. Winona Sands."

"Name sounds like a resort hotel. Wi-no-na Sands. Never met the lady but she sounds cool, 5-0. Though having to take a ferry ride to Daufuskie every time there's a booty call will get old quick, I'm thinkin'."

"I hardly know the woman, Mo."

I got up to refill my glass. Lately, I'd been way ahead of Ginn on that score. "Speaking of Alex, she hasn't been around much. She's been busy picking up the pieces. You two okay?"

"Her playing quarterback don't threaten my masculinity, if that's what you're asking. I know who I am. She does, too."

"Good to hear. Don't screw it up with her. She's pretty damn special."

"Don't need to sell me on Alex. I know at times it looks like she don't like you much, but she does. She worries about you. Wants you to find somebody and settle down. You ain't getting any younger. Maybe this Winona thing works out, if you don't get seasick visiting with her."

"I like her. But I'm questioning my judgment these days. My take on people was always one of my strengths. But I never suspected the Walshs were anything but harmless old hippies. I didn't like Brent much at first, although I should've known any friend of Don Henley couldn't be bad."

"Eagles, Fleetwood Mac. You white boys can have 'em."

"Actually, Henley had a line in a song that describes exactly how I'm feeling now. *The more I know, the less I understand.*"

"Lucky you got me around to straighten you out. And old Bosco here. You let him check out this Winona chick. If he gives his seal of approval, then she be fine." He addressed my dog. "That right, pal?"

Responding to his name, Bosco left my side on the sofa and rushed over to Ginn, who rewarded him with a home baked cookie. The dog took the bribe and tail wagging, went over to one of his many dog beds to work on it.

I said, "You think he really likes you or does he just know you always have a treat waiting for him?"

"Boy loves me. Even if his master needs his training wheels put back on, this dog is a fine judge of character."

He raised his glass and we drank deep.

Acknowledgments

As in the previous Riley King epics, I've taken liberties with the legal jurisdictions in the Lowcountry. Hilton Head does not have its own police force --- it is covered by the Beaufort County Sheriff's Department. There is no Judy's Island. It's the geographic equivalent of a composite character. The mayor of Hilton Head, John McCann, and Mayor Ron Pappas of Waxhaw, neither of whom bear any resemblance to the character in the book, were very helpful at detailing how small town government is structured.

Media producer and host Nancy Glass gave me great insight into the business of reality television. Novelist Reed Farrel Coleman, as always, is a font of great advice. And narrating the writers' columns of the great Lawrence Block was inspiring.

If you've been with Riley for a while, you've undoubtedly noticed that there's been a rock star cameo in the most recent books. These appearances are wholly fictitious, although I have been lucky enough to encounter these gentlemen in person in my previous life as a disc jockey.

My wife Vicky is responsible for the great cover art and is also a huge help in the marketing and promotion department. Camine Pappas is a great asset in making the graphics happen. Our Golden Retriever Duncan is dismayed that Bosco didn't have a bigger hand in solving the mystery this time around, but is busy dreaming up plotlines for the next effort.

Brilliant Disguise

About the Author

Brilliant Disguise is Richard Neer's eighth novel featuring Riley King.

His work of non-fiction, *FM, the Rise and Fall of Rock Radio*, (Villard 2001), is the true story of how corporate interests destroyed a medium that millions grew up with.

Neer has worked in important roles both on and off the air at several of the most prestigious and groundbreaking New York radio stations in history --- the progressive rocker WNEW-FM for almost thirty years, and the nation's first full time sports talker, WFAN, since 1988. He was instrumental in the birth of WLIR, the first suburban progressive station, in 1970.

Something of the Night was the initial offering in the Riley King series, then came *The Master Builders*, (May 2016). *Indian Summer* was published in the fall of that year. *The Last Resort and The Punch List* were followed by *An American Storm* and *Wrecking Ball*. *Three Chords and the Truth* features Jason Black, a new protagonist.

He shares a vacation home with his wife Vicky and Duncan Dog on Hilton Head Island.

Made in the USA
Columbia, SC
30 October 2022